Gambler's Luck

Gambler's Luck

H. B. Broome

A Double D Western
DOUBLEDAY
New York London Toronto Sydney Auckland

A Double D Western
PUBLISHED BY DOUBLEDAY
a division of Bantam Doubleday Dell Publishing Group, Inc.
1540 Broadway, New York, New York 10036

Double D Western, Doubleday,
and the portrayal of the letters DD
are trademarks of Doubleday, a division of
Bantam Doubleday Dell Publishing Group, Inc.

Library of Congress Cataloging-in-Publication Data

Broome, H. B.
Gambler's luck/H.B. Broome.—1st ed.
p.   cm.—(A Double D western)
1. Frontier and pioneer life—Texas—Fiction.   I. Title.
PS3552.R6598G35   1993
813'.54—dc20   93-19153
CIP

ISBN 0-385-42217-2
Copyright © 1993 by Horace B. Kelton
All Rights Reserved
Printed in the United States of America
December 1993
First Edition

1   2   3   4   5   6   7   8   9   10

For Adam,
Tara,
Richard,
Oliver,
Kendell,
Megan,
Rachel,
Griffin,
and future members
of their generation

Acknowledgments

While *Gambler's Luck* is a work of fiction, its setting is in San Angelo, Texas, in 1881. The author found material concerning certain events as well as background information regarding San Angelo and West Texas in general in the following books:

1. *Historical Montage of Tom Green County*, Tom Green County Historical Society, published in 1986 by Anchor Publishing Company, 221 N. Main, San Angelo, Texas 76903.
2. *Texas Ranchman, The Memoirs of John A. Loomis*, copyright © 1982, Mary Alison Wilson, published by The Fur Press, Box 604, Chadron, Nebraska 69337.
3. *Yesteryear in Ozona and Crockett County* by V. I. Pierce, copyright © 1980, V. I. Pierce, published by the Crockett County Historical Society, Ozona, Texas 76943, printed by The Talley Press.
4. *The Concho Country, A History of the Concho River Region of West Texas* by Gus Clemens, copyright © 1980 by Augustus Ducas Clemens V, Mulberry Avenue Books, 133 E. Mulberry Avenue, San Antonio, Texas, printed by Newsfoto Yearbooks, San Angelo, Texas.
5. *Old Angelo* by Joe A. Gibson, copyright © 1971, Joe A. Gibson, printed and published by The Minuteman Press, P.O. Box 1762, San Angelo, Texas 76901.

The author wishes to give special thanks for information received from the following individuals who, among other things, are West Texas ranchmen: Monte Noelke, John Cargile, and Houston Harte.

Gambler's Luck

One

LAD TRIMBLE opened his eyes to the half-light before dawn and felt a rush of fear. A whipping wintry gust stung his face. Startled, he raised from the ground, pushing the scratchy blanket to one side. Then he realized where he was, his heartbeat slowed, and he put his head down on the warmth of the cloth sack filled with dirty clothes that served as his pillow. Staring at the sky, he saw that stars still shone upon the West Texas landscape. This, the sixth day on the trail since leaving Austin, should be when they'd reach their destination.

A gust of wind made rushing noises in nearby mesquite trees, causing limbs to thresh back and forth. Coals in the almost dead campfire turned red, and sparks fanned into the air.

A man on the other side of the dying fire began to groan as if he were suffering the tortures of the damned. He coughed, snorted, and growled. He hawked and spat, snuffled, and made a revolting gargling noise. After these preliminaries, Elzie Huck, driver of the freight wagon, yawned as he stretched his arms out stiffly to both sides. He scratched his stomach energetically, and began to curse with little originality but considerable feeling. He fought free of his blanket and pulled his pants and shirt over rarely washed long underwear. Pawing about, he found his boots and a heavy jacket, and put them on. After this he jammed a sweat-stained ruined hat upon his head and began stumbling about the temporary camp.

Huck pitched some buffalo chips and dry branches on the smoldering coals, waited for them to catch, then placed a larger stick of wood on top of them as flames began to crackle. In a short time Lad smelled boiling coffee and frying bacon and dressed hurriedly. Like most nineteen-year-olds he had a constant appetite.

Elzie Huck ate his fried bread, frijoles, and bacon with the deliberation he gave to all his actions. He was not one to be rushed. "We done overslept," he complained. Drinking scalding coffee from a tin cup, he added, "One reason that happened is I'm working myself to death takin' care of a damn greenhorn like you. I'm flat wore out, to tell the truth."

Lad saw Huck smile as he spoke, and supposed that the teasing amounted to an early morning attempt at humor. He didn't mind, for it took his mind away from the sense of vulnerability he'd had ever since he'd arrived in Texas. He'd never been on his own before, and the new surroundings bewildered him. He realized just how protected his life had been up until the time he'd been kicked out of college. That had happened just before Christmas and now it was spring. It was, to be exact, March 12 of 1881, and he was bound for the Texas ranch of John McIntire, his father's wartime friend. Sent from home in disgrace with instructions that he not come back until McIntire had "made a man" of him.

The long train trip through the South seemed like a dream to Lad. The lush green fields of Tidewater Virginia and then the heavily forested Blue Ridge and Appalachian mountains had been left behind. He remembered his uncertainty at leaving the railroad station in Austin and the frustrating time he'd spent before running into the half-drunk middle-aged wagon driver who'd agreed to take him to San Angelo for a fee of five dollars.

He hadn't really slept at all at the end of the first day's journey. He'd never spent the night on the ground before. They'd been struck by a violent rainstorm on leaving Austin, and the wagon had bogged down whenever they came to a low place. When this occurred, he'd been forced to climb down from the wagon and shove while Huck whipped the team of horses as they lurched into their traces in the effort to bounce the wagon out of axle-deep mud. Finally they left the hill country behind and proceeded into a new and totally different world.

In Virginia, and wherever Lad had traveled in the South, trees and mountains placed limits on how far a man could see. They established protective borders and gave people accustomed to them a sense of safety. Fields of cotton and tobacco and other signs of the presence of mankind lay on every side. The freight wagon, only the day before, had crested a slight rise on the trail, and it seemed to Lad that he could see at least a hundred miles in every direction. The land looked as it must have a thousand years before, as if no human had ever set foot on it. A sense of incredible solitude overwhelmed him.

He rose, picked up his things, and put them in the wagon. Looking to the east, he saw the sun's rim shimmering at the horizon, making a clear white line, and above it pale blue shaded into purple. Lad stared west, the direction they would travel today, and saw low hills still shrouded in darkness. His focus moved from that far stretch of emptiness over sparse brown patches of prairie grass, prickly pear cactus in clumps, and an occasional mesquite tree with its delicate tracery of leafless fine black branches.

Elzie Huck hadn't shaved for over a week. A mat of white bristles covered his lower face, and straw-like greasy white hair streaked with brown covered his forehead. Turning from the empty metal plate, he opened his buck knife and carved a hunk from a twist of black chewing tobacco. His jaws worked on this for a few minutes before he began to speak moistly. "I told you yesterday that I circled around the Hudnall Ranch, but I didn't say why." He stopped to spit into the fire before continuing. "They're mean as homemade sin, the whole damn bunch. Dee Hudnall, the daddy, is meanest of 'em all.

"He's about as unpredictable a man as you'll ever meet. Can be nice as all get-out—all politeness—and then in a split second, he'll fly off the handle. The man has a God-awful temper. Frankly, if I had a choice of bunkmates between him and a rattlesnake, I'd choose the snake."

By this time Huck had loaded up his gear in the wagon. As usual, he put the coals from the fire in an iron kettle that swung underneath it; they would serve to get the next fire going. Lad helped bring in the team of horses which had been staked out with long lead ropes the night before, and the driver busily strapped them into the traces. Moments later they moved out on the trail.

Huck continued talking about Hudnall, saying, "Now that he has that young wife, those sons of his are fit to be tied. They sure don't want to have a stepmomma younger than they are, and the idea that she'll share in their inheritance galls 'em."

Lad sat on the worn board seat as the wagon jounced along. His companion said, "I'm curious. You told me your daddy sent you out here for some reason. What's the reason?"

"He wants me to learn something about ranching."

"I suppose you can do that in not more than thirty years or so."

Lad ignored the sarcasm. "When do we get to San Angelo?"

"I believe we're goin' through the Loomis Ranch about now. In four or five hours we should be in sight of the Concho River. We'll hit town by mid-afternoon."

After the isolation of the trip from Austin, six days without seeing anyone at all except when they went through a few small communities, the sight of the bustling activity in San Angelo came as a surprise to Lad. They bumped along over a wide, deeply rutted street between rows of stores and saloons. Most were frame and single story, although a few had masonry fronts. Several two-story buildings constructed of limestone gave the appearance of permanence, but most of the others seemed to have been thrown together hurriedly. Overhangs in front of these drooped here and there. Lad saw a barber pole in front of one place with an upper floor. Next to the shop was a door with a hand-lettered sign on it which said "Beds upstairs, 25 cents."

Loaded and empty wagons, most open but a few covered, had been abandoned on the street, some with horses and others without their teams. Horses stood at hitching posts and rails. Men tramped diagonally across the road, all wearing big hats, all wearing boots. Many wore holstered sixguns and a few carried rifles.

The town had grown in a haphazard way. A board sidewalk linked a number of the structures, but in some cases patches of hard dirt separated buildings. Many of the places of commerce had clumsy advertisements painted on large boards in front of them, but a few of them with masonry fronts had more professional signs, occasionally engraved in soft limestone. Sheds hung over the irregular board sidewalks, providing protection for customers from the constant sun as well as rare rains.

Lad looked curiously at the different business establishments: "Johnson & Taylor," "HARDWARE," and "Slapowski and Bro." When they turned onto a broad torn stretch of dirt with an incongruous sign saying "Concho Avenue," he saw a cluster of saloons and little else.

A surrey with a top went by. The man driving it wore a derby hat and a black beard that covered the top of his chest. A group of men in cowboy hats stood in front of a place with a sign saying "H. Wolters & Co., Star Saloon." They watched intently as Huck's freight wagon lurched by them.

"Drunkards," Huck said as they passed the Star Saloon. "Same bunch in there all the time. I asked at the Nimitz if they had room for you, but they was full. So I'm takin' you to the Tankersley Hotel. It's right down the street on the corner. And then you're on your own. Is someone from the McIntire Ranch goin' to be in town to find you?"

"My father wrote his friend, and Mr. McIntire sent a letter telling me where to meet his men. It's in my bag. And I sent a telegram from Austin, just the way Mr. McIntire had told me to."

"Sorry that storm slowed us. Whoever came to get you had an extra two-day wait."

Moments later Lad found himself with the sack of dirty clothes and his suitcase on the porch of what looked like a two-story house. A heavyset woman with a broom in her hand came out the front door. She wore a nondescript brown dress that reached the ground. Her graying hair fastened in a bun behind her head, and she wore gold-rimmed glass spectacles.

"Howdy," she said. "My name's Annie Tankersley. Come right in, son. You look like you need a room and a hot bath."

When he entered he found himself in a small sitting room with a fireplace. There was a counter where a wooden pen with a dark crusted nib rested by a small round bottle of India ink on a stained blue blotter. He leaned against the counter and filled out a registration card. After inscribing his name, Lad Trimble, he put down his address, "Trimble Grove—3 miles north of Shirley Plantation, James River, Virginia."

"Virginia," Annie Tankersley commented, looking over his shoulder. "Never been there, but hear it's awful pretty."

"It certainly is," Lad said with a rush of homesickness. "Our place is not far from Williamsburgh, which lies down toward the end of the peninsula."

"Don't know much about that part of the world. Been in Texas most of my life. The Tankersleys were among the first settlers in these parts. In the sixties this area was still full of Comanches, but our family took care to get along with 'em. Later, other whites came, for the grass was as high in those days as a man's stirrups. It's fine cattle country. As more ranchers and cowboys moved this way, the Indians got upset. So the government built Fort Concho to provide protection. It's one of a line of frontier forts, as I guess you know. Of course, once that happened, even more folks began movin' in. For a while things got a bit tense, which is understandable since the Indians for all of time had seen this as their home ground. Durin' those years there was many a time we'd come in to take shelter with the army until the Comanches settled down. But, as I say, except for a few terrible things that I'd rather not talk about, we mostly got along fine. Everything's changed now, of course, what with most of the Comanches having long since moved on."

Annie Tankersley instructed a Mexican woman named Lupe who worked at the hotel to show Lad to his room. As he left she called after him, "I've moved downstairs after my bad hip got to botherin' me on them stairs. Makes climbin' difficult. And all the other rooms are taken, so I'm puttin' you in the room I built for myself. Don't often rent it. Anyway, it's the best we've got, and I hope you'll be comfortable. Privies are out in the backyard: men are on the far right, women on the left. Got the yard fenced so I'll have a place for Buster. That's my dog. I'd advise you to go careful at first with Buster or he won't let you get to the privy. What you do, on your way out, is stop by the kitchen and get a scrap of meat from Lupe. Then give it to old Buster, and after that you'll have made a firm friend."

By the time she'd finished talking, Lad had reached the second floor, following the Mexican woman. She turned to the right and led him to the east end of the building. The door had no lock. She opened it for him and stood to one side, waiting for him to precede her.

Lad stepped into the room and looked about. It had wide-planked, pegged hardwood floors. On these were two hooked rugs. Yellow curtains hung at the windows and a colorful patchwork quilt covered the large double bed. The bedstead was made of brass and had large balls at the four corners. Lad sat on it, then sank back in exhaustion on the feather pillows. He had never been as tired in all his life.

Looking up, he saw Lupe standing at the door. He smiled at her and she returned it, then silently left the room. He stretched out upon the indescribable luxury of that old, soft mattress and groaned with pleasure.

Two

LAD LAY BACK in the long footed bathtub. Only his head showed above the steaming water Mrs. Tankersley had instructed Lupe to prepare for him. Gradually the aches and bone-deep pains faded away. Had any human being in history known greater luxury? He doubted it. He sat up when the water began to cool, scrubbed with a rough washcloth and lye soap, splashed back down, then heaved out of the long zinc tub. He put on fresh underwear, a clean white shirt, and lightweight gray wool trousers. After this, he padded barefoot down the hall to the end room he'd been given.

He dropped onto the mattress, turned over on his stomach, rolled restlessly to one side as he adjusted his head, allowing it to sink into the smooth softness of a real pillow, and fell fast asleep. Two hours later his hunger waked him.

Emerging from the front door, he found Annie Tankersley alone on the covered porch of the hotel. She sat in a rocking chair with a pretty flowered china teacup in her hand. A soft breeze wafted over them as he seated himself in an adjoining rocker. She didn't look at him or speak, but simply sat there, rocking and sipping. A dog barked in the distance and, closer at hand, another barked in response. Small birds darted through the darkening sky, swooping after insects, feeding. He had a similar craving, but at the moment didn't have the energy to search out a place to satisfy his hunger.

"You get a good rest?"

"Yes, ma'am. I certainly did. I appreciate the bath."

"We don't charge extra for that like others do. That's one reason I've got so many regular customers."

She sipped from her cup and made a slight face, as if she'd tasted something bitter. "How old are you?"

"Nineteen."

"Older than I thought. When you came in I figured you for a sixteen-year-old runaway."

Lad laughed. "No, I'm not running. My father sent me to Texas. I'm to stay for a while on a ranch west of town that's owned by one of his oldest friends, John McIntire. They served together under Stonewall Jackson during the war. I grew up on my father's stories of his close ties with Mr. McIntire, and of their adventures during the valley campaigns. They'd march as much as twenty or even thirty miles a day through the mountain passes in the Shenandoah Valley. That was when the soldiers under General Jackson came to be called 'Stonewall's foot cavalry.' "

Annie choked on her cup, making a worse face than before. "In case you're wonderin', this ain't tea. It's gin. Helps my old hip more than any medicine ever has. I recommend gin as a tonic for bone trouble. Gin has mostly alcohol in it, which is a purifier. It has juniper berries, a fruit provided by God to help his children."

Lad hardly listened as she spoke, for he kept thinking of McIntire's employees who were supposed to take him to the ranch—and worried that he might not be able to find them. When she finally stopped rambling on about her medical theories, he spoke. "I've got a letter Mr. McIntire sent my father, saying that he'd have a couple of his men meet me in San Angelo at a livery stable on Concho Avenue."

"I can't get used to callin' the town that. We've said Saint Angela for a long time, then San Angela, and now this other. Which don't matter, I don't guess. We're known as that wild little place across from Fort Concho, and hope to live down the bad reputation one of these days. But back to what seems to be worryin' you, about those fellas at the livery stable." She sat up straight, looking grandmotherly, and smiled at the young man.

"I suspect they'll be at the Elkhorn Wagon Yard. It's on Concho just west of Chadbourne Street. On the other hand, could be they went to Girdwood's Wagon Yard, which is down Oakes Street not far from here. This hotel's on the corner of Concho and Oakes. Since we don't have but a few signs on the streets, mostly we just point and say, 'Go thataway,' or 'You'll find it over yonder.' "

She smiled at him. "Take it easy, son. Don't worry about findin' those waddies this evening—you look worn to a frazzle. Why not wait till morning to find 'em? It's too late to start on your trip anyway. Besides, they'll be tickled to have another night in town."

She shifted her chair, causing the rockers to make a jittering noise as they slid around, so she could face him in the gathering darkness. "I've known Mad John McIntire since he came to the Concho country. He lost his land in Mississippi during Reconstruction, what with all the Yankees pilin' into the South with their new laws and taxes. Anyway, he came out here and got a good-sized ranch—but in rough country. It don't have that much water, but I suppose that's not out of the ordinary."

"Mad John?"

"That's what most call him. Of course, not to his face. When he showed up in the late sixties, the countryside was still full of Comanches. He found himself in one bloody fight after another before he got them off the land he wanted. The Comanches considered they had the right to hunt there. Hard to say what an Indian really has in mind, but it's clear they don't believe anyone has the right to *own* land. This is where they and their daddies and granddaddies have hunted since they drove the Apaches off it.

"Most of us didn't have too much trouble with the Comanches. We figured how to make peace and get along, but John had spent too many years at war. As far as he was concerned, he was faced with armed men who'd kill him if he didn't kill them first. He looked on the Indians, I guess, like they were nothin' more than a bunch of nekkid red Yankees. So he went to San Antonio and hired a hard bunch of men, and after that all hell busted loose. It went on for several years. John got his land all right—but in the process, lost his mind. Not all of it. But by damn, as my Canadian friend Harriet says, he went 'wild as a loon.' For years we've called him Mad John McIntire, and when you get to his ranch you'll sure see that it's more than a nickname."

"Do you know him well?"

"Lord, yes. Everyone out here knows everyone else. I know John and know his family. His wife is a flighty little bit of thing, can't be over five feet tall. That's Ellen, and she's the sort to give herself airs. Then, they've got a daughter called Beth who's a little younger than you. But when John took leave of his senses, his wife took her leave of him. She took Beth, most of their money, and for the last few years has been back in Vicksburg, Mississippi."

They sat in silence for a time. A lone cowboy rode down the street, leaning back in his saddle, stretching his legs out as straight as he could, pushing his boots into the stirrups, swinging them forward.

Then he reined his mount to one side and stepped down before the Star Saloon.

"I'll need to buy some work clothes," Lad commented. "I thought I could do that after I got here."

"There's a couple of general stores where you can find pants and shirts, slickers, boots, and all that." She looked at him, then added in her raspy voice, "I never heard of a man showin' up for a job on a ranch without his own saddle, but John will have extras. No use spending your money on that, for a good one can cost you fifty dollars. And you'll do well to earn twenty or thirty a month. He'll have some old spurs, I guess, and maybe leather leggin's. From the way you look to me—and the way you talk—I'd say you're in for a real education."

Lad grinned and nodded his head.

"Son," Annie said, "be sure to get yourself a good hat." She poured some gin into her teacup from a clear glass bottle which rested by her chair. Then, speaking vigorously, she emphasized, "Pay heed to what I'm sayin'. You'll need a hat with a wider brim than the one you had on when you showed up here this afternoon. The summer sun out here is fierce. It ain't like what you may be used to.

"Let me tell you a story. Maybe it'll make you understand how important this advice is. My cousin Frank got throwed off a horse one day. That kind of thing can happen to anyone, even a good cowhand, one who's been at home on horseback since he could walk. Frank's leg was busted bad and he couldn't crawl over to get his hat —which wasn't fifty feet away. Broken bones heal, or at least most do. Cowboys get tore up all the time. But there was no chance for healin' in Frank's case, for he died of sunstroke." She pursed her lips. "So mind what I'm sayin', be sure to get the kind of hat that'll give you some shade." As an afterthought she added, "And whenever you get throwed, for you will be—many a time—the first thing you do is find your hat."

Annie rose and went to the railing at the edge of the porch. "Sure is quiet." She stood there staring at the empty street.

Five or six cowboys came out of a saloon and then ducked back into it.

"Somethin's goin' on," she said softly.

"What do you mean?"

"I just figured out what's strange. This is Saturday night—by this time every week the town's full of soldiers. But there's not a one in sight."

She put the teacup down on the floor. "Don't want you to get the idea that I'm a drunkard. There's been too much of that in my family. It's in the blood, so I watch out so I don't get caught by the weakness. But at this time of day, it does seem to help my hip."

Lad felt rested and completely relaxed for the first time since he'd started his long trip. He sat in his sagging chair, enjoying the softness of his clean shirt, the feel of the cool evening breeze which carried the smell of wood smoke and of meals being cooked. His mouth watered and a faint cramping began in his stomach. He looked at the heavyset old lady who rocked deliberately back and forth beside him, her chair creaking as steadily as a clock's pendulum. She talked of random events, moving from one to another.

Lad interrupted her abruptly. "Where's a good place to eat?"

"They serve a good steak at Tucker's, that's the saloon in the middle of those others." She turned about, her eyes narrowing. "It's early yet. Best for you to go for your supper now, then come right back. Sometimes on Saturday nights things get out of hand. You understand me?"

"Yes, ma'am," he replied politely.

The day had darkened into night as Lad went down the steps of the hotel and crossed the bare dirt of the road. He heard hoofbeats and hurried, reaching the other side as three cowboys loped their ponies along the street before pulling up to a sliding stop in front of the largest of the saloons, one with a sign over it saying "Early Able's Place." Under this, in smaller letters, was written "Saloon, Gaming, and Dancing Girls." The men tied their horses to a very long hitching rail at which at least twenty horses already stood. He passed by this place, looking over the batwing swinging doors at the numerous patrons standing along the bar. He paused at the entrance, for near it stood a dark-eyed girl in her twenties, rolling a cigarette, pouring tobacco from a small white sack into a paper curled expertly in the fingers of her right hand. She rolled it, licked the paper, and smoothed the slightly lumpy tube. It occurred to Lad that he'd never seen a lady smoking before except for country women who liked a pipe now and then. He paused beside her, both of them illuminated by the lights from inside the saloon. A piano tinkled from inside, played by a man who had considerable energy as well as no concern for discords. For a moment their eyes met. The young girl had rouge

in circles on her cheeks and long brown hair pulled to one side. The
top buttons of her blouse weren't fastened.

"Howdy, sport. Lookin' for some fun?"

"Well . . ." he began uncertainly as she edged closer.

Holding the cigarette in her fingers slightly away from her pouting
bright red lips, she asked, "Got a light?"

"I . . . ah . . . don't smoke."

"Jesus Christ," the young girl snarled. She turned about, pushed
through the doors, and entered the saloon.

Feeling like a perfect fool, Lad proceeded down the street, passing
several other saloons until he found Tucker's. Only a few horses
stood before it, and he walked in, allowing his eyes to adjust to the
dim light.

Lad moved through the saloon to a table in a corner at the far end
of the rectangular room, away from the bar. Four cowboys playing
cards sat at a large round table that would have accommodated seven
or eight. Two others stood at the bar. The frame structure had a tin
ceiling with square patterns embossed in it, and coal oil lamps hung
from rough sawn rafters, giving off a yellowish, hazy glow. A fat
Mexican man with a large soiled cotton towel wrapped around his
ample waist came to Lad's table. He said in broken English, "You not
drinkin'."

"No, I'd like to order something to eat."

The fat man smiled, revealing several missing teeth beneath a
drooping mustache. "We only got one thing. I'll cook it for you
myself."

The steak, when delivered, looked like smoking charcoal on the
outside and, when a knife cut it, blood raw on the inside. It had the
consistency of leather. Lad had never tasted anything better in his life.
Hunger is the finest of all sauces. He ate everything on his plate,
devouring a giant baked potato and the canned tomatoes served with
it. The Mexican cook had brought him a small stack of steaming
tortillas and a plate of frijole beans cooked with small red peppers.
When he tried them Lad felt he'd put a live burning coal on his
tongue, and almost strangled. Grasping the glass that the cook had
filled for him, he tried to wash away the searing sensation, only to
choke on a draught of hellish liquid. Instead of water, he'd gulped
down bar whiskey.

Lad had been around firearms all his life. He knew how to care for
them, and at his home they had a special concoction with an acid base

that served as a bore cleaner. For a terrible instant he felt sure he had swallowed a mouthful of just such a substance. He ate a few tortillas and felt better.

One of the four cowboys at the round table rose to his feet and went outside. He stood at the open door, staring down the street, and then called over his shoulder, "You boys better git out here."

As they joined him on the sidewalk their eyes widened. "Son of a bitch!" one exclaimed. The bartender, the cook, and the men at the bar went outside. Lad joined them.

A group of almost a hundred cavalrymen approached from the west, moving down the road toward the saloons. Light from these establishments fell upon them, and as they came closer, the observers saw that all were armed, wearing wide bullet-stuffed cartridge belts with regulation black holsters for their army Colt revolvers. Over half carried carbines as well. The men wore black open-necked shirts, blue cavalry pants that tapered down and fit inside tall black riding boots that came almost to their knees. All wore hats with brims twisted in dozens of different ways. Some were up flat in front, others curled as a cowboy's hat might be, but most were merely rumpled.

A cowboy said, "Don't recall seein' anything like this before."

Another replied, "Me neither. Never saw 'em come to town with all them guns."

A boy of perhaps fourteen ran up and joined them. He was panting. "They was over to the Nimitz Hotel, lookin' for Tom Mitchell. Said they was goin' to hang him. But he wasn't there, so they said they'd by God see if he was in the saloons."

"Oh hell," the bartender said as he backed toward the bar. Moving behind it, he pulled a Winchester rifle from a cupboard beneath a rack of bottles, and called to the Mexican cook, "Pancho, blow out all them lanterns." Then he shouted, "Git in here and close the door." His voice was suddenly hoarse. "Tucker's Saloon is closin' for the night."

A volley of gunshots splintered glass, and then all hell broke loose.

Three

FOUR TROOPERS burst through the door, Colts in their hands. Without a word they began firing into the rows of bottles on the shelves. Glass slivers showered in all directions, mirrors shattered, hollow-sounding explosions detonated in the saloon, bouncing wildly through the air.

"We're lookin' for Tom Mitchell," one of the troopers howled. The bartender ducked out of sight, and all the others in the room hurled themselves on the floor. More soldiers piled into the room, swinging chairs left and right. They rushed the huddled cowboys, who instantly fled. One of them flung himself through the flimsy glass of a back window, smashing it into a thousand pieces. The others quickly followed suit and dived after their leader. They landed on their arms, heads, and backs, some smashing into rusty trash barrels in the alley and others hitting cordwood that the cook had stacked for his stove. The firewood gave way, logs collapsing, cowboys rolling, arms and legs flying left and right as they tumbled onto the hard ground.

Lad crawled under the round card table and saw high boots and blue-clad legs pounding by, heard the shouts and crashes. A coal oil lantern was knocked from the rafter and it burst into a ball of flame. Seeing this, other troopers grabbed the remaining lanterns from the nails from which they hung, and hurled them at the walls. Soon Tucker's Saloon filled with a reddish haze and black smoke coiled in the air.

Terrified, Lad moved from his hiding place. He saw the soldiers retreating. One of them swung a lantern back and forth, then tossed it underhanded over the bar. The instant it hit, a flash of blue-white light flared out and flames blew across the entire wall where bullets had broken whiskey bottles. Unbroken ones began to explode in a startling chain reaction, sounding at first like a battery of Gatling guns in the heat of battle, and then like a glassy series of bombs blasting. The wall turned instantly into an inferno.

Flames engulfed the back door and windows, and a horrifying conflagration fell like a nightmarish curtain blocking the front door. Lad alone remained inside, backing panic-stricken from the blaze through swirling smoke and fiery embers. Glancing about, he saw licking red streams rippling up wooden support beams and out across rafters. The tin roof began to buckle and as the metal sagged, flames above it flickered and then burst into incredible red and orange flowers. In a moment of hypnotized madness, Lad stared at them: they were so unexpected—and so curiously beautiful. He broke free of his trance and picked up a chair, threw it through the front window, and an instant later went headfirst through the jagged hole.

Rioting soldiers surged in front of the line of saloons, screaming demands that the townspeople surrender Tom Mitchell to them. They flooded down Concho Avenue, roaring curses, firing rifles and pistols left and right into buildings.

Lad made a run for it. He sprinted across the street to get away, but blue-clad men came from the shadows and grasped him by the arms.

"Hang the son of a bitch," a tall man with broad shoulders bellowed. His blue-black face contorted with frustration and rage. "Whoever's got that rope—bring it here. If we can't find Tom Mitchell, we'll hang this one. Them cowboys been gittin' away with murder! We got to stop it." A number of troopers stopped in their tracks—caught by the sound of his words.

The tall man roared out, *"Are we goin' to stand for them killin' us buffalo soldiers like dogs?"*

The mob milled about indecisively, then several voices responded, shouting "No!" The men, caught up in the mob violence, suddenly seemed to change. As hysteria took hold, several screamed, "Hang him, hang him." Others took up the cry, joining in the bloodthirsty litany. Dark-clad soldiers crowded around the tall trooper, and two soldiers pinned Lad's arms behind him.

At that moment a shotgun roared like a cannon. An instant later it boomed again. The manic soldiers stopped in their tracks and whirled toward the sounds. They saw a most improbable sight.

A grandmotherly lady strode down the center of the street. She stopped deliberately, broke open a Greener double-barreled shotgun, and shoved two new cartridges in it. Snapping the barrels back in place, she waddled with dignity directly into the mob with an absolute certainty that, like Moses striking out through the Red Sea, she'd find a passage.

At least a hundred soldiers, most of them with black faces, made way, parting as she entered the path that formed in their midst, and they stood in consternation, unsure of what was going on. Many had torches in their hands that they'd been using to set fires, and these were held aloft, lighting the way of the dumpy woman who wore a ground-length sweeping dress.

Annie Tankersley pulled back both hammers of her shotgun and held it hip high, swinging it left and right as she progressed.

One trooper, his clothing smeared with soot, his shirt torn open to his waist, began to shout at her, cursing vilely. He fell instantly silent when the old lady raised her shotgun and pointed it directly at him.

"Mind your language. You ought to be *ashamed* of yourself!"

"We're after Tom Mitchell; he murdered old Sam."

"Well," Annie replied, "this boy ain't Tom Mitchell. And I suggest that you soldiers git your tails back across the river to the fort where you belong."

She walked to the men holding Lad's arms. To them she said, "This boy is in my charge. He hasn't harmed a soul, and I'm takin' him with me. Do you understand?"

The muttering soldiers gathered in a menacing circle, surrounding the heavyset elderly lady and the white-faced young man beside her.

Annie Tankersley raised the shotgun skyward and pulled one trigger. The close-by burst set ears ringing, and the circle widened as men pulled back.

Annie's voice rang into the night air, carrying like a church bell's clear chime, reverberating in the sudden quietness. "A shotgun can rip a man's stomach out, not to mention his lights and liver. At this range, a double-barreled Greener will knock a hole in you the size of a bushel basket." She thumbed the lever to one side, broke the weapon open, and shoved another cartridge into place.

"Turn him loose," she said ominously as she cocked the hammers once again. The men holding Lad instantly obliged.

They began to growl and swear. But they could never harm a woman. Confusion spread among them.

"Come along," Annie said. And then she and Lad walked away from the mob.

At a distance, cowboys hiding around corners watched the strange scene that took place before their eyes. Several saloons burned out of control with no one fighting the blazes. Many windows had been shot out, but so far no one seemed to have been seriously hurt.

Some officers on horseback could be seen loping down the street toward the stupefied mob.

"Oh hell," a trooper said, seeing the officers approach. The soldiers turned toward the officers, suddenly looking sheepish. Several glanced over their shoulders at the grandmotherly lady and the slender youngster with her as they disappeared into the shadows.

"They were going to *kill* me. They *would* have killed me if you hadn't stopped them."

Lad sat at a table in the kitchen at the rear of the Tankersley Hotel while his savior bustled about, baking cookies. She stood before a large black iron stove with bright nickel trim. At one side lay a device used to remove the round iron lids so kindling wood and small logs could be added to the fire. Less than a foot long, it had a spiral handle to dissipate the heat, and a blunted triangular tip that fit in the slots in the heavy round lids. While waiting for the fire to reach what she judged to be the right heat, she completed her work. She mixed lard and sugar and flour along with elements from her secret recipe, and then pressed the mixture with a wooden rolling pin into a roughly oval flat shape on a flour-dusted bread board. After this she took an empty can, one that had a worn label showing it had once held evaporated milk, and used it as her cookie cutter, busily pressing out rows of circles in the limp dough. She rolled the lacy remainder in her hands, patted it into an irregular lump, and stuck it in a corner of the greased cookie sheet.

She pushed this into the cavernous oven—it was large enough to roast a thirty-pound turkey—and sat in a chair beside Lad. These ordinary actions seemed to calm the boy, she noted. He'd been in shock, sitting with her wordlessly until a moment ago.

Annie said, "Sometimes men get worked up. Something builds in them like pressure in a boiler, and they have to let off steam or explode. There's a difference between men and women, has to do with their makeup, held over from God knows how long ago."

After a pause she continued. "Let me tell you what lay behind the meanness that broke out tonight. The Mitchell brothers rode into San Angelo from their ranch on the Colorado River to celebrate a while back. After a spell they ran into a nigra soldier who was drunk.

"They took him around with them from one saloon to another. The soldier kept wanting to sing, and they said they'd pay him to do that. First thing you know, a quarrel came up about how much they owed for the entertainment. Tom Mitchell pulled out a Tranter six-shooter, an English make with a double trigger—one for cocking and the other for shooting. The soldier grabbed for it, and the gun fired —shot him right through the head."

She sighed. "Tom said it was no more than an accident—but he *did* point that Tranter at the man's head."

Annie looked at the boy's pale face and her heart went out to him. Rising, she moved to his chair, leaned forward, and took him in her arms. He clasped her tightly, holding her awkwardly.

His face was pressed into the top of her ample bosom, and this muffled his words. "I was afraid."

"Of course you were."

They sat side by side again. The aroma of the cookies spread its overpouring sweetness about them. Three tallow candles in a brass holder in the center of the table gave off a soft light as she put the cookies on an off-white platter, one that had been her mother's. She'd had it for so many years that hundreds of tiny, almost imperceptible cracks crazed all across its ivory-colored surface. Faded pink roses made a delicate wreath around the oval border. She and Lad ate cookies and sipped coffee which she served in her best china, Spode cups that matched the one she used out on the porch each evening for her gin.

Lad gradually felt a little better. In the warm homelike kitchen, the savagery of the street seemed unreal. "I've never seen anything like what happened tonight. It was as though I'd gone back in time. I've read of occurrences like these in the Middle Ages, when life meant nothing."

"You have an odd way of talkin', but I sort of like it," Annie said with a smile. She leaned forward and patted his hand. "By tomorrow this will have passed clear out of your mind."

"If I live to be a hundred, I'll not forget one thing about tonight." He searched for the right thing to say, but could only comment, "I don't know how to thank you."

She smiled and wrinkles gathered at the corners of her eyes. "No need to do that."

"Oh yes there is. You took a terrible chance. I never saw such bravery, not in all my life."

"Those soldier boys weren't about to touch a hair on my head. I knew I could buffalo them buffalo solders." She chuckled at her clumsy joke.

She cleared the table and brought out a worn deck of playing cards. Absently, she began to deal in preparation for a game of solitaire, slapping them down face up in parallel rows. She began moving cards about, holding some, looking at the others, caught up in her game.

Lad sat while normality gradually came back in the room, replacing horror. Filled with the wonderfully hot crisp cookies, he sipped his coffee, feeling relief flood through him.

"Fiddle!" Annie said, scowling at the table.

Lad knew little about the game of solitaire but he judged she'd not been successful. Acting on impulse, he pulled the cards from in front of her. He riffled them, cut the deck several times, and then, in a practiced way, arched the cards in each hand. They fluttered in a dazzle through the air, before merging in a gambler's flamboyant shuffle.

"My stars!" Annie exclaimed. "How on earth did you do that?"

He spread the cards in a broad semicircle, face down. "Pick one," he said, "but don't let me see it." When she had, he swept the cards into a stack, slid her selected card, still face down, under them, then shuffled and reshuffled the cards repeatedly. After this he dealt them, face up, so swiftly that Annie could see only a blur of red and black rectangles flurrying onto the table. When all fifty-two had been dealt, Lad, with a certain theatricality, rose. "The card you chose"—he paused for effect—"is this one." He touched the three of hearts in the midst of all the others.

Annie's mouth fell open. Awed, she asked softly, "How in the Sam Hill did you know that?"

"Am I correct, is that the card you selected?"

"Yes," she replied, genuinely astonished.

"Well, Annie, it's the simplest old trick in the world. I glanced at the bottom card before I started. It was the ten of spades. When you slid your card over, you'll remember I put it under that. So, all I had to do was pick the card that came after the ten of spades."

"But you must've cut the cards and shuffled 'em seven or eight times."

"I took care not to separate the ones in question." Then, smiling at her perplexed expression, he said, "I have what my mother used to call 'quick hands.' "

"You're a professional gambler?"

"Lord no. I was a student at Washington College, which is Washington and Lee now. It's in Lexington, Virginia, in the valley down from Roanoke and over the Blue Ridge Mountains from Lynchburg."

"They teach card sharkin' at that school?"

"No, but it was—a hobby. And one that got me into trouble. I'll tell you about it one of these days. They threw me out, and my father sent me here, as I think I told you."

Annie Tankersley remarked, "I notice you didn't say 'Papa.' "

Lad's features tightened. "My father's a very formal person. If you ever met him you'd see that right away."

"And your mother? What does she think of your leavin' home?"

"She died when I was ten."

"I'm sorry." Annie fidgeted, embarrassed. Then she changed the subject. "What kind of business is your family in?"

"We've been on the same land for generations. We cultivate tobacco and other crops and raise Thoroughbreds and saddle horses. Some years back we began training hunter-jumpers."

"Sounds like you know a bit about horseflesh."

"I've worked with them since I was a little kid." Lad seized the opportunity to focus on the past. It relieved him to move his thoughts from the present and talk of familiar things, to relive for a moment times from his childhood. "We had a horse trainer, an old fellow named Jessie who'd been a slave. Jessie knew an awful lot about teaching a horse how to take fences, and he would let me help him. When I was only five or six he began working with me, using jumps not over a few feet high. He started me bareback, worked on my balance and things like that, and this went on a long time before he'd let me try it with a saddle. It took a while for me to find how important the rider can be in helping the horse. If the rider hesitates or if he's afraid, the horse senses it."

She let him talk, enjoying his soft Virginia drawl, his aristocratic accent. Annie decided she'd never seen a living soul so out of place in West Texas as this kid. When he rode out of town with those cowboys tomorrow he'd be in for a rough surprise.

Four

EARLY THE NEXT MORNING Lad walked up the dusty road between the staggered rows of simple buildings. A rooster crowed exuberantly, the familiar repetitive high sounds vibrating through the coolness. Everywhere he looked he saw bottles, parts of chairs, a few lost hats, and broken glass. Hundreds of brass shell casings littered the ground, silent reminders of volleys fired at random by outraged troopers. Several structures had been badly damaged by fire, and all that remained of Tucker's Saloon was a gutted blackened shell. A few wagons clattered by, but no townspeople had yet appeared to inspect the results of the previous night's riot.

The rim of the sun cleared the horizon behind him and he followed his long shadow, which wavered ahead of him. At Chadbourne Street, he saw a sign on which the name "Elkhorn Wagon Yard" had been hand-painted by an unskilled hand. Following Annie Tankersley's instructions, he'd check here first and then try Girdwood's Wagon Yard if he couldn't make contact. The often folded letter in his suitcase, which he'd read so many times he'd committed it to memory, instructed him to meet the men from McIntire's ranch at a livery stable on Concho Avenue. This appeared to be the only business fitting that description.

The sprawling wagon yard covered half a block, and fences connected with lean-tos all around the perimeter completely enclosed it. Inside lay a series of pens and corrals, many with horses. Heavy open freight wagons, covered wagons, a few hacks and buckboard-style buggies, and one graceful, old-fashioned shay rested alongside the interior pens at various angles.

Lad went through an open lane in the main building that was large enough for wagons to drive through, not seeing anyone. He called out hesitantly but received no answer. He walked through the dirt-floored passageway, smelled the not unpleasant but definitely pungent odor of a place where horses have been stabled for years and where cleaning the stables has never been a priority.

Emerging from the building, he walked past numerous small pens where cow ponies and draught horses fed on hay or merely stood near the troughs, heads down, waiting patiently. He saw a variety of unpainted small frame sheds built all along the inside of the fence and realized that the Elkhorn Wagon Yard served as a place of lodging for visiting cowboys and wagon drivers. From what he'd heard of their pay, they'd not be able to afford to go to the Nimitz or Tankersley hotels. A number of men lay curled on their sides, rolled up in blankets or bedrolls, sleeping on bare ground inside the sheds.

A middle-aged fellow with a face that looked like whitleather walked up to him. "Can I help you?"

Lad asked about the men from McIntire's ranch, explaining he was to meet them.

"So you're the long-lost Virginian! My God, if you'd a' been one more day gittin' here, them cowboys would have drank theirselves to death. Come on, I'll show you where they're at."

He proceeded ahead of Lad in a rolling gait, for he had one leg that must have been four inches shorter than the other. Gimping along, he said, "Lord, wasn't that a *ruckus* last night? Them soldiers was out for blood. Thought they'd burn down the whole damn town."

They arrived at a doorless shed. In it lay several sacks of feed and two cowboys. One sprawled awkwardly on his back, mouth open. He looked as if he had died a painful death. The other was on his hands and knees in a corner, retching horribly.

"Howdy, boys," the leather-faced man announced cheerfully. "This here's the feller you come to git." Turning to Lad, he remarked, "I don't believe they'll be up to travelin' for a spell."

Lad had more than enough time to return to his lodgings, where Annie Tankersley prepared a fine breakfast for him, chatting amiably as though nothing out of the ordinary had happened the night before. After receiving her detailed instructions concerning things he would need, he went to a store on Chadbourne Street and bought a hat, boots, pants, and shirts. He stood in the remarkably comfortable boots.

The storekeeper gazed intently at Lad's feet while pushing and pressing on the boots with both hands, as solemn as a doctor examining his patient. He cleared his throat and gave his professional opinion. "These here are a perfect fit. You're likely to come in from a long workday and forget to take 'em off before you go to sleep."

Lad stood before a tall pier mirror, looking at the high-crowned hat with its very wide flat brim standing out stiffly around it. He couldn't keep from smiling at the sight of his reflection. "I look like an idiot," he remarked.

"Let me put some shape to it," the store owner said. He had a smoky wood-burning stove in the back of the room with a teakettle bubbling on it. Holding the hat over the kettle, he allowed hot steam to hit both sides of the brim and the crown. Then he curled the brim up on both sides of the hat's front, and with professional care he crushed the crown, creased it carefully, put matching dents left and right, then molded it as carefully as if he were an artist working on a clay sculpture. He backed away, looked at the hat with a critical eye, then leaned forward, held it over the steam, and pushed and pressed it until, after a good ten minutes of these efforts, he appeared to be satisfied.

He had Lad put it on his head and beamed from ear to ear at the results, saying, "Now you look like a sure 'nough Texan."

The image in the mirror surprised Lad. His appearance had definitely changed. He wore a wide belt, denim pants, and a blue cotton shirt. Looking down, he took in his shiny new brown boots, and then his eyes rose to the curl-brimmed hat. He hoped he looked like the other cowboys but wasn't sure. Uneasily, he felt as he had once in college after dressing for a costume ball. Now, as then, he felt as if he were in disguise.

A girl in the back of the store stood watching him. He saw her amused expression in the mirror over his shoulder. Embarrassed, he turned and for a moment their eyes met. She smiled in genuine amusement, a dimple deepened in her left cheek. She had sun-streaked blonde hair tied loosely at the nape of her neck with a light yellow ribbon. The girl appeared to be fifteen or so, slender but with the beginnings of a woman's soft curves. He noted her mouth: it was large with very full lips. She was extremely pretty, and he couldn't take his eyes from her.

Her face colored and she turned away. When he looked back a moment later he saw her standing at a counter unfolding a length of calico. A vacant expression had replaced the sudden humor he'd seen.

On reaching his hotel he saw three horses hitched to the rail out front. Two wiry, disheveled cowboys, who looked as though they hadn't changed their clothes in a month, sat in rocking chairs on the porch with Annie Tankersley. He recognized them as the men he'd seen in the shed at the Elkhorn Wagon Yard earlier.

She said, as he came up the steps, "Lad, I'd like you to meet Boots Ramsel and Jim Pucker. I've known both of 'em for years, and am pleased to find you're in good hands."

The two cowboys, one by one, leaned forward wordlessly for a brief handshake, their calloused hands feeling to Lad as though a steel rasp had scrubbed across his soft palm.

"I been tellin' Ramsel and Pucker about your experience with them hunter and jumper horses, the ones you train to leap fences."

This provoked a smile on the weathered faces of the two men. Pucker said, "We don't have many fences, but we got a horse for you to work on. Might get him to jump over bushes or jackrabbits."

"You must be talkin' of Claude," Ramsel remarked. "Claude's a five-year-old gelding that's never seen a day of work. Can't keep him in a corral. Goes right over the top rail of any pen. If we can catch Claude, you'll have a time with him."

Both cowboys laughed at that, but only momentarily. Pucker leaned forward, clutching his head in agony. Ramsel said, "Ma'am, if you'd be kind enough to point out the privy, I do believe I'm goin' to be sick again."

Observing his friend's hasty departure, Pucker said, "This town is a good deal more fun at night than it is in the mornings."

When they finally summoned the strength to depart, the cowboys took a length of mecate, a thin, hairy rope, and tied Lad's suitcase and cloth bag behind his saddle. The suitcase balanced precariously behind him, and the bag swung down on the right side, bouncing at each step his slightly swaybacked mare took.

"We knew we'd have a greenhorn," Ramsel said, "so we brung you the tamest horse we got. Her name's Sister, and she must be at least fourteen years old. But she'll put up with anything or anybody."

Lad sat in his Mexican saddle somewhat uneasily. It had a wide flat-topped saddlehorn, and a high cantle. Leather peeled from its dried surface.

The three men proceeded in a trot down Concho Avenue. "We ought to get there in five or six hours," Pucker said. "The old man is right anxious to see you; we don't have much company."

Without another word, they went to the wagon yard where Pucker explained he'd left something important. A few minutes later he returned with a bottle which had only a few inches of whiskey left in it. He choked down half of this, handed the bottle to Ramsel, who finished it and pitched it into a barrel beside the road. Both men looked terribly pale.

They turned north, proceeding up Chadbourne Street on the way to Beauregard, the road leading out of town going west. This took them past several general stores, including the one where Lad had done his shopping earlier. He noticed the same young girl with blonde hair he'd seen in the store coming out on the sidewalk carrying a parcel wrapped in brown paper. She wore a long faded blue skirt and a white blouse. In spite of the coolness of the morning she wore no coat.

A large man who'd been seated in a buggy stepped down heavily from it, strode toward the girl, and grasped her roughly by the arm. He pulled her from the board sidewalk to the dirt road and without any warning drew back his hand and hit her with his closed fist so hard that she'd have spun to the ground if he hadn't held her.

Lad and his companions jerked their horses to a stop, startled by the sight. The big man held the girl by her upper arm with one hand and with the other deliberately slapped her face. A cracking noise sounded as he delivered each of three swift stinging blows. Grasping her by both shoulders, he began to shake her violently back and forth.

Without thinking, Lad swung down from his horse, dropped the reins, and started toward them. But Ramsel and Pucker spurred forward, riding on both sides of him. Each leaned down and grabbed Lad. They lifted him until the toes of his new boots scarcely touched the ground. Pucker said sharply, "For Christ's sake, boy, what do you think you're doin'?"

They dismounted and led Lad to his mare. "Mount up," Ramsel said grimly. "It don't do to get between a man and his wife."

"That there," Pucker added, "is Dee Hudnall. He'd as soon gut you as look at you."

Lad sat his horse once again, riding between the two cowboys from McIntire's ranch. Turning in his saddle, he looked back at the girl. She sat limply in the buggy, blood smeared from her nose over her mouth. A flaming handprint showed its vivid red mark clearly on the

side of her face where she'd been slapped. Strangely, she wasn't crying. She looked straight ahead, her eyes glazed and dull.

Lad stared at the broad-bodied man standing by the buggy. He
leaned over to pick up his hat which had fallen to the ground. His
knobby head was completely bald and his olive skin shone slightly in
the morning light. His eyes, pig-mean and as lusterless as marbles,
fixed on Lad—as if memorizing his features. A ripple of disgust
twisted his face, and he whipped around, stepped up into the buggy,
and grasped the reins. He wrenched his horse around, then pulled a
whip from its holder and lashed the horse's rump. The hack bounced
across ruts, swinging from side to side as it bounded down the road
in the opposite direction.

As their three horses fell into an easy traveling trot, Ramsel said,
"I've heard of the youngster. She's named Martha Ann but most call
her Mattie. They say she ain't all there in the head."

"Which might explain the reason she'd marry a man like Dee Hudnall," Pucker responded.

"Why would she marry a man old enough to be her father?" Lad
asked. When the others didn't reply, he added, "It seems unnatural."

"Ain't nothin' natural about Dee Hudnall," Ramsel said laconi-
cally.

By mid-afternoon they had reached rough country. The sun lay behind clouds and a sharp wind kicked whirls of dust into the air. The
trail they'd been following disappeared, and now the men struck out
over a series of small hills, descending into brush-choked low places,
then climbing one incline after another. At the top of one they saw a
vast plain studded with random mesquite trees.

"When do we get there?" Lad asked.

"We been on the ranch since we crossed Spring Creek," Ramsel
said.

"Won't be long now," Pucker added. "We're almost home."

Two hours later they reached a long low mountain with a rimrock
crown along its jagged crest. After riding around it they leaned forward as their horses lunged up a slope, then they crossed the flat that
lay in front of the McIntire Ranch headquarters.

Boulders and big rocks littered the side of a steep hill which stood
off to the right of a large house with several chimneys protruding
from its wood-shingled roof. A long bunkhouse lay about a hundred
yards behind this, and near the bunkhouse were several shacks and a

small barn with a shed built on one side of it. As they came nearer Lad made out a sturdy corral built of cedar posts.

At that moment he heard an unearthly squalling, a high-pitched piercing wild sound that raised the hackles on the back of his neck.

All of their horses shied, even old Sister, the placid mare carrying Lad.

"God in heaven," Boots Ramsel exclaimed, clutching the reins as his young horse leaped sideways.

"Look yonder," Pucker said, pointing to the right.

Lad saw a man's head bobbing as he descended the steep hill, winding between rough boulders. The sounds became clearer, and he recognized them vaguely. He'd heard them once before in his childhood while on a trip with his father to a settlement near Grandfather Mountain in North Carolina. A branch of the Trimble family had a summer place there. The strange music brought back memories of cool fresh air in heavily wooded huge mountains during that long-ago summer. The area had been settled by Scots, and on that trip—he'd been eleven at the time—he'd first heard the raucous howling that only bagpipes can utter.

The piper came fully into view, and the warlike notes of "Scotland the Brave" grew ever louder as he drew nearer. The sounds skirled and echoed from the rocky slopes, shrill notes clashing with hoarse ones, with a resulting jarring dissonance that clashed about the astonished ears of the three riders and their skittish mounts.

"It's the boss," Pucker exclaimed.

Lad stared with disbelieving eyes at the approaching elderly man who, at first glance, appeared to be wearing a very short skirt. He strode forward with purpose, muscular calves rippling. He wore a woolen kilt of a woven tartan design, primarily of blue and green, a greenish gray coat of rough Harris tweed that only reached to his waist, and a fringed tartan sash which crossed his chest and trailed over his shoulder. A round green cap adorned his head. Lad received other impressions as sensible old Sister slowly backed away from the apparition. He saw a dangling purse flopping at the old man's loins and a black-handled knife protruding from colorful high socks above tasseled shoes.

McIntire clomped forward, now not forty paces away, one elbow pumping air into the bag that issued a glorious assortment of howls from the clutched bundle of pipes.

"It's finally happened," Ramsel rumbled. "He's gone clean out of his mind." At the moment the words left his mouth he fell silent, for his startled mount reared straight up, forefeet pawing the air, neighing a high-pitched whinny. Ramsel whipped his hat off and slapped the top of the horse's head with all of his might. The animal took immediate offense, plunged forward, and threw his ears back, then, in spite of being weary from the day's ride, bucked halfheartedly before the rider regained control.

Ramsel's language scalded the horse, which tiptoed sideways, giving the clear impression that he planned to get even one of these days.

"It was merely a welcome," said Joshua, the old cook who'd worked for John McIntire for years. "I keep tryin' to explain that the boss wanted to do somethin' special, that's all. He's talked of nothin' else for days but the fact of this young feller, the son of his oldest friend, comin' to stay with us. Then he got to talkin' about them damn valley campaigns, and I had to listen to how they went through them passes at night and surprised Yankees asleep and then ran for it, and then done it all over the next night, and burned them bridges, and had fewer soldiers but always had more at the point of the fight, and many another story that he's told me four hundred times at the very least. Anyway, what I'm tryin' to get you to understand is that . . ."

"Hold on." Pucker waved his hands in an effort to gain the floor. "Joshua, it ain't that I don't like to hear all this. Normally, as you know, I'm always willing to be a good listener. But my health won't take it right now."

"You and your damned health," the cook complained.

Lad sat on a cot in the bunkhouse, not really listening to the banter that followed. Crisscrossed ropes on a wooden frame supported a thin striped mattress which had been stuffed with feathers. A cotton blanket covered the mattress and a heavier wool one lay folded as his pillow.

Ramsel said to Lad, "The boss is known far and wide as Mad John McIntire, and it'll take you a while to get accustomed to his ways."

"He didn't utter a word. Just bowed from the waist when he'd finished playing that song on his bagpipes and went to his house," Lad answered.

Joshua said, "Well, that's his way. He don't say a whole lot. But he's tickled pink that you're here."

Lad lay down on his back, looking up at the dusty rafters, and when he closed his eyes he saw the face of the pretty blonde with the deep dimple on just one side—was it the left? He tried to picture her, but the images shifted and when he saw the girl's face again in his mind's eye, it had blood smeared across it and an angry red welt disfigured her cheek. He thought of her husband, Dee Hudnall, and remembered the way the man had glared at him. He could still see the menace in the bald man's cruel eyes. Lad shuddered.

He remained very still, thinking of the girl named Martha Ann, the one called Mattie. Fascinated, he recalled the way she'd looked when he'd first seen her in the store, remembering her smile. He wondered about the girl's life, simply not able to imagine her being married to the bull-shouldered middle-aged man in the buggy. The thought of her lying in bed with Hudnall turned Lad's mind blank. Surely, he decided, her purpose was to keep house. Somehow, this idea made him feel better.

In his imagination Lad was back at the store—standing beside Mattie. He saw himself beginning a conversation—leading her to the bench outside where they could sit. He wanted to talk to her. He said to himself: I'm going to find that girl. He felt a certainty about this.

Five

FEW OUTSIDERS knowingly rode through Dee Hudnall's 300,000-acre ranch, and no one had so little sense as to attempt to approach his protected headquarters without an invitation.

The property sprawled over uneven terrain some thirty miles southeast of San Angelo. It had served as hunting grounds for the Comanches, and before them for other tribes for thousands of years. Most of it still looked as it had during those times. Grass brushed the bellies of horses walking through it in some areas of Hudnall's land, for it hadn't been used by white men for grazing purposes until recently. It had cedar, hackberry, live oak, and juniper trees as well as mesquite. Several rocky creeks ran through it, roaring after spring rains and going almost dry by autumn. Rough low hills came into view near the ranch's center, and a long box canyon which ran from east to west hid within one of these. The Hudnalls lived here. Well guarded.

Entering the canyon on the western side, invited visitors passed through a narrow section. If they looked up they'd see one or two riflemen observing their movements. The passageway widened after a few hundred yards and extended irregularly until at its broadest point it stretched almost half a mile from one side to the other. Near its end they would see the pens and corrals, a barn, and a collection of frame dwellings.

The largest of the houses faced west from its position before a steep hill, almost a cliff, at the end of the canyon. It had begun as a dog-run shack, two rooms connected by a primitive hall. Each had its own fireplace and their chimneys protruded from the weathered shake cedar shingles. Later additions sent a wing to the north—where the three Hudnall sons had their bedrooms—and another to the south, which now housed the living room, dining room, and kitchen. Then, on the south side, the house turned in an L shape with an extension going from the house back toward the hill. Hudnall had his office, a small sitting room, and his sleeping quarters in this wing. A variety of different types of chimneys rose from higher and lower sections of the roof. There were no porches on the original house or on any of the later additions, due to the fact that the Hudnalls didn't believe in sitting in plain sight if they could avoid it.

Only about ten of the fifty armed cowboys who worked for Hudnall stayed at the bunkhouse near the barn. The others lived in line camps located at distant points on the ranch, tending the cattle.

Smoke rose from a small kitchen at one end of the bunkhouse. Inside it the air smelled of sweat and dirty blankets mixed with the odor of burning wood, coffee, roasting beef, and bread being baked. Hudnall's men ate well. They received good pay too, considerably more than regular cowboys. They knew the boss had enemies and that he often had gunslingers as well as his three boys with him when he left the ranch. But after their initial sense of uneasiness at going to work for a man with Hudnall's reputation, they gradually relaxed. Within a few weeks after going to work, the job seemed to be very much like others they'd become accustomed to on other cow outfits.

Most of Hudnall's employees took a certain amount of pride in working for the wealthiest rancher in the area. They often heard rumors concerning how he'd made his money. There were stories that he'd gotten his start as a gambler in New Orleans. Others told of cattle he drove from South Texas to the railhead in Dodge City, Kansas, and how his herds tripled in size on the way, and how other herds and their drovers failed to arrive at all.

In the bunkhouse this Sunday morning the men lay about. Sloan, the new cowboy who had joined them the day before, sat quietly, listening, as the skinny middle-aged top hand called Dutch concluded the instructions concerning his duties.

"Don't go near the big house, that's important to remember. Hudnall is careful." He paused for emphasis before adding, "He's nervous and has guns all over the place—which is a bad combination. The only people allowed there outside of the family are me and Jay Lute—and we only go when Hudnall sends for us."

Dutch rubbed his jaw reflectively. "Never knew a man like him. He don't trust nobody—not even his own kin. But, back to what I was sayin', you'll be all right if you do your job and stay away from him."

"I met his three sons when I arrived."

The others made no comment at first. A small wiry fellow sat on the edge of his cot, working the stiffness out of a new rope. "They're full growed but stay at home and do as their daddy tells 'em. Which puts their nerves on edge, I guess, 'cause when they're with us they take turns givin' orders."

"Is that girl I saw his daughter?"

Several laughed. Dutch said, "No, you just made the same mistake a good many have. That ain't his daughter, that's his *wife*. She's his third. The other two are dead—Hudnall's women don't last long. This one's younger than the last of his boys. I'd say she's seventeen years old or thereabouts. They been married for two years. She's one of them damn farmer's kids who lived on a little bit of dirt, off some miles to the east of the fort. They say she's simpleminded—I wouldn't know—never heard her say a word."

Dee Hudnall stood in the bedroom in his pants and sock feet, looking through a drawer in the chifforobe for a shirt as he prepared for his trip. Mattie, wearing a blouse and skirt, sat on the edge of their bed watching him warily.

Hudnall turned about, a tan shirt in his hand. A hulking man, almost hairless, he had veins that seemed near the surface of his slightly oily skin, bulging as they twined under the surface like thick bluish ropes. He was a heavy man, his stomach protruded but it had hard fat. He had an unusually large bald head with noticeable ridges, and small ears which protruded, making him look as if he were intently listening at all times. His broad fleshy nose, thick lips, and the prominent bones surrounding his eyes gave him a primitive, savage look.

He gazed intently at Mattie with a flat dull stare. She averted her eyes, looking down at the floor.

"I haven't talked to you about this until now. Wanted to wait 'til I'd calmed down. I been thinking about the way you sneaked away from the Nimitz Hotel in San Angelo. Were you meetin' that young fella at the dry goods store?"

"I don't *sneak*—only kids do that. Just felt like shoppin'. And I don't even remember the man you're talkin' about."

"Don't lie to me, Mattie."

She didn't show any expression at all, but simply sat there, waiting, as he examined her face during the long pauses that always took place during these interrogations.

"You remember him all right. I had Lute follow you; he told me about it. You never talked to him, but you don't normally talk to anyone, come to think of it."

Hudnall sat down beside her, putting his arm around her waist, and his tone lost some of its coldness. "I'm sorry I hit you, honey, it's just that you know I can't stand for you to go around those young bucks. You don't have any idea how a gal like you can stir men up. Some women have a way of walkin', a way of teasin', that can cause trouble." His eyes narrowed. "I've seen you do that in front of my own boys."

His face turned pale and he spoke softly, the way he did sometimes before striking out at her, and she drew back. But this time nothing happened.

He hesitated a moment, then pulled her awkwardly across his lap until she looked up at him, half lying on his arm.

She didn't resist, allowing herself to be drawn against his chest. As he touched her face and ran his calloused right hand over her body, she stared over his head at the ceiling.

"Still built like a child. You need to put on some weight, girl. You need to fill out some. It's a shame you're barren—I was hopin' for some more boys out of you."

She didn't reply to his constant complaint. She wondered if she'd spoiled his plans; the other wives had died in childbirth. Perhaps he hadn't intended for her to stay around to be in his way this long.

"Lord, Lord, honey, you mean the world to me." He continued caressing her with his rough, thick-fingered hand. "But we got no time right now for more of this. I'm going on a trip with Lute, Dutch, and the boys. We'll be back in a week or two."

He moved away from her, leaned down for his boots, and pulled them on. Rising to his full height, he stretched, then kissed her full lips. He backed away, looked at her, and began laughing. "Here I am at forty-nine with a seventeen-year-old wife. No wonder I'm a little jealous. Surely you can't still be mad about how I acted—I've told you I'm sorry I hit you."

He buckled on his cartridge-filled gunbelt, adjusted the Colt in its worn holster, and grabbed his hat from the table as he walked from the room, not aware of the hatred in her eyes.

Hudnall led. He rode a few lengths ahead of the others. His three lanky sons trailed, talking to one another at times. Dutch rode with them, sitting a sorrel with a blaze face. Dutch kept fine-looking animals in his string. Lute as usual was nowhere in sight. Dutch decided that he must be over the hills to the north, scouting for trouble.

An hour later they saw Lute on foot in the distance, motioning to them. They spurred into a faster trot and rode toward him. As they topped a small rise, a freight wagon came into view with a team hitched to it. Lute's nervous bay tugged at its reins, which had been tied to a tree nearby. Near the wagon they saw pale threads of smoke rising from a fire that had almost burned out.

When the five men rode into camp, Lute waited at one side, staring fixedly at the driver who waited near his wagon. The riders pulled their horses to a stop and sat there, looking down while the short fat man with stubby white bristles all over his face smiled nervously, moving from one foot to the other. His clothes looked filthy, as if he hadn't changed them in months. Faded red longhandled underwear showed under his shirt in spite of the mildness of the late March day.

Loftin Hudnall, the oldest of the boys, said, "Damned if it ain't Elzie Huck. How you doin', Elzie?"

Huck tried to smile but his chin trembled.

Jay Lute walked about fifteen paces to some brush where he kicked at freshly butchered remains, shoving an animal's head and some entrails with his boot. He picked up a bloody hide that lay under several inches of dirt, and dragged it behind him as he returned. Facing Hudnall, he said, "This man slaughtered one of your calves."

Lute went to the wagon and threw back a piece of stiff brown canvas. Under it lay the remains of a small side of beef. "Looks like he had a steak for his dinner, just before I showed up. When I got down from my horse, he sat there lookin' scared. I could tell somethin' was wrong."

The five men dismounted, dropping their reins. Their well-trained horses stood as if tied to the ground.

"You oughtn't to be on my property," Hudnall said in measured tones. "And you damn sure made a mistake when you killed that calf."

Elzie Huck tried to smile, saying in a joking way, "Everybody knows you got the tenderest beef in West Texas, Mr. Hudnall. Besides, *you* know me, I drive by here all the time. Sometimes I can save a few hours if I cut through your range."

He looked about at the unsmiling, deadly serious faces, and began to babble. "As far as the calf goes, travelers have to eat. I didn't shoot a steer, just a little calf. Not as though I was a rustler or somethin'."

"That's exactly what you are."

"Hell, Mr. Hudnall, I'm friends with your boys. I drink beer at the Star Saloon with Loftin and Hobie and even, sometimes, with Julius, your youngest. We're friends. Besides, Mr. Hudnall, *everyone* knows old Elzie Huck. I drive the freight wagons to San Antonio and back all the time. I got some money—here, just a minute—I'll find it." He dug through his pockets hurriedly and finally came up with several dollars. "How much is that calf? Is this enough?"

"Unhitch his team," Hudnall said over his shoulder to Dutch and Lute. "Then tie that fat little son of a bitch to one of the wagon wheels while I figure out what needs to be done."

Huck struggled a moment, trying uselessly to tug away from the strong hands that grasped him and threw him back against the wagon. "What are you doin'? Damn, boys, you don't have to do that." Huck's whine broke into a soft wet whimper, and he fought to keep from crying out.

The two cowboys tied the shaking fat man with quick efficiency, as though they'd thrown a calf during branding season. After they'd finished, Dutch and Lute walked about fifty yards off to one side and hunkered down on their bootheels. Dutch rolled a cigarette and lit it while Lute simply rested expectantly. Neither man said a word.

The Hudnalls, father and sons, moved away from the wagon until they reached a fallen hackberry tree. Hudnall sat down on the trunk, and his boys sat in a semicircle before him.

Dee Hudnall said patiently, "As you know, we got blame near four hundred and seventy square miles of land on this ranch. You can ride for three months and not cover all of it. If the word gets out that a rider can steal our stock without us doing a damn thing about it, why, we'll be out of business."

The father changed his position and put his hands on the rough bark of the trunk. The sons sat on the ground looking up at him.

"The only way to hold on to what's goin' to be yours someday is to make sure that everyone finds out that it's a terrible mistake to rustle our stock."

Loftin spoke up. "Papa, Elzie's no more than an old fool. But he's harmless. He didn't think of it as rustlin'."

Hudnall snapped, *"I* think of stealin' my stock as rustlin'." Then, relaxing once more, he said, "Boys, I'm tryin' to help you, to teach you how things have to be done."

He pulled his Colt from its holster. The long-barreled Peacemaker had a worn wooden grip. He held it out to Loftin. "You're the oldest. I believe this is your job."

"God a'mighty, Papa, Elzie's a friend. Like he said, we drink beer together sometimes."

"Hobie?" Hudnall held the six-shooter by its barrel, offering it butt first to the middle son, who sat, head down, not responding.

Hudnall's face hardened. Standing, he said, "I won't ask the baby of the family to be the only man among you."

Julius rose also. His face was as hard as his father's. "I'll do it."

"No," Hudnall snarled.

He walked over to the wagon where Elzie Huck stared with unbelieving eyes.

"I'll pay for that calf, Mr. Hudnall. I'm real sorry. It was just that I'm so damn tired of frijole beans all the time. Can you understand that? And I promise never to set foot on your ranch again."

Hudnall raised the single-action revolver, thumbing the hammer back, locking it in place. In the heartstopping silence, the metallic click sounded clearly.

Huck began to beg, his eyes round in disbelief, staring as Hudnall deliberately raised the barrel, pointing it straight at his chest.

Huck's shriek ripped from his wide-open mouth as he saw the certainty of his execution.

The Colt exploded and its bullet slammed into the victim, jerking him backward. He slid sideways, hanging from the ropes that tied him to the wagon wheel. Bright red blood cascaded from a great hole in the center of his chest.

Hudnall backed away. His sons stood as if hypnotized. Lute and Dutch walked forward to join them.

At last Hudnall holstered his sixgun. "Bury him right where he is. Put the head of that calf on the mound as his marker. Then hitch his team to the wagon and turn it loose. They'll probably be found in a few days. Somebody'll take the wagon back to the owner in San Angelo, but no one will know what happened. Men disappear out here from time to time."

He said as he walked away, "Let it be known that Huck may

have rustled some Hudnall stock. You won't have to say anything more."

He removed his hat and rubbed his hand over his big bald head. Tersely he said, "I ain't proud of you boys."

Six

LAD'S FIRST DAY on the McIntire Ranch began with disaster. The cowboys assembled at the big corral after the kid who worked as the wrangler brought in some fifty horses, excited as a result of their wild run from the pasture. They swirled around in clouds of dust and dirt clods, kicking at one another, squealing and snorting.

The cowboys sauntered into their midst, with the horses wheeling and charging left and right. One after another, the cowboys roped their choices.

"I'm gonna git old Dan this mornin'," Ramsel hollered, flicking his loop deftly around the head of a plunging buckskin.

Lad tried several times but failed in his attempts. Pucker came over to help him. He whipped out a wide loop which he swung from one side to the other, holding the rope down low, almost letting it touch the ground. He floated it backhanded over the head of a big dun that rushed by, pulled the rope behind his hips, grasped it firmly on both sides as he sat back on it, dug in his heels, and snapped the horse around. Then, moving down the rope hand over hand, he slid the noose up high on the horse's neck. The animal, aware that the time for play had passed, passively followed Pucker as he turned toward the saddle shed.

Lad stood by as Pucker slid a bridle on the horse's head, forced the bit past bared teeth after a momentary struggle, and fastened the straps.

"This here is Happy," he said to Lad. "Don't know how he come by that name. He has a temper now and again, but as a rule is fine."

He flipped a worn saddle blanket on the horse's back, then swung a heavy saddle up, the stirrups and leather flinging through the air and slamming solidly in place. Soon Pucker had the long leather belt through the cinch strap, yanked hard on it, jammed a knee in

Happy's belly so he wouldn't swell up, and in seconds the cinch, made of multiple strands of thin rope, had been fastened. "Found you a better saddle than the one you rode from town," he commented, moving back from the horse but still holding the reins.

"If you like, I'll top him off for you. Happy ain't been rode much lately."

Lad unwisely declined. He took the reins, stepped into the saddle, and his career as a cowboy began. Happy danced six or seven steps, jumped sideways, flattened his ears, jammed his head between his front legs, and went all to pieces. Lad would have been thrown instantly if Happy hadn't kept jumping back under him. As it was, he lasted some ten or fifteen seconds before cartwheeling off and landing on his back.

The cowboys stood or hunkered down, watching. They passively observed as Lad got thrown a second time.

He recovered slowly and rose to his hands and knees, head hanging down. Then he staggered upright, ready for another attempt.

Happy reared and flailed with his forehooves, but Lad caught the reins, yanked the horse down, grabbed hold of the saddlehorn, and wrenched himself into the saddle. Happy bowed up into a knot and then leaped high into the air before settling down for some serious bucking. He pitched in high leaps in a straight line across the big corral. For a moment it appeared that the tenderfoot might stay on, but then the horse began sunfishing—twisting in mid-air and landing stiff-legged. In seconds Lad catapulted off and thudded into the worn snubbing post in the center of the pen. He fell in a heap beside it—apparently dead.

The cowboys fell down with laughter at this. They hooted and hollered, never having seen anything as hysterical in their lives.

Happy, although riderless, kept bucking, in the process smashing Lad's hat deep into fresh manure. The hat hung on the hoof of a forefoot momentarily, giving Happy new cause for alarm. The heaving dun careened through the scarred earth of the corral until it flew off. This drew more cheers from the observers.

There had been numerous comments about Lad's brand-new clothes, but almost all had reserved their particular disdain for his stiff-brimmed spotless hat. And it did stand out in contrast to the sweat-stained limp headgear that the others wore—each with a distinctive twisted shape, all with upturned slightly ragged brims. Now the tenderfoot's hat was unrecognizable and looked to the cowboys as if it was almost broken in.

Lad pulled himself up by clinging to the snubbing post. His shirt had been shredded, and abrasions on his chest bled freely. A dark welt colored the side of his face. He managed to limp back to the saddle shed while the cowboys watched him wordlessly, enjoying the show.

Lad drew near to Pucker and said, "Well, if you don't mind topping him off, as you said . . ." On hearing this, the cowboys grinned and chuckled.

The dun had lost his temper completely by now and refused to cooperate. Ramsel managed to catch the reins at last and after a brief battle, seized the horse by the ears, jamming one in his teeth, "earing him down." Lad watched this in astonishment.

Pucker took the reins and, with Ramsel still biting the ear, prepared to mount. When he got his left foot in the stirrup, Ramsel fell away.

Pucker had Happy's head bent around sideways toward his left knee, holding an extremely tight rein as he mounted. By the time he got his right leg over, he'd pulled Happy's head almost back on top of the saddlehorn. Pucker slammed the rowels of his spurs high into Happy's shoulders several times, and after a few jolting efforts on Happy's part, this part of the fun ended.

Lad, badly bruised and shaken, and wondering if every one of his ribs had been broken, took the reins in both hands, pulled the horse's head around as Pucker had, and stepped into the saddle. The big dun backed ten or twelve steps before settling down.

A mixture of raucous comments and a few cheers met this achievement, but most of the men looked disgusted. Lad flushed with embarrassment and didn't look at his catcalling companions.

He hadn't been introduced to more than a few of the seven cowboys who lived with him in the bunkhouse. They had in common a fixed look in their eyes. Most had mustaches, and all had weathered faces, the product of a lifetime spent out of doors.

One picked Lad's manure-begrimed hat from the dirt and dipped it into the horse trough, then cleansed it roughly with his hand. He reshaped it as best he could and handed it wordlessly back to its owner.

Happy edged sideways away from the hat as Lad reached down for it. He put it on his head, feeling cool rivulets run down his face, and followed the others out of the corral, heading toward the northern horizon.

Lad stayed close by Boots Ramsel and Jim Pucker through the day. He noticed that Pucker wore spurs with large dull rowels attached to downturned short shanks, but Ramsel dispensed with these, favoring instead a quirt which hung ready for use by a loop around his saddlehorn. Both had long coiled ropes attached to the pommels of their saddles, and oiled canvas slickers securely tied behind the cantle with long leather tie strings affixed to the back jockey.

They teased him constantly but in a friendly way. Evidently they'd been appointed by McIntire to be responsible for the greenhorn. He hadn't met the ranch owner as yet except for the brief encounter when he'd first arrived.

"The boss's family came back last Thursday," Ramsel observed. "They been gone for almost two years; went to Vicksburg, Mississippi, where they used to live. So Mad John's stayin' at home today. He'd ordinarily be with us. Anyway, he said to apologize to you for his lack of hospitality, it's just that he's getting reacquainted with his wife and daughter. By the way, you're supposed to have supper with them tonight."

Lad contemplated this information. He felt a slight shyness at the news he'd been given. "Were you on the ranch when they lived here before?"

"Lord, yes. Pucker and I rode out here lookin' for work four years ago, and haven't any more ambition than to be at the first job we could find."

"How old is the daughter?"

Ramsel said, "Don't start gettin' any ideas about courtin' that gal. Her mama's got strong feelin's about cowboys; that's why she took her away from Texas. But, answering your question, she'd be about your age, I guess."

All the men split into small groups, heading out through ravines and over hills. Today they'd simply try to get a count on the stock that lay in this section of the ranch.

The spring roundup had already taken place—Lad soon learned that he'd missed that big event. After the harsh winter every year, the cowboys from many ranches would assemble, each outfit served by its own chuckwagon. They'd go out together and sweep through hundreds of miles of prairie, gathering stock that had scattered in the icy winds that swept down all the way from Canada, over the Great

Plains, and on through the Panhandle of Texas into the western part of the state.

Each spring the widespread wandering groups of cattle would be gathered into a giant herd. Then, with galloping horsemen around the perimeter waving coiled ropes and hollering to hold them together, other cowboys on cutting horses would separate the stock by brands. This process took time, and frequently the segregated steers and cows and calves and a few great-shouldered bulls would get mixed up again, requiring a repetition of the work. But finally each ranch's cattle were cut out, the assembled herd dividing into half a dozen smaller herds that were driven back to their respective ranges.

The cowboys who took part came from as far west as the Pecos, from as far north as the upper branch of the North Concho. Some came from the Devil's River area. Over the years, the men became well acquainted with one another and, although this annual ordeal involved brutal fourteen-hour workdays, they enjoyed it.

In the wild chases through the shinnery, scrub oaks, and underbrush, invariably a horse or two might go down. Each morning the men roped their mounts from the remuda held by their wrangler, and had their daily rodeo as horses not ridden much during the winter put up violent protests. As a result, broken arms and ribs and collarbones were not uncommon. A few fights added to the injuries. Noses and eyes showed insults. Bruises, sprains, and backaches were to be expected. This was the finest time of the year, Pucker and Ramsel assured Lad, and it was a damn shame he had missed it.

Lad drew a deep sigh of relief that he had.

They rode at least thirty miles that day by fits and starts, occasionally spotting a little bunch of spotted Mexican cattle mixed with a few longhorns. When this occurred Pucker made a quick count and wrote it down with a short lead pencil in the tally book he kept in his shirt pocket. He spoke of the foreman, recovering at the moment from a broken leg back at the bunkhouse, a man named Lew Cutter.

"Cutter thinks a noonday meal is for sissies. He does permit us sometimes to stop while we knife open a can of tomatoes which, by the way, is what we'll have to do today. Anyway, what brought him to mind is that he follows the old way when it comes to keepin' count of cattle. He has a tally string tied to his saddlehorn, and he slips a knot at every even hundred. Naturally, usin' that system, he has to keep a lot in his head, so on days when we're gittin' a count, he don't talk at all. One thing I learned early was never to say a damn word while he was starin' at the stock with his hand on that tally string. It was as much as your life was worth to interfere with his concentration. Old Cutter does have a temper." He smiled with amusement at some memory.

Pucker added, "I knew a Meskin once who kept his tally with ten pebbles. Kept them in one hand and shiftin' a pebble to the other on even hundreds."

Ramsel said, "It really don't matter except to the owners. If we find seven thousand or nine thousand head on this part of the range in the next four or five months, they'll just figure that the rest were out of sight or had moved on. But this way they keep us busy."

Jap Turner, a spindly little man with badly bowed legs—and squinty eyes which gave rise to his name—loped over to them. "We're close to Bat Cave. Reckon we should show it to the boy?"

Pucker drew his horse to a stop. "Without the boss here to fuss, and with Cutter down with a broke leg, there's no one to tell us we can't have a little fun if we like." The others agreed with this reasoning.

Without another word they wheeled about and headed northeast. On the way they had to descend single file into a steep arroyo. They made their way through the rock-strewn draw, and up the other side. Soon they could make out a long flat hill, what the men called a butte. It had great stones forming the rimrock lining its crest. It stood before three other hills which due to their distance looked blue.

"The cave's in the skirts of that butte," Jap Turner told Lad.

After riding for half an hour they entered a fold in the uneven land. The horses held their heads down low as the men rode with loose reins, letting them pick their way through rocks and a surprising array of different kinds of cactus.

Ramsel, in answer to Lad's questions, identified some of these, pointing out tasajilla, soto, and catclaw. "That over yonder is what we call stick cactus; the Meskins' name for it is corodencia, I think. And this on the other side is cholla." He pointed to his right and said, "That's Spanish dagger, what the Meskins call lechequilla, I believe. Of course, most of what we have is prickly pear, and I expect there's a dozen varieties of it. I swear, one of these days the prickly pear's goin' to take over this country. That and the damned mesquite."

Ramsel smiled. "Things with fangs and thorns seem to do best out here. It's a damn shame there's no market for 'em."

They came to a grassy flat and decided to make a midday stop for their meal. Slamming pocketknives into dented tomato cans and sawing irregular holes in the tops, they managed to extract their first course. With no more than hardtack as added sustenance, washed down with water from canteens, the lunch didn't take a great deal of time.

Nonetheless, they all leaned back to rest afterward to allow their digestion time to function. During this lull, Ramsel said, "Some of us ran across Bat Cave—that's a name we gave it—while out on a roundup a few years back. We'd camped not far from here. During those days this part of the ranch was overrun by coyotes, and they'd drive you crazy at night. The coyotes got to bayin' at the moon, and it's a right scary sound. You'd hear one makin' that high-pitched caterwaulin' at one side, then another would join in off to the other. We were sittin' around the fire, and their howlin' just kept on— sounded like there must a'been around twenty or so of 'em out in the dark. Pucker said, 'I never heard of men bein' attacked by coyotes,' and I said, 'Well, there's always a first time.' And old Pucker just snarled at me, the way he does sometimes. Later on they kept wakin' him up and he got mad."

Ramsel began to chuckle. "So Pucker jumped up and chunked a boot out into the dark past the campfire's light, tryin' to scare 'em off. Well, they must've drug that boot off, for when daybreak came, we never found it.

"Anyway," Ramsel continued, "it was early that next morning, a clear day without a cloud in the sky, when all of a sudden we saw what looked like rain—the way it looks in the distance, with shades of gray comin' down at an angle. But it made no sense at all on a clear day like that, so Jap and Pucker and I rode over toward it. As we got closer we realized that what we'd seen wasn't rain at all, but a cloud of bats comin' back after a night they'd spent outside feedin' on insects. We saw *millions* of bats," he said emphatically.

The four men rose and began walking uphill. "It's not far," Ramsel said, gasping for breath from the climb. Like most cowboys, he rarely walked for fifty yards if he had a horse available, and he was far from being in good condition.

They stopped while Jap stomped on some dead brush. He picked up a branch, knocked small growths from it, and then nodded with satisfaction. "We'll need a torch once we git inside," he explained to Lad. He tied a rag which he'd brought from his saddlebag to one end of the crooked greasewood stick, and said, "We're nearly there."

The men walked past a large boulder and a moment later they reached a great jagged hole, a yawning crater some thirty feet across. They went down into it, holding on to rocks to keep from losing their balance as they slid on loose rocks and sand until they reached the first level. At the far end they saw a large black, forbidding opening and made their way toward it single file.

"When we discovered this, it took us a spell before we worked up the nerve to explore it," Jap said. "I recall Pucker sayin' that it looked to him like the front door to hell. But we've clambered into it several times since and haven't come across any devils so far."

"We weren't all that brave," Ramsel remarked. "As I recall, we let you down with a rope tied around you. Then we put two ropes together so you could get clear to the bottom, and after about half a day, we figured it was safe."

Jap Turner grinned as he said, "My daddy didn't raise no damn fool. But I'll admit that first time was a bit hairy." To Lad he said, "Watch your step—the first part is kindly steep. It's sort of a big chimbly."

"Chimbly?" Lad repeated, eyebrows raised.

Pucker muttered, "Jap ain't educated. He means 'chimney.'"

Lad nodded.

Jap stopped at the rocky entrance to Bat Cave and sat at the edge of the hole for a moment before cautiously sliding down it. He checked his rate of descent with his bootheels and by holding on to rocks at the sides of the steeply angled shaft.

The others followed his example, the ones below complaining at the showers of fine gravel and dust that those above them dislodged. During this entire time, Pucker's clear voice sounded heartfelt and unusually profane complaints, pausing only when it became necessary to breathe.

The channel made various turns, and their boots kept slipping as they made their way down.

On reaching the bottom, Lad saw it was a narrow passageway. At the point where it widened, Jap Turner waited for them. He managed to light a rag on the end of the greasewood branch and held this flare high over his head.

The smell of smoke mixed with a strange musty odor, one unlike any in Lad's experience. And then he became conscious of something else: the encrusted floor crunched and rustled beneath his feet. The odd feathery accumulation at places reached his ankles.

"The first time we was here," Jap said, "old Pucker had to walk on one boot and one sock foot, since the coyotes had drug away the boot he'd chunked at 'em. Then all of a sudden he commenced to cuss and raise all manner of hell about what he was walkin' in."

Ramsel's deep laugh rumbled, echoing faintly back a moment later.

Lad stared up as they reached the more or less level floor of a large cave. He'd been in caverns in Virginia, but had never seen anything like this. In the flickering torchlight he saw innumerable weeping long tendrils, slender pointed cones, stalactites, hanging from the cave's rough ceiling. As though striving to meet them, stalagmites rose from the rocky floor, looking slightly wet. Their thick rounded ends shone with reflections of the pale yellow flames.

With an indrawn breath of horror he saw the wrinkled, wing-folded, leathery bodies of countless bats hanging head down from the walls and upper surfaces of the cavern. And he realized he was walking on bat droppings that had accumulated over the centuries.

"Let's show him the bottomless pit, Jap," Pucker said.

Their guide raised his torch and inched toward the back of the absolute darkness that seemed to curve just beyond the glimmering rays. Shadows blended with light from the flames, changing the appearance of the cavern from one second to the next.

"Over here," Jap called. "Watch your step."

The other three shuffled behind him, moving cautiously on the uncertain footing, treading on brittle, powdery layers mixed with stones and debris and dust from the ages. Then they stood at the crumbling edge of a sheer drop, gazed over it, and saw total blackness.

Several minutes passed before Pucker picked up a large rock and pitched it over the side. They stood in the uncanny silence of the underground cave, surrounded by foul-smelling air, and at last they heard a faint splash.

"There's an underground river down there, by God," said Jap. "No doubt about it. If they was only some way to pump it out, we could keep more stock out here. As it is, the cattle stay close enough to the creeks to git to water once a day, and most of the land this far away don't get grazed."

"Jap says he plans to sell this information," Pucker said.

"Does Mr. McIntire know?" Lad asked.

"We never told him," Jap said. "And don't you go discussin' it neither. One of these days Pucker and Ramsel and I are goin' to be rich men because of this water."

The two men he named began laughing. Ramsel said, "That's a pipe dream, Jap. Besides, if you was rich, your gold pieces would soon go into the pockets of bartenders and whores in San Angelo."

Seven

BATTERED BY THE DAY, Lad stood in the corral and stripped off all his clothes, ignoring the curious horses that stared at him. He climbed into a big stone trough, and winced as moisture entered the abrasions along his ribs. Sighing with relief, he sat in the cool water, splashing about, and then leaned against the edge, putting his face against a smooth stone, feeling the leftover warmth of the sun. He emerged dripping wet and flicked off the water as best he could with open hands.

Lad put on clean underwear and the clothes he'd brought from Virginia: a soft white shirt woven of linen and long stapled cotton, and a pair of gray lightweight wool trousers. After fitting a thin black leather belt around his waist, he leaned against a cedar post of the corral's fence while he pulled on dark socks and slid soft leather English shoes on his feet.

Chickens clucked in the henhouse near the barn, and swallows swept through the last light of evening. A fat black and white Scotch terrier trotted by, swollen dugs wagging as she proceeded slightly on the bias, followed by five clumsy puppies. The bunkhouse had been built using crude pier and beam construction. It crouched a foot off the earth, and the dogs went under it.

Lad wrapped his discarded dirty clothing into a bundle, put this under one arm, and followed them. Bending down, he could make out the long-suffering mother on her side with the greedy puppies crowding against one another, squirming and blindly rooting about as they sought their supper.

He felt his own stomach growling, and entered the bunkhouse. The men fell silent at his changed appearance. As he dropped off the grimy clump of clothing on his cot and turned to leave, the cowboys made wry comments about his clean clothes, adding scathing remarks concerning anyone who'd toady up to the boss. Lad paid no attention, not really hearing them. He could think of little other than finding something to eat.

Lad walked from the bunkhouse toward the two-story dwelling which sat on a rise overlooking the pens, corrals, barn, and outbuildings. The imposing frame house, painted light gray with dark green shutters at the windows, had a wide veranda across the front and down one side. A neat white picket fence protected the yard from livestock. Lad paused, feeling a fleeting shyness about meeting strangers and particular apprehension about the reception he might receive from Mad John McIntire. In his mind's eye he saw the way the kilted old man had looked, marching down from the heights with his bagpipes.

He trudged up the slope, went through the gate of the picket fence, and walked on flagstones to the steps. He ascended them, then crossed the porch to the front door. As he raised his hand to knock, it opened.

Mad John McIntire summoned his guest into the house without uttering a word of welcome. The old man had a grizzled mustache and a neatly trimmed beard with faded red shadows in its grayness. His almost completely white hair, thinning on top, still grew luxuriously over his ears and behind his head where it hung over his collar. Creases ran down beside his mouth from either side of his hawklike nose. He wore an open shirt and an old set of trousers tucked into high-topped cowboy boots with short loops flopping down on each side.

"My wife and daughter will be down shortly," McIntire said in an accent that hinted of his Scottish heritage. He motioned toward a chair and asked, "Could I prepare you a drink?"

Lad declined but his host ignored him. He said, "This is Scotch whiskey, and there's nothing like it in all the world. I've only got twelve bottles left, but there's a keg aging in my gun closet."

The hot whiskey burned its way down to Lad's empty stomach. He smelled its unforgettable smoky aroma, then leaned back in his chair, allowing the warmth to spread. Dazed by fatigue, he managed to pass on his father's best wishes.

"There was a considerable amount of confusion around here after you arrived," McIntire said, apparently as a halfhearted apology for not having seen his guest sooner.

An embarrassing silence followed. The two sat in the stiff living room, a place that gave Lad the impression that it saw little use. He waited for his host to speak, looking at yellow flickers from candles reflecting on their glasses.

The old man looked lost in melancholy as he held his drink, staring into it. Without preamble he said, "I rarely play the pipes anymore. I learned them as a boy before we came to this country in the early fifties."

He skipped from one topic to another. He spoke of his life growing up near Utica, Mississippi, before they moved to "the new place not far from Vicksburg." Moments later he fell into a tale about the war.

Lad had often heard his father's friends do this, constantly returning to that obsessive topic. Whenever men who'd served in the conflict sat together, they'd invariably relive those few years that had been so very much more vivid than all the decades lived before or after them.

"What was left of our company joined with Lee's men. We figured each day might be our last, and this went on for all those long, long months during the siege of Petersburg. That came after the fall of Richmond, and it was as close to hell as the eyes of man have ever seen. Some nights, when we'd been under cannon fire all day and with the shells still falling, I'd play my bagpipes, and all our boys would cheer. I carried the damned things through rain and snow, strapped on my pack, for nigh onto five years. Can you believe a sane man would do such a foolish thing?

"Grant's army shelled us constantly, and finally our lines began to break. We couldn't get supplies—for the Yanks cut the railroad lines going west—and then their cavalry began to seal off our lines of retreat. That's when we fought our way clear. Lee planned to join with General Johnston's troops out to the west. After that we'd wheel about and face the enemy. Lee knew the terrain, the roads and trails and rivers. He knew the woods. He'd fought long odds so often before, and we thought he could bring it off at least one more time.

"God, how we tried. We fought all day and night and all the next day—with bluecoats coming at us on all sides. The scouts came in, and it was clear the Yanks had us outnumbered ten to one. We passed through a little community, I seem to recall it had a girl's name, Amelia, I think it was, and at the creek on the far side of it we could hardly see for the smoke from our rifles and theirs. By then we had lads dropping their weapons and collapsing from exhaustion. None who survived will ever forget the experience. When we got together later we called that 'the time we finally spent poor Dixie's bottom dollar.' "

He touched his waist on the right side and looked down. "I took a bullet in my side and thought at first I was dying. It knocked me flat, and as I lay there with my hand on it, feeling the hotness, I realized the bullet had passed clear through. You can't imagine how it bled. Blood ran down and filled my boot clear to the top when a man helped me to my feet. We made it to cover and lay down behind some fallen trees. The air was black with smoke and shells and bullets, and I could feel the life draining out of me. Later I thought back, and considered it a rare and strange thing, for I'd gone through the war without a scratch, through all those years of skirmishes and battles, until then. There we were, not all that far from Appomattox Court House, and I'd been hit one day before the war ended.

"Your father and I'd seen a lot together. He was the best friend I ever had, and he carried me home with him, back to your place on the James River. It took months before I got my strength back. You were a little tyke then, I doubt that you'd remember anything at all about those times. As I got better, we'd ride on the few Thoroughbreds that your family had managed to keep hidden in the woods—all through the war.

"We traveled on one occasion some thirty miles or so to Williamsburgh and passed the night at Carter's Grove. The next day on the way back we stopped at Shirley Plantation, where General Lee had been raised as a youngster."

He examined his visitor carefully in the light that fell from the candles in the brass candelabra on the oak table between their chairs. "You don't favor your father. Must take after your mother. Was she from Tidewater stock too?"

"Yes, sir, she was his second cousin."

"I know about all that inbreeding in your world, and can't say I approve of it, although God knows it doesn't appear to hurt horseflesh."

A vivacious lady clad in rustling green taffeta came down the stairs, followed by a girl in a dark blue linen dress with ivory buttons lining its front. A white lace collar framed her face. She had dark hair and eyes which she kept downcast.

Both men rose to their feet while the old gentleman said with some pride, "May I present Mrs. McIntire—and this is my daughter, Beth."

Mrs. McIntire, an elegant stick-thin woman with great energy, showed considerable interest in their guest. She was immediately taken by his easy manners, his soft Virginia accent, and by his appearance. She spoke of their dreadful journey from Vicksburg down the Mississippi to New Orleans, and then by boat to Galveston. From that point on the trip had been one horror after another, she exclaimed. They finally arrived without their luggage, which she sincerely hoped would follow by freight wagon.

"Vicksburg wasn't at all as I'd remembered," she said. "Before the late unpleasantness we spent so much time planning parties—and going to them. There were balls and picnics and things like that all the time. Well, that's gone forever. All the men are *working* now—can you imagine? It was a great disappointment to me, for I had such plans for Beth."

Later they moved to a long mahogany table in the dining room where an old black woman named Rose served them. She and her husband, Ludlow Tate, lived in the small shack behind the main house. "Don't know what we'd do without them," McIntire and his wife agreed.

Tonight they dined on leg of lamb with mint jelly, lima beans cooked with ham hocks, hominy grits, and thin biscuits which steamed when broken apart. Lad fell silent as the butter was passed, listening to the McIntires' comments on the minor events of their day. He hadn't had a meal like this in a very long time and gave it his full attention.

"My," Miss Ellen remarked, "but I do love to see a young man with an appetite like yours."

Beth kept taking quick looks at him from under lowered lids. Once their eyes met and her face flushed.

McIntire talked of a cattle buyer he'd seen the week before, and spoke of a Mexican rancher who kept inviting him to his spread near Durango. "But I'm too old for lengthy travel," he said.

Abruptly he pushed his plate away and straightened in his chair. Looking at Lad, he said, "You're not suited for life on a ranch. Your hands are as soft as a girl's—you've never really worked a day in your life."

Stung by the words, Lad stiffened.

McIntire ignored the effect of his comments. "I heard about your being thrown time and again this morning—until Jim Pucker took the starch out of your cow pony and got him settled down." The older man shrugged. "I don't say you couldn't learn how to cowboy, but you've come to it late in life. You've been educated to be a gentleman, and a gentleman these days is as useless as a tit on a boar hog. From what I read in your father's letter, you didn't do a very good job of learning your manners in that fancy school. Got kicked out for foolishness, card playing and gambling and the like, is what I understand. Now, I can't take that seriously; it certainly doesn't sound like the sort of thing that would cause offense out here in Texas. But my old friend felt it reflected on the family's honor, and it enraged him. You know far better than I how precious the idea of honor is to him."

"Mr. McIntire," his wife said emphatically, "this is our guest! I'm mortified that you'd speak to him that way." She glared at her husband. Her daughter looked disconcerted.

"Don't mistake me," McIntire said to Lad. "You're more than welcome to spend all the time you like here on the ranch. But if you're thinking of finding a new profession, I can't think of anything for which you're less suited. It strikes me that in fairness I should be honest with you."

Lad didn't know what to say. Fortunately, he didn't have to for McIntire rose from the table. He put his hand on Lad's shoulder, and the gesture took some of the sting from the things he'd said. "You're a fine-looking boy and must know how flattered I am to be of some use to your family." With that, he bowed slightly to his wife and daughter and departed. They heard his bootheels thudding on the stairs as he went to his bedroom.

"I can't imagine what came over Papa," Beth declared.

"He hasn't changed one whit," her mother snapped. Then she put her hand to her head. "I'm awfully sorry, Mr. Trimble, but I feel faint." With that she rushed toward the stairs and left the two young people alone.

Lad moved from the table. "I think I better leave."

"Please, don't go, not for a little anyway. Let me pour you another drink—I'm told it's good for the digestion."

Lad smiled as she led him back to the living room. He accepted the glass of Scotch which she put beside him and sipped from it.

Beth had seemed shy during dinner, but without the constraints put on her by her parents, she relaxed. Soon she was regaling Lad with stories of her mother's disappointments in Vicksburg. As she spoke he gathered that family members and close acquaintances called Beth's mother Miss Ellen, and Miss Ellen had decided she couldn't bear living alone on the ranch any longer after so many years of what she considered privation. And so she took her daughter with her back to Vicksburg where, as the daughter of Senator Thomas Gaines, she had enjoyed a privileged life.

"Mama had simply been miserable out here," Beth said, and explained that homesickness caused her to imagine things would once again be in Mississippi as they had been during prewar years. But as soon as she arrived, the pain of postwar reality struck her.

"We stayed in a large white house on what was left of the Gaines plantation, and there were a great many other relatives living there. We had no servants except for Rose." She related how the men worked in the fields, the women cooked and washed. Survival had been their primary concern for years, and they'd made progress. Gradually things improved. But their former way of life remained a distant memory.

"Mama wrote home to say we'd come back, but that Papa had to promise to build a house in town for us sometime. So he bought some property far enough west of the rough part of town but close enough so we could shop in the stores whenever we chose, and we could go to church. But now that we've moved back, he says that the bottom has fallen out of the cattle business and he hasn't any idea when he'll be able to build."

She sighed. "I don't care as much as Mama does about living in town, but I'd like at least to visit now and then. The important thing is to see different people, to talk to other women and girls."

"And men?"

She grinned. "Oh yes. There must be ten or twenty men in San Angelo for every unattached lady—not counting the officers at Fort Concho—so I'll have my choice of suitors. If I'm really lucky I may meet one who can both read and write."

"I'm sure you'll find many gentlemen callers."

She laughed good-naturedly.

The two continued in this vein for half an hour and then Lad said good night.

She followed him as he left, and for a few moments they stood together in the fenced yard before the house. They looked up at the moonless sky and saw millions of brilliant, glittering stars.

"I've never seen night skies like those out here," Lad said.

"I suppose it's because the air's so dry, although I couldn't say. But the stars aren't like this anywhere else I've ever been." She moved closer. "I'm not like Mama—I love it in Texas."

He felt slightly dizzy from the effects of the day and the whiskey. "I'm tired."

"I could tell you were." Beth turned toward him, brushing as if accidentally against his arm. She seemed to expect something from him, some word or gesture.

Awkwardly he backed a step away. "I hope we have the chance to talk again soon."

"I do too, Mr. Trimble." With that Beth turned and fled into the house.

Lad walked in the moonless night along the path leading from the gate down the long slope toward the bunkhouse. A warm glow filled him as he thought of Beth. Mixed with this was a sense of shame and confusion. During recent nights he'd had impossible fantasies which tortured him. His head had filled unwillingly with thoughts of Mattie Hudnall, the girl he'd seen in the store, the one with full lips, high cheekbones, and long blonde hair. He had a quick vision of how she'd stared at him with those pale green eyes and then smiled, the dimple on her left cheek deepening. He hadn't been able to take his eyes from her thin, tight blouse outlining small, high breasts.

The contrast between Mattie and Beth was so sharp that he wondered how he could think of them at the same time. Chagrined, he stumbled into the bunkhouse, feeling his way along carefully in the darkness, through the sounds of a few groans and of snoring, to his narrow hard cot. He lay down and only moments later sank into exhausted sleep.

Eight

MATTIE SAT ALONE at the kitchen table, drinking coffee from a chipped cup. She wore an old print dress, washed so often that its pattern barely showed. The black stove behind her had a smoke-darkened pot of coffee and a large iron kettle of frijoles. Only rarely was either of these empty. On occasion she would absently add coffee grounds and water to one and dry frijole beans and peppers to the other.

She heard a kid goat shriek as Ramón wired his hind legs to the crosspiece between two cedar posts near the barn. Then came a gargling noise and she knew his throat had been cut. They'd have cabrito tonight. She'd bake it the way the boys liked it, with the outside crisp and slightly burned and the inside pink and moist. She didn't mind cooking; it kept her from thinking of Hudnall.

She still remembered vividly when her father had been forced off his small farm. The eldest of the children, she'd taken care of her sisters after her mother's death. That day she helped load the old wagon, wondering where they'd gotten the big new mule. On the way east they moved off the trail and stopped on Hudnall's ranch.

She saw her father thank Hudnall for the mule, then pocket some money handed him. And then he asked her to get down from the wagon.

She left her three small sisters behind and walked uncertainly toward the gaunt, bent form of her father and the big-bellied broad-shouldered man who stood next to him. He had thick lips and looked at her intently, causing her to drop her eyes. When she first saw him she knew she'd seen him before. He'd come to their farm and talked to her father. She recalled the way he'd stared at her as she hurried past him on the way to the shelter of their small ramshackle house.

"She's a good girl, Mattie is. You say you'll take good care of her?"

The two talked for five or ten minutes as the realization gradually came to her that she was being left behind. Fearful, she started to run, but her father grasped her sleeve and pulled her back.

"You're near about full growed, Mattie. It's time you thought of your future. Mr. Hudnall here is goin' to be your husband."

A few months later a cowboy brought an itinerant preacher onto the ranch, and a brief wedding ceremony followed. But she'd been in Hudnall's bed from the first night under his roof. Even in the far wing of the house, Hudnall's sons would have heard her cries that night. She grimaced, thinking she'd probably sounded much like the kid goat she'd just heard. And she'd been every bit as helpless.

His three sons didn't speak to her at all except for an occasional shouted order or oath. At these times, she'd be dismissed as Hudnall got them together and thundered at them. Once Loftin, the eldest of the three boys, said, "Hell, Papa, we don't mind your havin' a woman, that's understandable for any man. But did you have to *marry* her?" Then Hudnall's curses made the air blue.

Only a month ago, she had heard Hudnall bellowing, "I hadn't intended to leave her a damn cent, but after the way you boys been actin', I've had the lawyer draw up a will, and she's to get *half* of everything I own when I die—which won't be for one hell of a long time. I ordered that will drawn up so as to teach you boys a lesson. You're to show your respect for me by mindin' your manners around her. Besides, the day will come when you may be goin' to her, hat in hand, for a loan." She heard Hudnall's raucous laughter and the mutinous murmurs from his sons.

That was the first she'd heard of the will—a few days after Hudnall had beaten her in the street in San Angelo in front of everybody. She didn't know why the public battering should have bothered her so, since he whipped her regularly in private. But it did.

She moved to the open window, noting the light green tender new leaves on the mesquites. A soft warm breeze blew through her hair. Spring had come. A thrill began in the pit of her stomach at the unaccustomed thought: Someday I'm going to be *rich*. She couldn't get used to the idea.

Since she'd overheard the conversation she'd changed her ways with Hudnall, trying to respond to his nightly embraces in spite of her revulsion. He would never know how she despised him, how his touch repulsed her. Thank God, she said to herself, he's still off on his trip. He'd been gone now for three weeks.

The cowboys came into view in the distance, dry dust clouds drifting behind their horses. She stood at the front door and squinted west into the low sun, but couldn't see Hudnall's thick form in their midst. As they drew nearer she sighed with relief. One more night without him.

She went to the bedroom and combed her hair, staring at her face in the speckled mirror. She thought again of the soft-spoken young man she'd seen in that store, the one with the slightly curly dark hair and the courteous manners. In all her life she'd never seen a man like that. And she could tell instantly that she attracted him. She stretched her arms over her head, then turned toward the kitchen. Ramón by now would have butchered the kid goat, and it was time to prepare supper.

Later Loftin came to the house. "Hobie and Julius," he said, referring to his brothers, "been actin' so damn contrary that none of us can stand bein' around 'em no more. I told 'em they'd been too long without a woman and sent those boys off to Early Able's saloon in San Angelo. His sign says he's got dancin' girls, but I never seen one of 'em come downstairs and dance with nobody." Loftin laughed at his joke.

"I'll have your supper ready in just a little."

Loftin pitched his hat into a corner and unbuckled his gunbelt. After hanging this on a peg, he moved behind her. "Mattie," he said softly, "this here is the first time we'll have the house to ourselves. I got the same problem as Hobie and Julius, and I figure that by now you must feel the same way as I do. A married woman is used to it regular—and you been doin' without."

"Don't talk that way."

He stood directly behind her as she faced the stove, and put both arms around her waist, pulling her body against his.

She stamped her heel on his instep and broke free. Loftin's face twisted with pain and surprise. He leaned over to touch his injured foot and then straightened, scowling darkly at her.

Calmly she said, "Am I goin' to have to hit you with this poker?" She reached to one side and grasped the smoke-blackened iron rod used to stir the coals and kindling wood in the stove.

He moved quickly, seizing the poker and wrenching it from her hand, then threw it to one side. The steel rang sharply against the wooden floor.

Mattie backed against the wall and Loftin followed. He placed an arm on either side of her and shoved his knee between her legs.

"Don't," she said, her voice muffled.

"Now, honey, it's time you learned what a *young* man is like."

The door to the kitchen—which had been open—slammed shut explosively. Loftin whirled to find the hulking figure of Dee Hudnall standing ten feet away, his face white with rage.

Loftin instinctively backed away. "I was just teasin' her, Pa. We're always horsin' around, ain't that right, Mattie?" His voice shook.

Hudnall grated out his words. "I heard every word you said." His eyes widened until the whites showed, as he screamed, "I know *exactly* what you had in mind, you stupid little bastard!" He turned toward Mattie, eyes ablaze.

"You led him on. I know you did. That's how you women are—never content with one man, always flirtin'—always causin' trouble."

"It—it ain't true," she stammered.

He slapped her face and she fell sideways, breaking her fall by grasping a chair but then sliding to the floor.

"Loftin, you git off this ranch. I killed Elzie Huck for takin' a calf, and you've set out to take my wife. Son or not, I won't stand for that." His chest rose and fell as his breathing labored. "I'm tryin' to control myself." He seemed unable to continue, but regained his composure although his voice shook with emotion. "I know I'd regret killin' my own flesh and blood. *Git,* I said, and stay out of my sight till I send for you—if I ever do. Go to the South Camp, but before you leave, tell me one thing. Have you had your way with her?"

"God no, Pa. I told you we was just foolin' around."

"Have either of the other boys?"

"No, sir, none of us would even think of such a thing. I swear . . ." His words trailed off as Hudnall advanced on him.

"I'm on my way, Pa. I'll stay at the South Camp, but please believe me."

He grabbed his hat and gunbelt and bolted from the house.

Hudnall jerked his head toward the bedroom. "Mattie, you git in there. You know what has to be done."

"I didn't lead him on. I'll put my hand on the Bible and swear it."

He followed her into their quarters. "Don't lie—or I'll git even madder."

Hudnall deliberately stripped her as she waited dumbly, knowing what would happen. When she stood naked before him, he pulled off his wide leather belt.

"Bend over that chair," he said hoarsely.

As though hypnotized, she did as he directed. She put both hands around the arm of the chair, and clutched it so tightly that her knuckles turned white. With eyes shut tight, looking into darkness, she waited. And then the pain was so intense she thought she'd faint.

Hudnall lashed her buttocks until they bled. She fell writhing on the floor, and he hit her legs and then her back. She didn't scream or cry out. Not once. At each blow her breath hissed between her clenched teeth.

Leaning over, Hudnall rasped, "You know I can't stand the thought of you with any other man—but most of all, *not with my sons.*"

He growled, "Go clean yourself up."

She put on a robe and went outside to the windmill. The short wooden tower held turning wooden blades, and she heard the groaning sound the sucker rod made as it went up and down. Leather pads brought water up to the tank. She opened a tap and washed her face. Mindless of cowboys who might be watching in the deepening twilight, she raised the robe and started to wash her wounds, but it hurt too much. She smoothed the robe over her legs, washed her face repeatedly, and returned.

"I've made a decision," Hudnall said as she dropped the robe to the floor, oblivious to his presence, and slipped into a clean nightgown. "I can't leave you here when I'm not around. And I have business that requires me to travel. Some time ago I began building a house west of the Concho River in San Angelo, and it'll be ready before long. I won't have you out here with them boys. They're in their bull stages. I should a'known this would happen."

His face twisted and he began to scream at her. "You damn Jezebel! You whorish little bitch! Gittin' in heat, rubbin' up against poor Loftin that way. Hell, of *course* he couldn't keep from gittin' roused. It ain't *his* fault. Of all the women I've known, you're the worst." He ran his tongue over his thick lips, leaving them wet and shining. "Anyway, by God, you're *mine.*"

He breathed heavily, pacing up and down in the room. "Git in the God-damned bed," he rumbled. "Stop crouchin' on the floor holding your knees like you was ten years old. You're a woman now, a grown woman with a *husband.*" He walked over, raised a hand, and she quailed before him.

He backed away, lowering his arm. "Go on, now," he said, his voice suddenly gentle. "You know I love you, Mattie. I have to teach you how to behave, it appears. God knows, your pappy didn't teach you a damn thing. The only sensible thing he ever did in his whole damned life was to sell you to me. I got you for a mule and fifty dollars. And it ain't been much of a bargain neither." His face contorted. "Barren little bitch."

He sat beside her when she crawled into bed and pulled the sheet over her. She was curled into a knot and her shoulders shook silently.

"There, there," he said. "No need to cry. We just got ourselves a situation here that needs correctin'. Here's what we're goin' to do. When I spend time in town I take some rooms at the Nimitz Hotel. There's a little parlor and a bedroom. They serve passable food, and that's where you and I'll be by tomorrow. You'll live in the hotel until the new house in town is finished. When I'm away, Ramón'll stay behind to run errands for you. There's a shed out back where he can sleep."

He sounded like a parent comforting a frightened child who had awakened from a nightmare. Petting her gently as he spoke, he continued in this vein as she sobbed into her pillow. "You'll be safe in the new place. There won't be nothin' on earth to scare you."

His words took on a steely ring as he added, "There won't be no men for you to fool around with neither. When I ain't there to keep an eye on you, Ramón will be. He's the quickest man with a knife I've ever seen, and honey, I've seen quite a few."

In spite of Lad's determination to prove to John McIntire that he could master whatever tasks might face him, he continued to suffer daily setbacks. These began when his horse regularly bucked him off each morning. After riding all day, his back and legs cramped and he could scarcely walk. But after he'd been working on the ranch for six weeks, his endurance improved, his hands and muscles toughened, and he felt better physically than he could ever remember.

The cowboys had, with a certain amount of tolerant teasing, picked out a string of horses in the remuda which he could ride. A few would crowhop a little when first mounted, but he stayed on—a fact that gave him an exaggerated sense of satisfaction. He didn't make excuses, but the fact was that Thoroughbreds, the horses he'd ridden since childhood, didn't pitch. This violent behavior was something he'd never experienced until his arrival on the ranch.

The wrangler had managed the week before to bring in the big gelding the others had laughed about, the one named Claude. The animal had an unusually shiny golden coat and a dark flowing mane and tail. He held his head back on a curved muscular neck, ears forward, eyes alert, nostrils wide. Lad decided this must be the most disdainful horse he'd ever seen. Claude stood over sixteen hands high and rose above the smaller mustangs and quarter horses in the remuda.

"Except for his coloring, he looks like a Morgan," Lad said to Boots Ramsel. "They make fine hunters when they've been trained. You see them in Virginia."

"Claude came from the Three Rail Ranch on the North Concho—which is some south of Virginia," Ramsel said. "None of us ride him since he's so damn unpredictable. Loves to jump anything in sight, be it a fence or a bush—and goes out of his way to find things like that. You can be tryin' to rope a steer, standin' in your stirrups, leanin' forward, and Claude sees a little tree. The next thing you know he takes a leap sideways, bounds into the air, and you're hangin' on to the saddlehorn for dear life—if you haven't fallen off. Once or twice we tried to keep him in the pens so we could work him out of his bad habits, but he jumps right out. So when Pucker and I heard from Annie Tankersley that you'd grown up on jumpers, we decided you and Claude was made for each other. That's even clearer since we've had you around here awhile. Neither one of you is worth a damn around cattle, so by puttin' the two of you together we're not wastin' anything."

He smiled, laugh wrinkles crinkling around his light blue eyes, which shone with amusement as he added, "I said to the wrangler, 'Pete, we got a boy that wants old Claude in his string.'"

Lad managed to get his rope around the big horse's neck, who flung his head high, backing away into a corner. After several unsuccessful efforts, he cinched the saddle in place, put his foot in the stirrup, and mounted. Claude skittered sideways, dancing so lightly that it seemed his feet barely touched the surface of the torn ground of the corral. With his head drawn back by the tight reins Lad held, he fell into a rocking short gallop and moved slowly about in a large circle before responding to Lad's soft voice and to the steady pressure of the bit. He stood at last, pawing at the earth, his nostrils fluttering as he made low unhappy whinnies, obviously not pleased with the situation.

The day was awkward, for, when Lad least expected it, Claude would rear straight up and paw the air, or he'd bolt to one side or the other.

"Claude don't buck much. He ain't impatient, and instead of tryin' to git rid of you all at once, his strategy is to drive you crazy over a period of time. A day on Claude will age you by several months," Pucker said to Lad with a straight face. "Most of us have tried it once or twice." Then, speaking seriously, he added, "But be careful if somethin' comes up and you take him into a run. He can jump sideways so fast he'll go clean out from under you. He'll bust your neck if he can."

That night, with the help of the wrangler and two other cowboys, Lad put a set of rawhide hobbles on the unhappy horse and kept him in the corral. During the next week, after supper, Lad would work with Claude, taking the work as a challenge. He would put a halter on him to which he'd tied a fifteen-foot lead rope. After removing the hobbles, he'd force Claude to move in a wide circle around him. At first a few cowboys watched the exercise, making caustic comments, but then they got bored and left Lad and the big gelding.

During the second week of these exercises, Beth started coming down to watch. She sat on the top rail during the hazy half-light just before night fell, feeling the cooling south breeze, watching Lad and the horse.

Lad now had a slender branch from a sapling which he used to tap the animal to keep him moving in a circle around him. Then he'd have Claude reverse directions. He'd found a cavalry saddle which, while larger than an English saddle, was much lighter than the heavy western ones.

By the third week he began riding the golden horse, using this saddle, taking him in the same circles, around and around. Usually Beth watched. He put up four small fences in the corral, made from boards that lay behind the barn, and then took Claude over these.

He sat erect in the saddle, supporting his weight with his bent legs, feet braced, heels down, in the shortened stirrups. At the low jumps, he'd lean forward and stand in the stirrups. The horse took the barriers gracefully, rocking back into a restricted short gallop due to the pressure of the reins which Lad held low in both hands, just in front of his waist with his elbows firmly at each side.

The following week Lad worked the horse outside the pens, posting to Claude's trot, moving up and down—a sight that Beth hadn't seen before. Pete, the wrangler, observed this and almost choked with laughter. A number of the other cowboys fell into the habit of coming outside to watch.

Ramsel said, "It's a different way—but I've heard of it. The boy has good hands and balance, he has a good seat. In spite of bein' hopeless around a rank bronc, he can handle a horse fine. I've noticed that out in the pasture since the first day."

But Pete snorted, "It may look stylish, but it sure would wear you out if you tried that all day."

On Saturday after their supper, the cowboys hunkered down on their bootheels or sat in chairs they'd pulled outside, watching Lad work with Claude in the lengthening light. With summer's approach, the days had grown longer. The western sky had strange colors across it: pastel shades of pink with vivid orange shadows. In the east the blue turned from blue to a dark velvet lavender shade. A fresh wind cooled them as they watched Lad patiently train the horse.

Lad put Claude into a lope, riding him in a big circle and then in a slow figure eight. From the corner of his eye he noticed a small group of people standing in the front yard of the main house, apparently observing him. John McIntire had told the cowboys earlier in the day that Harley Bragg, the owner of the neighboring ranch which lay some miles to the north, would be his houseguest, and apparently he'd arrived.

Lad felt the energetic action of Claude under him, impatient at being restrained by the bit, big muscles flowing smoothly. On a sudden impulse he swung him toward the two pens next to the corral, but still held the horse in check. Claude pulled his head back, ears pointed forward. As they neared the pens, Lad loosened the reins and touched the animal with his spurs. Claude burst forward, sailing over the fence into the pen. At impact, Lad pulled the reins and kept control. The animal seemed to dance in a restrained, choppy canter, then—released again—took the fence on the other side. The observers cheered as they saw the horse arch over two more fences, clearing the pens then circling about in a rocking lope, toward the big corral with its unusually high rail fences.

Lad gave Claude his head, holding all his weight in the stirrups and leaning forward well over the horse's shoulders as the big golden gelding soared in a steep angle over the six-foot barrier. He regained his seat, clapped his spurs into Claude's sides, and in a cloud of dust rushed toward the other side, flying over it as well, although a back hoof flicked the top rail.

The cowboys outside the bunkhouse began howling and yelling, and even Mad John McIntire could be seen waving his arms excitedly. His wife and daughter hugged one another and cheered. All of them seemed to be astonished by what they'd seen. However, their guest remained slightly away from them, motionless and aloof.

Claude bowed his neck and settled into a high-stepping canter until Lad managed to pull him to a walk. He dismounted, tied him to the hitching rail, and walked up to the low picket fence at the main house where the McIntires awaited him.

"That's quite a show you put on," McIntire said enthusiastically. "I'd like you to meet our neighbor. This is Harley Bragg who owns the Y Bar Ranch that lies to the north of ours. He's ridden most of the day to get here, and will be staying with us for a time."

Bragg appeared to be in his early forties. He wore a dark suit, an open-necked shirt, and western boots. On being introduced to Lad he inclined his head slightly, but didn't offer to shake hands. In the late afternoon light, Lad noticed that he wore thin black leather gloves, which seemed odd. The man had left his hat inside and had long dark hair, worn in the old style, and a bushy black mustache. His eyes looked suspiciously at Lad.

"Miss Ellen tells me you're from Virginia," Bragg said tersely.

"Yes, sir," Lad replied.

At that moment Beth and her mother approached, both talking about how fascinated they'd been to see him on the horse, taking all those jumps through the pens. Beth said, "The cowboys told me that Claude could jump out of the corral, but I didn't believe them. I certainly wouldn't have thought it possible with a man on his back! I swan, I never saw such an amazing sight."

Beth moved close to Lad, excited by the things she'd seen, obviously proud of him. She put her arm through his as they walked toward the house, leaning against him and talking with enthusiasm. Lad glanced over and saw Harley Bragg's face darken as he observed them.

In the parlor, after having served tea and cookies, Miss Ellen babbled contentedly. She told Lad that their neighbor came from old Southern stock. In fact, she said, impressed by the information she passed on, he was related to General Bragg.

"Many's the soldier who died because of the incompetence of your relative, Harley," John McIntire stated. His wife flushed with chagrin at this, but Bragg simply shrugged.

"Errors happen in wartime. There's no general alive who never made a mistake. The only people who avoid them are those who never made decisions—and even they get criticized. For example, look at what people say of General McClellan."

The men strolled away from the women, into the dining room. The dishes had been cleared from their evening meal, and they stood at the Sheraton sideboard which had a cut-glass decanter and glasses in a silver tray with an ornately worked silver piecrust rim around it. Mad John poured glasses of Scotch whiskey for them while he explained that Lad was the son of one of his oldest friends. He and Lad started speaking about ranch affairs, McIntire asking questions and Lad answering as best as he could.

During this exchange, Bragg grew increasingly restive. Lad saw him rise from his chair and pace back and forth. His left arm didn't swing when he walked, and it appeared to be stiff. This wasn't out of the ordinary since the majority of the men Lad had noticed on ranches suffered from a variety of old injuries. At last Bragg interrupted, saying, "Young man, if you'd excuse us, I've come over here to discuss a matter of importance with Mr. McIntire, and I need to do it in private."

Slightly embarrassed, Lad nodded and turned to leave the room. But he had hardly reached the door when Bragg began speaking impatiently. "John, I don't want to beat around the bush. I've come over to seek your permission to call on Miss Beth. I'm a widower, and she's of marriageable age. You'll have to admit, if we put our properties together, we'd have one of the biggest ranches in Texas. Of course, the main reason I want your permission is that I'm greatly taken by Miss Beth. As you know, before she left for her long stay in Mississippi I spent time over here. And I believe that we came to an understanding."

Lad heard a low sound from McIntire, but couldn't make out the words.

Beth ceremoniously led him to a chair in the parlor and sat on the rug at his feet. Her mother's hands worked busily on needlework. She had put on a pair of gold-rimmed glasses for this finely detailed task, and at times looked over their rims at the two young people, smiling at them.

Moments later McIntire came into the room followed by Bragg. He said to his wife, "Mrs. McIntire, Mr. Bragg has done us the honor of asking if he might call on our daughter. He says they have already reached an understanding."

Miss Ellen looked startled, but not nearly as startled as Beth. The girl jumped to her feet in confusion, and stood there, looking helplessly at her mother.

"Well, Beth, this is interesting news," Miss Ellen finally said.

Beth looked wildly about and said, "Papa, there's been some mistake. Mr. Bragg used to come see us when I was sixteen and we'd talk, but not ever about anything serious." She added weakly, "There was never any kind of understanding between us. I'm awfully sorry, Mr. Bragg. I have a great deal of respect for you but . . ." She stopped for a moment, then cleared her throat. "The thing is, I've already got a gentleman caller."

Suddenly a look of great relief flooded her face and she smiled. "I'm seeing Mr. Lad Trimble."

A vein swelled on Bragg's temple. His face turned from scarlet to purple.

"Please calm yourself, Harley," McIntire said. "I've known you for years and am aware of your temper."

Speaking with difficulty, Bragg said to Beth, "Do you mean that you're seeing this young pup?"

Lad stood up stiffly. He certainly had not been "calling" on Beth, and assumed she was using this as an excuse that she'd come up with on the spur of the moment. In his own opinion, it was ridiculous for an elderly man like Bragg—who must be all of forty or more—to be thinking of courtship anyway. Feeling a bond for a girl of his own generation, he decided to help her out of this awkward situation.

He decided friendly diplomacy would be his best tactic. "I'm nineteen, Mr. Bragg, and don't believe you can consider me a 'pup.'"

He would have said more, in fact had planned to, but Bragg took three strides forward and slapped his face as hard as he could, snapping Lad's head to one side.

Lad felt the heat of rage surge throughout his body. His voice quivered as he said, "I don't believe Miss Ellen would approve of more of this in her home." He spun on his heel and walked toward the front door. When he reached it, he turned and said, "Mr. Bragg, if I could have a word with you outside."

Miss Ellen cried out in astonishment, and begged Bragg to apologize.

"I am the offended party," Bragg said. "We'll settle this matter with dueling pistols at first light in the morning." He stared coldly at Lad. "We'll meet on the heights above the house at dawn."

Turning to one side, he said to McIntire, "I believe you have a brace of dueling pistols?"

"I do." A wild light shone in McIntire's eyes. "I'll have the pistols loaded and ready."

Beth screamed out, "This is madness!"

McIntire said to Lad, "You better try to get as much sleep as you can. You'll need a steady hand. In the old days I saw a number of these affairs."

"I'm not too interested in shooting him," Lad began to say. "I'll admit I had in mind trying to whip him, but . . ."

"It's a matter of honor now," McIntire declared. "I will see that it's done properly."

Beth and her mother began to cry.

Nine

AROUND MIDNIGHT the wind grew stronger, causing the bunkhouse to tremble ever so slightly. Moaning noises came from the eaves of the roof, and the rafters made strange creaking and popping noises. Lad lay awake, staring into the darkness. Others in the long room slept, some snoring, others tossing at times. Perhaps he dozed off for an hour, although he'd have sworn he never closed his eyes. But once it thundered, a crash followed by a flare of lightning which brightened the windows, and he realized he'd been having a troubled dream but couldn't remember anything about it.

A pounding rain hammered the roof momentarily, large drops cracking against the windows, but then stopped. Leaks in the roof dripped after this. Lad prayed for violent weather. Surely men didn't duel in storms. He could feel and smell the wet wool of blankets and the air's dampness—and his own fear.

When total blackness where the windows should be turned to squares of dull gray, he sat up on the edge of his bunk. A knot of anxiety burned at the pit of his stomach, and for a moment he thought he might be flattened by an attack of nausea. But the wave passed, leaving him weak. He put his hand on his forehead, wondering if he had fever, but his head felt clammy and cold. He had never been this afraid in his life.

Filled with dread, he put on his clothes and went outside, splashing through puddles from the night's showers.

Joshua, the cook, had built his fire in the outdoor oven and was already baking biscuits. A large black coffeepot was boiling, and Lad breathed in the familiar aroma. It brought back images of the past, and he was instantly caught up by a swelling of homesickness that eclipsed any he'd ever known before. He longed for the safety of childhood.

Lad kept wondering: Is this my last day on earth?

"What you doin' up this early? I ain't even rang the bell." Joshua began to talk of the trouble he'd had in finding dry wood for his fire. "Had to take off all them logs on top 'til I found some I could use."

Standing near the cook, Lad glanced up the slope and saw movement at the main house. John McIntire in his Scottish garb walked out, carrying a bundle in both arms. He left the house and went toward the rocky heights beyond it. Moments later another figure came out. Lad saw Harley Bragg in his black suit, the tail of his coat flapping in the brisk wet wind as he went in the direction McIntire had taken. Mist and haze hung heavily, and the figure disappeared into the predawn shadows.

"Want some coffee?" Joshua inquired.

Lad shook his head, unable to speak at first. "There's something I have to do," he murmured after moistening his dry lips. The busy cook paid him no attention.

He returned to the bunkhouse, unbuckled his spurs, and took them from his boots. He didn't want to run the risk of tripping on them. Taking a deep breath, he departed for the heights above the main house.

Low-lying clouds hovered about the craggy hill and fog sank into the rocky gullies and draws that creased its side. Wind blew feathery wisps into the spidery branches of mesquite trees. Lad's boots slipped on the wet rocks underfoot as he ascended the hill. Nearing the top, he wound through the upright flat stones of the rimrock and then emerged to the mesa's uneven floor.

When he passed the last boulder he heard an alarming squawk, a harsh discordant squealing as if a dozen infuriated tomcats had suddenly started fighting. Then the tones modulated and, as the first ray of sunlight pierced the dawn's gloom from the eastern horizon, he made out McIntire's form.

Dressed again in a blue and green kilt and wearing patterned knee socks, the old Scot had on his head a green cap with a red topknot and, perhaps due to the rain, he wore his rough tweed coat, a blend of green and gray shades. It was short, only reaching his waist, and over it he'd draped a tartan sash which hung diagonally across one shoulder and down to his hip on the opposite side. Puffing energetically into the mouthpiece, he pumped the bag with one elbow while his fingers fluttered along the holes as he played a wild melody.

Mad John McIntire strode back and forth, mindless of his flapping kilt. With his bagpipe skirling, its warlike howls echoing from the boulders on both sides, he stared straight ahead, captivated by the moment.

Harley Bragg stood, legs slightly apart, scowling belligerently.

Reluctantly, Lad gave up his idea of approaching with an outstretched hand. He realized he'd not have an opportunity to make the speech he'd mentally prepared, the one stating that they should each forgive and forget whatever slights might have caused this misunderstanding.

He heard slight crunching sounds, footsteps on loose gravel, and an instant later Beth stumbled around the face of a boulder, her face pale. She stood there, breathing heavily.

McIntire carefully put down his bagpipe and walked to a flat rock on which a polished mahogany box rested. He summoned the two men and opened it, revealing the rounded wooden handles and long barrels of a brace of dueling pistols.

When McIntire addressed them, his normally rich Scottish brogue somehow intensified, and the r's rolled so that they had to pay close attention in an effort to follow his speech.

"These belonged to Gordon McCabe, an old friend of mine who lived in New Orleans. Before the war I'd often visit Gordon. An affair of honor required the use of these pistols, and Gordon didn't survive. To my surprise, I found he left them to me in his last will and testament." McIntire smiled. "Until this morning I've never had occasion to put them to use. These are muzzle loaders, of course. I've had a long experience with this type of firearm and have taken particular care in measuring out the powder for the primer in the firing mechanism and for the charge. But it's a damp day, and you never can tell with these things. When I heard it raining some hours ago, it bothered me, but I've kept them in their box, so it's my hope that neither will misfire."

Lad didn't feel reassured. McIntire saw him examining the weapons encouched in the dull gold velvet of their fitted case. "Have you ever fired one of these?" McIntire inquired.

"I've seen them, but never held one before."

"How about you, Harley?"

Bragg said, "I have experience with such weapons."

"In other words, you've faced a duel before."

"Yes," Bragg answered shortly, his face impassive. "What are the rules to be?"

McIntire replied, "Well, since you claim to be the offended party, although I don't know that I agree to that, you get to pick your weapon, and young Trimble will take the other. After that you'll stand back to back and take five paces as I count. Then you'll stop and not turn until I say, 'Commence'—which will be the signal for you both to wheel about and fire."

"It sounds irregular," Bragg complained.

"This is my first time, damn it, Harley, and seems to me as good a system as any other."

Beth came nearer. "Don't do this, Mr. Bragg. Lad doesn't want to fight you."

Bragg's face took on a fierce look. "I hadn't realized you were present, Miss McIntire. You shouldn't be here."

Beth hesitated, seeming uncertain, then turned about, her face ashen. She began to walk away, but on reaching the edge of the mesa where the path twisted down through stones twice her height, she stopped. With her back to them, she stood watching the men as if mesmerized.

The two men took their weapons and stood back to back. McIntire's resonant voice began to count, and they paced deliberately away from one another. As the Scotsman called out "five" they stopped, each with elbows at their sides and their hands holding the pistols aiming skyward. In the distance Beth cried out, but nearer at hand, McIntire shouted, *"Commence."*

Lad whirled and saw Harley Bragg pointing a black bore at his face. He brought the blue steel dueling pistol to bear in his outstretched right hand—split seconds seeming to take forever. It had a hair trigger, and as he tried to aim the wavering long barrel at his opponent he heard a metallic click, a slight fizz, and his weapon prematurely exploded, kicking violently. He'd never known a handgun to make such an incredible noise.

At the very instant that he staggered from the surprise of the blast, a vicious warbling cracked past his ear—and he realized he'd missed death by inches.

A cloud of acrid black smoke rose from the muzzle of the barrel which he still pointed forward. A mist hit his cheek and fine raindrops began to fall. Through the veil of gunsmoke and the growing downpour, Lad stared with disbelief at his antagonist.

Harley Bragg dropped his weapon and grasped his left arm. A stream of oaths came from his lips. His face twisted into a dreadful mask, and he began to make horrible noises as he wrenched at his arm in apparent agony.

Lad stood transfixed, watching the spectacle as Bragg threw his head back, mouth open wide, vile curses splitting the morning's silence. And then he saw the most grotesque sight of his life.

Harley Bragg's black-gloved left hand slid out of the sleeve—*as his entire arm fell to the ground.*

"My God," Lad gasped. His vision blurred, the world whirled, and he felt himself sinking—then falling. He blurted out in horrified astonishment, "I shot off his arm!"

Bragg stared down near his feet as though in shock. Curling fog rose behind him. He began cursing again. He kicked the appendage, and spun around to face Lad. "You little son of a bitch, you *ruined* my wooden arm."

Lad heard voices. He was lying down. He opened his eyes and felt Beth holding his head at her soft breast.

"What happened?" he inquired.

"I think you fainted," Beth replied.

"I have not received satisfaction," Harley Bragg declared.

McIntire stated, "Oh, yes you have. Each of you fired your weapons, and you got hit. If you hadn't already lost that arm at Antietam, you'd sure as hell have lost it now. So I declare this duel to be officially over."

He picked up his bagpipes, but before putting the stem in his mouth, he added, "Harley, I'd be greatly obliged if you'd stop your cussin' in front of my daughter. That arm didn't cost you a cent—the ladies in Richmond gave it to you as a gift when you got out of the hospital."

Lad rose unsteadily to his feet. He said to Bragg, "I'm really sorry."

"That's all right," Bragg said. "I never wore the damn thing except when I felt like dressing up. Usually I just pin my sleeve."

After Harley Bragg stormed out of his house, John McIntire sent for Lad. They sat in the kitchen, drinking coffee, looking out the window as rivulets ran down the multi-paned windows.

"It's always a rare sight to see rain in these parts," McIntire said. "I can't tell you the joy I feel at these times. Tomorrow I'll walk out and observe small things that only follow a shower: little red velvet cochineal bugs, a few small flowers that spring from sand and rocks, which seems an impossibility, but new life shows every time this happens. The grass will turn green. These are small celebrations of a very important event, for we totally depend on rain—something that in my childhood in Scotland I took entirely for granted."

Lad hardly listened. He was thinking not of the rain but of the fact that he was alive. In a husky voice he said, "I still don't know what provoked the quarrel."

"Bragg is an impetuous man. I've known he had his eye on Beth, but he may be too old for her. On the other hand, there's some merit in what he says. We *could* combine our ranches. He's got more land, but I've got more water. Anyway, the two of us have gone together and bought four thousand sheep. We've got Mexican herders, and are interested in the experiment."

Lad paid little attention, still weak with relief at his escape that morning. Quiet elation flooded through him.

"The point is, Bragg and I have a good bit at stake in staying friends. After all, a man needs to get along with his neighbors; and in spite of Bragg's acting as if he'd let the unpleasantness between the two of you be forgotten—I know him well. He won't forget. It'll fester until he comes after you again. And the next time he'll carry a sixgun and won't be bothered by rules."

"He accepted my apologies, and . . ."

"No," McIntire interrupted. "He may have acted that way, but his pride's hurt. He said to me that he couldn't stand the idea that I'd keep you on the ranch—this close to Beth. That puts me in a very awkward spot. After all, your father is the best friend I ever had. He saved my life, took me to your place when I was near death, and there's no way to repay him. I know that Beth popped off about your being the man she'd chosen to call on her, but I suspect, Lad, that she's feeling a little desperate. She has a horror of being an old maid, but a worse horror of marrying some old cowboy. Her choices out here aren't too attractive for her. And then you came along.

"You may not be aware of it, but my wife and daughter on first sight of you decided you were the best-looking young buck they'd ever laid eyes on. With your manners and the easy way you talk, you had the two of them captured."

He waved his hand for silence. "I know that this conversation is embarrassing, and I'd drop the subject if it weren't for a terrible dilemma I've got to face. Your dad sent you out to me, trusting me to make a man of you. Now, I know that you might learn a little about ranching, given the time. But in all frankness, you haven't shown a hell of a lot of interest in it—and may be about as useless a hand as we've ever had on the ranch. What I'm about to say is this: I've given my word to your father that I'd take you on and help you find a direction to your life. I can't go back on my word."

The old Scot looked at Lad with a canny smile. "However, *you* can make a decision that will take it out of my hands. You can simply decide to go home. That'd solve my problem—and I suspect you'd be happy to get back to school. It may be that after a time your father will permit you to help on his place. Or maybe you can study for the law or something like that. You have family connections that would help you make something of yourself in a number of different ways. But, as I say, this is a choice you'll have to make."

Lad sat quite still, listening to the older man. The contrast between his careful reasoning now and his bizarre behavior at other times seemed inexplicable. He decided that McIntire sounded as sane at that moment as any man he'd ever heard, and he welcomed the advice.

"As for my daughter, she's hardly met you. I can't imagine that she's formed any deep feelings. This is the kind of weakness that young girls have—which can go as quickly as it comes. But if you hang around, that could be an added complication."

And so, after a brief period, Lad agreed. He reluctantly accepted a salary payment in the form of two twenty-dollar gold pieces. McIntire also insisted that he take the horse named Claude, the old spurs, the saddle and bridle and other gear, including a slicker in case the rain should start again. And by mid-afternoon, Lad found himself prepared to leave.

Beth came down to the corral to say goodbye as he saddled Claude. He'd packed all his belongings he could in large saddlebags. The remainder had been stuffed in a fat roll protected by his new slicker, which he secured behind the cantle with long leather tie strings.

"Will I see you again?"

"I hope so," Lad said awkwardly. He mounted and looked down at her. "Well . . ."

She turned and ran toward the house.

Pucker and Ramsel also sauntered to the pens before he left. Jim Pucker said, "Take care of yourself, Lad. We're comin' to town in a week or so, and if you're still around we'll introduce you to some mighty nice gals that won't cause people to shoot at you." He grinned as he spoke.

Ramsel lit a cigarette with cupped hands and then, squinting as the smoke rose past his eyes, said, "Some of the boys just got in last evening from San Angelo. They'd gone with the wagon to get Miss Ellen's and Beth's luggage that finally showed up from Galveston. Anyway, they saw Dee Hudnall and one of his gunslingers arrive in town together with that girl Hudnall married. Be sure to ride in a wide circle around him. They say he killed Elzie Huck not long ago for butcherin' one of his calves. Of course there's no proof, but I wouldn't put it past him."

"Elzie Huck's *dead?*"

"That's what they say." Ramsel pulled at the cigarette and drew the smoke down deep into his lungs. "Be careful to stay out of Hudnall's way."

"I'm not eager for any more duels."

Pucker and Ramsel burst into laughter.

Lad rode east with the warm sun at his back. Ahead he saw dark clouds flickering with lightning. He planned to find a telegraph station and send home for money for his trip. As the hours passed, he thought of his time on the ranch. He felt an ache at the thought of Beth, and tried to put her out of his mind. But then he pictured Mattie Hudnall, saw her as she'd been in the store, the way her eyes met his, and he drew a deep breath.

He resolved to take a room at Annie Tankersley's hotel and spend most of his time there. After his experiences that day, he didn't think he'd risk any more excitement.

Ten

LAD RODE EAST, watching the clouds ahead of him moving in the sky, and banks of high black thunderheads boiling restlessly. Sheet lightning glowed almost continuously and thunderbolts sizzled down at angles, making brilliant jagged patterns. At times two or three struck simultaneously, and moments later he'd hear sharp cracks as if the heavens were exploding. Between these bursts a constant deep rumbling, like hundreds of distant kettledrums, vibrated through the air. By the time night fell, when he'd planned to make camp, the rain began. So he kept riding, looking for a place of shelter.

Lad dismounted and unwrapped the new slicker from around the bulging blanket which held those of his belongings not in the large saddlebags. He tied the fat bedroll behind the cantle, aware that everything he carried would soon be sopping wet, and stepped back into the rain-slick saddle.

Touching Claude with his spurs, he headed in what he hoped was the right direction. The slicker helped, although his clothes were already soaked. Water kept running off the brim of his hat, and more of it ran down his neck and trickled down his back. Pulling the stiff oilcloth collar up, he ducked his head.

He could hardly see with his head held down under the drooping felt of his sodden hat brim, but he kept looking for trees, for an outcropping of rocks where he could crawl, for any place to get out of the downpour. An hour later he saw a light off to his right and reined Claude toward it. As he neared, he saw in the lightning's flare the charred remains of a building that had long since burned down. Only the foundation remained. Near it stood a dull whitewashed frame dwelling. Several large old mesquite trees spread their heavy branches over it, and the wind whipped these back and forth, knocking and scraping on the loose shingles of the uneven roof. In the background he made out the dim outlines of a barn and pens.

After he tied Claude to a tree limb, he walked to the back door. When he drew near it he saw a tall man holding a heavy Colt down by his side. Lad kept his eye warily on the sixgun as he approached. Light from the entryway fell out upon him, illuminating the torrent, making the rain glisten. He felt as though he stood in a thicket of crystal rods while he waited, shifting his weight from one foot to the other.

The man standing in the open doorway had a large head and a friendly smile. He said, "Howdy, stranger." With that he cocked the six-shooter but kept it pointed at the ground.

Lad swallowed with difficulty before managing to reply, "Good evening."

"Fine rain we're having," the man with the pistol said, standing on the sill, protected from the storm except for wind-driven spray.

Water flooded down on Lad. Rivulets streamed over his shoulders and smaller ones dripped from the front of his hat. "Yes," he replied.

"Well, come on in the house. Get in where it's dry."

He stood to one side, allowing Lad to pass, remaining behind him on their way through a small hall, past a kitchen, and into a long room. Lad saw a splendid dining table on his left. It had in its center a soup tureen and various serving dishes. The table had been carefully set for one with what appeared to be Dresden china or perhaps Meissen ware as well as elaborate silver knives, forks, and spoons. The room had several coal oil lamps which revealed an unexpected interior. The simple house from the outside showed that it had in all likelihood been built for hired hands, but its furnishings clearly indicated that it now served a different purpose.

Lad looked about and saw a long dark sideboard, a heavily carved piece of furniture, probably German. The combination dining and living area had a couch, various easy chairs, and hundreds of books. The overall effect was one of warmth and comfort.

Lad took off his hat and dripping slicker and the man holding the Colt saw that he was unarmed. He turned to one side, carefully uncocked the pistol, then walked in sock-clad feet to a corner of the room where he put the handgun on a stack of papers in a rolltop desk.

"Forgive my caution. Few riders pass this way and some, I regret to say, have bad manners." He smiled broadly and held out his hand.

"My name's Montgomery Blackwell DeLong, although the Mexicans call me Huérfano, which is their word for orphan. I'm not bereft of parents, of course. They call me that because I live in this abandoned, solitary condition. My mother's very much alive and, may I add, is highly critical of me. She's long been distressed that the Gypsies didn't steal me when I was a small child that time they stayed for a few weeks by the river. She deliberately encouraged me to go down and watch as they struck their tents and broke camp, and years passed before I realized her true intentions. It almost broke my heart."

He opened his bright blue eyes quite wide at this odd statement and watched the blank expression on his guest's face with quiet enjoyment.

Lad barely had the opportunity to introduce himself when it became apparent that his part in the conversation was to listen. He did so with growing bewilderment, wondering if the man had lost his mind. DeLong spoke again, rambling on about the rain, mixing comments about his lonely life out on the barren prairie, all the while smiling, unable to conceal his pleasure at having an audience.

Lad had never heard such an unusual Texas accent before. The man's tongue seemed to be unaccustomed to speech. This, however, was obviously not due to choice but to the remoteness of the place where he'd spent his entire life. DeLong began to tell one tale after another, employing an actor's skill. He would pause dramatically, head drawn back, and then come to a preposterous conclusion.

After Lad gathered that he was not only invited to pass the night but that his host would be mortally offended if he declined, the two put on slickers and went outside. Lad retrieved his saddlebags and bedroll from his saddle and returned for a moment to the house, pitching them on the floor of the entryway at the back door. Then he rode Claude to the barn where he pulled off the saddle and bridle. He rubbed him down with some dusty gunnysacks that lay in a corner of a stable, poured oats into a shallow trough, broke up some hay, and left the horse contentedly munching. He and DeLong ran through the rain back to the house where they dropped their hats and slickers on a table in the kitchen.

DeLong served Lad with a large cup of steaming coffee and invited him to put on some of his own dry clothes which he pitched out on a bed in the spare room where Lad would stay. Lad had to roll the sleeves of the shirt and turn up the pants legs, as though he were a child wearing a grownup's things. But, with dry socks on his feet, he padded back to the living room feeling infinitely better.

Absolutely delighted to have company, DeLong began with that day's complaints. It appeared that he owned this ranch. "I run it with the help of a foreman I call Minimum Tom. Old Minimum has a ragtag passel of cowboys, most of them from Old Mexico. They wander up on foot, and after a while, some manage to do a fair job." After this he elaborated upon the foreman's shortcomings. Feeling he might have overstated his case, he then described the foreman's skills and unique abilities.

"Let's do something about your wet clothes," DeLong said, interrupting his monologue. He strode to the kitchen and put more wood in the cookstove. Lad extracted some of his extra shirts and pants from the crumpled, dripping bedroll and then picked up the sodden clothing he'd worn that day. With DeLong's assistance, he hung all of these on a rope they strung over the stove.

"These will be dry by morning—if you're able to start off on your journey then. Frankly, I hope you can't. I'd like to think that the storm might keep on for days, but they usually pass in a hurry. In fact, the slightest hint of moisture normally stops right at my property line. It's a lifelong mystery to me why my neighbors always get rain while my land suffers from eternal drought."

Lad wondered that the man should complain of arid conditions when he'd almost drowned in the downpour riding through his ranch.

DeLong droned on. "Guess it's the Lord's way of keeping me humble, making sure that I stay busted and hopeless." By now Lad had stopped listening carefully to this drawled litany of discontent. He could see that the man wouldn't exchange places with anyone else on earth.

DeLong, in spite of his size, moved quickly and had deft hands. He set another place at the table and in a short time served Lad with an astonishing dinner.

They began with a delicate thin soup followed by a salad course—made primarily of watercress from Spring Creek, which ran through the ranch. Then they had tender medallions of veal and some form of pasta, all of it covered by a rich tomato sauce in which many different herbs had been blended. DeLong explained in minute detail how he'd prepared every dish which he offered.

After dinner they moved to easy chairs by a wall with books in shelves from floor to ceiling.

"I am the most miserable of men," DeLong began, "living out my life on this Godforsaken desert. Nothing but cactus and coyotes—and starving cattle that die just as it's time to go to market. No woman to comfort me, no friends. At my time of life I need to turn from sitting around campfires with busted-up cowboys. I yearn for a life of culture and need to be in the company of gentlemen who read poetry. As a rule the only folks I see don't say more to me than 'Howdy' when they drop by and then nod when they leave. Of course, my Mexican friends will talk at great length to me. And some of the Indians will too. But I don't understand much of their conversation."

He leaned back in his chair, prepared for a marvelous evening.

Lad told of his time on the McIntire Ranch, not mentioning the duel or that he'd been asked to leave. He simply stated what was on his mind, that he was on his way to San Angelo and intended to return to Virginia.

"Watch your step when you get to that town. In my drinking days, back when I depended on bottles of what I used to call 'old step-steady,' I hung out in those torn-up shabby bars. There's some dangerous men in that settlement, Lad. On the other hand, I know some wonderful characters in it.

"When I was a down-and-out drunk I'd sit on the edge of the sidewalk and talk to a greasy old fellow named Horacio Escoba, a fat Meskin with hair hanging down from under his sombrero—it came almost down to his eyes. He's kind of funny-looking for a Meskin since he has freckles. Escoba carries a bucket of tamales and peddles them. Good tamales, too. Most folks think he's the village idiot, and that's how he stays out of trouble. Just grins and puts up with all the insults. But I got to know him. So, while you're in town, try one of his tamales and tell him that Huérfano DeLong sends his best regards."

Lad rode down Concho Avenue in the early afternoon. The day had cleared, but the dirt road had turned into an almost impassable sea of mud. Several wagons had been abandoned, sunk almost up to their axles. Claude's hooves sank out of sight at each step as he slogged through it, trying to pick his way gingerly around dull brown muddy puddles.

Lad found to his surprise that the Tankersley Hotel had no rooms available. A number of travelers had taken shelter, waiting for the roads to clear, so he went to the Nimitz where he rented a very small room at the end of a narrow hall on the first floor. It was located at the front next to a saloon, and drunks could be heard hollering just out the window. He could see why his room hadn't been rented.

After dropping off his belongings, Lad searched for a telegraph station but learned that he'd have to go to Fort Concho. He rode Claude through a low-water crossing, the horse slipping in the slick mud and almost falling as they ascended the bank on the far side of the river. After this he made his way south to the fort.

Lad rode into the area slowly, not knowing where he should go. The fort had no wall or protection and sprawled on the flat muddy land. Normally this would have been dry and dusty, and Lad saw few signs of vegetation. He dismounted when he reached the fort's perimeter and talked to a group of off-duty soldiers who sat in the shade of a lone mesquite. He saw a bare parade ground and a forlorn, lonely flagpole. The soldiers saw him look at a line of two-story dwellings and told him that was "officers' row." On the other side, he saw a very long barracks with a narrow porch all around it. "That's where we live," one of the enlisted men said. Upright posts at intervals supported the overhang of the barracks roof.

The cavalrymen pointed out the post headquarters and also, with some pride, the Fort Concho Hospital, an imposing stone structure with a cupola on top of its second story as well as three protruding chimneys.

When Lad reached the headquarters building, a sentry gave him directions, and a short time later he introduced himself to a bearded corporal who kept assuring him that the telegraph wires could only be used for official purposes.

Lad began to tell his story, that he had enough money to last almost a month, but not enough to pay for passage to Virginia. Gaining the man's sympathy, he explained that he had to get back home.

Lad put a silver dollar on the counter and said, "I sure need your help, friend." The corporal slid this smoothly into his pocket and took out a short stubby pencil and a piece of paper.

"What's the message?"

Soon Lad's brief communication was tapped out, dots mixed with dashes forming the letters for distant operators on the telegraph wire: "Lost job. Send money for trip home in care of Mrs. Tankersley,

Tankersley Hotel, San Angelo. Want to work for you or go back to school. Lad."

The soldier looked at him. "I have no idea if this will get relayed all the way to Williamsburg, Virginia."

Lad worried about that too, and also wondered who might carry it the final miles out along the James River to deliver it to his father.

The corporal said, "I never sent a telegraph message like this. I don't know how long it might take to send money out here, which I guess is your only hope since there's not even a bank in town."

"My father has friends in the banking business. They can surely find a way to get some money to me—maybe from San Antonio."

"You goin' to sit around and wait for it?"

"Don't know what else I *can* do."

The corporal shrugged. "Well, good luck." He grinned sardonically. "When you run out of cash I guess you can come out to the fort and enlist in the army."

Eleven

AFTER RETURNING from the fort, Lad stabled Claude at the Elkhorn Wagon Yard, remaining with the horse for a time. He found a semicircular, rusted steel currycomb, and spent almost half an hour grooming the satiny coat, scraping off dried mud, and finishing the job by brushing Claude from one end to the other with a stiff-bristled brush. He fed him some grain, then turned him out in the main corral with a number of other horses, watching as Claude headed for the water trough.

Old saddles hung nearby, suspended by mecate tied to their horns. Bridles with dried-out reins, pieces of harness, and old ropes had been looped around pegs in the walls. Lad liked the smell of leather and of horses.

Reluctantly he left and began slogging through the mud, walking east on Concho Avenue. He felt a prickling of fear as he recalled the riot on his first night in San Angelo.

This afternoon it looked as though it were a different place entirely. Instead of a horde of soldiers and townsmen and cowboys crowding into the town for a weekend, only a few serious-looking men struggled along the drowned streets. The dusty rut-filled roads had become barriers of puddles and slimy brown sludge. Wagons tilted where they'd been abandoned, and low places looked like small, dirty ponds.

Lad passed through swinging batwing doors into Early Able's Saloon, the one where the pretty girl at the door had spoken to him when he'd passed it the first night he'd arrived in town. He certainly hadn't any intention of seeking out the company of the women he'd heard about, the ones who worked upstairs, but curiosity prevailed over his better judgment. A tingling of excitement made its small quick circle within him.

Why not? he asked himself. Why not go in and look around? There'd be no harm in that. Besides, he had money in his pocket— and might as well enjoy waiting around until he heard from home.

Like most people, Lad could always find a good reason for his actions.

He took a place toward the back of the combination saloon, gambling hall, and whorehouse, finding a table that rested slightly away from the others. He sat there, looking about, getting his bearings with the aid of a few lanterns which shed irregular circles of light on the surrounding shadows. At the front of the saloon he could make out a long bar made of carved oak, stained so dark with lampblack that it looked almost ebony. A brass rail ran in front of it, and men put their boots on this as they threw down drinks. Spittoons rested at intervals on the floor near the rail. Splatters around these attested to the indifferent aim of tobacco chewers.

A number of men lined the bar while others drank seriously at tables, with bottles kept close by their thick tumblers. Others walked upstairs, accompanied by girls in red or green or bright blue dresses. A piano sat off to one side, but the piano player hadn't arrived yet and it remained silent.

A haze of tobacco smoke drifted just above the heads of the celebrants, of the drifters and cowboys and peddlers trapped in the town by the unusual circumstance of a rain so hard that the trails and roads couldn't be used. Nature herself had made it impossible for them to go back to work. This circumstance gave rise to a sense of celebration, as though it were a holiday, a free day in the universe.

At times, for no reason at all, a cowboy would howl. Others cried out greetings or insults at friends or acquaintances. While some drank silently, most laughed, catcalled, and talked. Glasses and bottles clinked, bootheels clumped on the unstable board floor, and a general hubbub filled the air.

A girl drifted down the stairs, saw Lad sitting by himself, and joined him. A second looked over from the bar, winked at him, and then she too threaded through the tables while men patted her behind. She didn't appear to notice these friendly attentions. After ten or fifteen minutes, two other girls joined the group.

And so it was, an hour later, that he found himself seated at a table with four brightly attired girls who gaily chattered as he held his whiskey. He didn't drink from it. The girls kept insisting that he buy one round after another. After holding his own glass for a time, he'd slide it on the wooden tabletop over to the slightly overweight, pretty girl at his side, the one named Mary Lou, and she would take it cheerfully.

"I got a hollow laig," she stated proudly, "and can drink you or any man under the table." With that she threw the rotgut down without a shudder, although she did turn slightly pale. She wiped her mouth with the back of her hand and began to tease him.

"Let's you and me go upstairs, sonny. For a dollar, you'll have the ride of your life."

The other girls whooped and began to describe with gusto various baldly stated propositions. They did so without the slightest embarrassment, obviously enjoying the effect they could see that these had. They stared in his face, cooed obscenities, and then said, "Don't mind us, we're just havin' fun with you."

One commented with a grin, "Well, it's true that we're just havin' a good time, sittin' around talkin', but *I* have to earn a livin'—and think it's grand there's a relaxin' way to do it, one where I can lay on my back." The other three squealed, pretending to be shocked. "We're not like her, darlin'," another declared. "We don't make love for money. We do it out of affection."

A friendly rivalry existed among them, and they considered this nice-looking youngster to be a challenge. But he simply sat and smiled, listening to their banter.

He didn't like the taste of whiskey but managed to drink one glass with about two inches of fiery brown liquid in it. Surprisingly, the second drink went down more easily, as if he'd anesthetized his mouth and throat with the first.

Relaxed by the alcohol and his tiredness, he began to speak to the girls, allowing the words to flow. If there was one thing he'd learned in Virginia, it was the art of useless social patter. At college he'd spent most of his time, when not playing cards, in perfecting this skill.

"Lord, I love to hear this boy talk," one said. The others leaned forward with real or pretended fascination, as if hanging on his every word. His drawled soft speech particularly pleased them, and they'd make wry comments about it while nudging one another at some of his remarks, laughing at times when he had spoken in all earnestness with no attempt at humor.

Lad hadn't drunk so heavily that he didn't realize that much of their appreciation for him stemmed from the fact that he'd been spending money like water, as though he had an inexhaustible supply.

Flattered by the attention, Lad hardly noticed that he'd downed several more glasses of whiskey. With each one he felt that he gained fresh insights, that his mind was much more receptive to impressions. In fact, he was quite surprised that his uncertainty had vanished, having been replaced with a deep and peaceful wisdom. He would have enjoyed discussing philosophy, but decided that this might not be suitable under the circumstances.

"Ladies," he said as he rose to leave them, "I've sworn to remain pure." At this they burst into gales of laughter, but he motioned for silence. "But if I should ever change my mind, I certainly intend to seek your assistance. However, I fear I may need a certain amount of instruction."

Mary Lou, the slightly overweight girl on his left, leaned forward. The loose, low neckline of her dress revealed twin hillocks, a wide expanse of white bust which rose and lowered at each breath. Lad could tell she was inordinately proud of this feature. "Honey," she said, "I'm better qualified as a teacher than just about anyone you could ever find. I've been in this business since I was fourteen years old, and there's no trick in it that I haven't tried—or had tried out on me."

Lad stood beside the table, smiling at the girls. He nodded in farewell as he picked up his hat, noting with satisfaction that it now looked as battered as those worn by the cowboys in the saloon. He strolled by several tables where professional gamblers played cards with townspeople and drovers and a few cowboys. He touched the money in his pocket, sorely tempted to try his luck, but resisted the enticement.

When he reached the Nimitz Hotel, he went to his room. A three-legged stand with a round marble top standing at the wall beside his bed held a pitcher of water and a basin. He cleaned up as best he could, splashing water on his face and hair after washing his hands. He touched his lips and, to his surprise, noted their numbness. While he didn't feel at all hungry, he decided he'd better try to find some supper.

After changing into a clean shirt, he went to the small lobby. It had leather-covered armchairs and one long couch across from the unoccupied counter where, during the day, a clerk usually stood. Several deer heads had been mounted and these hung from the walls together with one large painting of a Hereford herd bull with a massive head with great downturned horns.

On the other side, through opened double doors, lay a dining area with a large oval table in its center where a few candles glimmered faintly. All the lamps had been extinguished, and at first he could hardly see anything else. But then he noticed a few small tables, one in the corner and two along the walls. The dining room had thin white curtains with fabric ties holding them apart at the night-blackened windows, and he saw a few candle flickers reflect on the mirror-like glass.

Lad hesitated, wondering if he might be too late to be served. As he stood at the entry, a Mexican maid came from the kitchen with a tray and began clearing the platters and plates from the abandoned larger table. One man sat alone at a table near the door, a black hat on his head. He smoked a cigar, leaning back in his chair.

While Lad stood there indecisively, the Mexican girl approached him, beckoning with her hand.

He followed her to a table in a corner, pulled out a chair, and sat down as she moved a candelabrum with three candles in it from the area she'd just cleared. She put this before him and said, "We got some mutton left, plenty of frijoles and cornbread."

Lad nodded, relieved that he didn't have to go back into the muddy street. As he leaned back in his chair he saw the man in the black hat rise to his feet and depart.

Lad still felt the effects of the whiskey, and his head spun slightly. As his eyes became accustomed to the dim light, he saw in the shadows across the room that another table had candles on it, but these were guttering out and gave off little light. He noticed a person cloaked in shadows sitting there, a woman. She turned her chair slightly and faced him. In the faint yellow glow he saw with a start the face of the pretty blonde girl he'd thought about so often.

She didn't drop her eyes, but kept them fixed on his. Slowly a smile filled her face, causing the dimple on her left cheek to deepen. She rose from her chair and joined him, sitting down on the other side of his table.

"My name's Mattie Hudnall."

"I know."

"You do?"

"I saw you in the general store when I first came through town. I asked about you."

"That's nice."

Lad hadn't eaten since breakfast, and the effects of the liquor on an empty stomach affected his coordination. Not only that, his words sounded slightly slurred. He made an effort to speak more distinctly as he spoke vaguely of his day.

The Mexican girl arrived with his dinner and put it down before him. She looked inquiringly at Mattie.

"You want something?"

"Could I have a cup of coffee?"

The girl nodded. Glancing at Lad, the waitress asked, "How about you? Want coffee, some whiskey?"

Lad's nerves needed a tonic. He felt slight twitches in his fingers. "I believe I would like a whiskey. Make it a double."

The girl shrugged, as if saying, "Why not," then walked away, wide hips swaying.

"Do you have a room at this hotel?" Mattie asked.

"Yes. I tried to get one at Tankersley's where I stayed before, but it's full." He waited for her to say something, but when she didn't, he added, "I suppose you've got a room here too."

She nodded, accepting the coffee cup the Mexican girl brought to her, but kept her eyes directed toward Lad. She silently watched him drink his bourbon, then turn to his dinner. She observed attentively the way he handled his knife and fork.

"I can't figure out why I'd come over to sit with a perfect stranger. You must think that's peculiar."

He shook his head. "Not at all. I'm glad you did—it's a lonely feeling being by yourself in a place like this."

"That's for damn sure," she stated with emphasis.

Lad said, "This may not be a proper thing for me to say, but I've thought about you ever since that day I first saw you."

She looked startled. "Why?"

He smiled. "Because you're so pretty, I guess. You're different-looking somehow." Slightly embarrassed, he picked up his glass.

Lad had two more drinks after his meal. Mattie sat very still as he talked, telling her something of his story. He explained briefly that he'd sent home for money; he'd be leaving soon for Virginia.

The conversation drifted aimlessly, yet a tension ran under its surface. At one point, interrupting herself, Mattie remarked, "You've got such nice curly hair. It's brown—kind of like your eyes." Then she looked down into her cup. "I don't know what made me say a fool thing like that. I generally don't talk to no folks at all. Guess I'm kind of out of practice."

She didn't say anything about her life. She didn't mention that her husband Dee Hudnall had left town for a few weeks, but that Ramón remained behind, guarding her night and day. Even now he'd be prowling around outside, watching the front and back doors of the hotel. In the darkness of the night she'd look from her window on the second floor and see him across the street, leaning against a wall, his cigarette glowing red as he inhaled.

"I'm afraid I must have drunk a little too much. I'm not accustomed to it and . . ." He stopped in mid-sentence, having forgotten what he'd meant to say.

"Let me give you a hand."

With her assistance, he returned to his room. Several times he stumbled, but she put her arm around his waist. Once she laughed out loud and said, "I can't imagine why I'm doing this. I don't even know you."

"Ma'am," Lad said gravely, "I'm mortified that you should see me in this condition—and am deeply grateful for your help."

"I swear," she said with a sigh, "I haven't run into anyone like you in all my life."

When he entered his room, she withdrew the arm she'd had around his waist but remained very close, her body almost touching his, her hand resting on his arm. He felt it tremble. On impulse, Lad leaned his head down slowly toward her upturned face—prepared to stop if she objected. But she didn't.

Very gently he kissed her full soft lips.

He looked down at her widened eyes and heard the sharp intake of her breath.

"Thank you," he murmured.

"My pleasure," she answered, backing away, and fled down the hall.

The end of May brought hot constant winds from the south. Memories of the rain-swollen river and muddy streets seemed a dream. Dust swirled again as wagon wheels banged through potholes. Lad, in the short time he'd been in the town, felt surprisingly at home. Since he was always ready to buy drinks for those around him, the regulars at the bars hailed him when he would enter. But time passed slowly.

During the afternoons he would stroll by the river, thinking of his impending journey back to Virginia. Once, after having walked for miles, he sat down to rest on the grass in the shade of tall swaying pecan trees. Wind pushed through their branches, making them rustle.

Someone had planted bamboo at the river's bank, perhaps as an experiment, and it had grown into a choked grove. He heard noises from it and listened curiously. Moments later three children with dirty blonde hair crawled out of it, saw him, and ran. When they'd gone out of sight he rose and walked to the deep green thicket. The children had worn a narrow path that wound into the midst of the limber bamboo. He followed it, having to crawl at several places, and found an enclosed space, an irregular circle about eight feet across. The ground underfoot was covered with fallen leaves and a soft clover-like growth unfamiliar to him. He smiled, thinking of his own childhood, of the fun of finding a hidden spot like this. Then he leaned over and retraced his steps, slender swollen-jointed bamboo stalks brushing against his arms and back, leaves touching his face.

He wandered beside the North Concho, remembered the trip made by Beth McIntire and her mother from New Orleans to Galveston, and decided he'd enjoy going home by boat. He'd never been on an ocean trip, and the prospect excited him.

He had moved to the Tankersley Hotel, and during lulls in the day would sit on the porch with Annie Tankersley, telling her of his plans.

"What if your dad decides not to send you the money you need to get home?"

The thought had never entered Lad's mind. For a moment he was shocked at the idea, but then said, "There's no fear of that. I'm his only child; he's always provided for me."

"You told me he'd lost patience with your wasting time in school. I thought his idea was for you to hold a job—and learn about life in the real world."

"I believe I've learned that, ma'am. This time in the West has been an experience for me."

Annie looked at him over the rims of her glasses. "I'm certainly glad that, at the age of nineteen, you've learned all about life."

He grinned. "Well, I suppose there are a *few* things yet to be experienced."

She changed the subject. "They say Dee Hudnall's started building a big house out on the west bank of the North Concho. A peculiar house in some ways, without any windows at all on one side."

Lad shifted in his chair uneasily.

"Lupe is friends with Josefina, the girl who works at the Nimitz.

She tells me you've been passing time with Mattie Hudnall—that you usually have supper with her there."

"Don't you remember I stayed a few days at the Nimitz Hotel when this place was full—right after the storm?" At her nod, he added, "Anyway, that's when I met her."

"Josefina tells Lupe that you've taken to visiting in her sitting room."

Lad's face showed his surprise, and he didn't respond.

"Son, in a little town, folks are aware of every move that takes place. If I know of this, you can rest assured that others do too."

"I don't know what you mean. There's nothing wrong with passing the time of day . . ." His words trailed off into silence. He cleared his voice nervously. "I assure you that we've just talked. She's lonely, staying all by herself—and I am too."

"That may be, but she's married. Not only that—her husband's a dangerous man." Annie's blue eyes looked intently at him. "I'm tellin' you this for your own good: stop seein' her."

"I don't understand."

"I think you do." She winced suddenly and put her hand on her side. "Gettin' old is no fun, Lad. Seems like there's a new pain every other week. This one's been gettin' worse, though. Old Doc says it must be my gallbladder, but what does he know?"

She heaved a deep breath, trying to compose herself, and said, "That girl is trouble. Mattie may look and act like a little kid, but she's hard as nails. She'd have to be to make it as Hudnall's wife. I don't want you to get yourself into trouble."

"No fear of that. I'll be leaving soon—already have my plans. I'm going to take the stage to San Antonio, then another to Galveston. I understand a boat goes from there to New York, but it makes quite a few stops—and one is at Norfolk."

"How much money do you have left?"

"Enough to last for two more weeks if I'm careful."

"Might be a good idea to start lookin' around for a job."

He set his rocker into easy motion, smiling uneasily at her. "Lord, Miss Annie, I hope it hasn't come to that. Surely I'll hear from home this week or next."

He sat on the railed veranda, rocking gently, feeling the heat of the wind press past his face. Annie had, with effort, risen to her feet and departed.

Lad thought of Mattie Hudnall. He'd never known such an excit-

ing girl. They'd talk each night of inconsequential matters. He realized the risk—but had always enjoyed mild flirtations. A small coil of
excitement built within him as he recalled the way she'd clung to him
as he'd left her the night before.

She'd said, "My husband's comin' back soon—and you're goin'
away—so tomorrow night may be the last we'll have. But be careful.
Ramón may have heard about you comin' over to see me. He's been
watchin' me like a hawk. Wait until after ten tomorrow night. I'll
leave the door unlocked." Then she'd wrapped her arms fiercely
around his neck.

Lad opened his eyes. It was only four in the afternoon. Six hours to
wait.

Twelve

LAD STOOD across from the Nimitz Hotel, his back against a wall. A bright moon shone and he could see the outline of the scattering of buildings. He hid in the shadows, looking to see if Ramón might be waiting, mindful of Mattie's warning. But he saw no one at all. At one time two men rode by, saddles creaking, hoofbeats sounding through the clear night air. One of them spoke and the other laughed.

Summoning his courage, Lad moved quickly across the road, ran up the stairs and into the hotel. The clerk wasn't behind the counter. A few men sat at the tables in the combination dining room and bar. Unnoticed, he reached the stairway and made it to the landing. Breathing rapidly, he paused, then went to the second floor. When he reached her door he tapped lightly with his fingers.

The door opened quickly—she'd been standing behind it. Mattie closed the door and locked it, then whirled around. Her hair had been let down and it hung loosely upon her shoulders. She wore a thin cotton nightgown with a light robe over it.

Excitement churned through Lad. She stood very close to him.

"You're late. I was afraid you wouldn't come."

He didn't answer but simply stood there, speechless, his heart racing.

She put her arms around his neck and drew his face down to hers. At the touch of her open lips on his, an urgent whirl spun through him. He pulled free and looked into her glazed eyes. Over her shoulder he saw a bed through an open door. Some of her clothing lay on it. A few garments lay on the floor where she'd dropped them. A candle on the table by the bed cast a soft haloed light.

Faint sounds came from the hallway outside the door—a board creaked, half-heard footsteps started, stopped, and continued. They passed directly by the room, then hesitated again. Mattie sprang away from him. She tiptoed to the door and stood with her ear to it, then crept back, white-faced.

"It's Ramón—do you think he followed you?"

"I don't think so." The tension built until it seemed to have a physical presence. Lad sensed that if he put out his fingers he might actually touch it.

"What'll we do?" he asked.

"I don't know."

She put her finger to her lips and motioned with her head. They retreated to the far corner of the sitting room. Mattie pulled him close and murmured, "I'm going to dress and go downstairs. He'll follow me. When he does, you can get away. There's a window at the end of the hall, and it's a short drop to the roof of the kitchen. Nobody will see you."

She put her arms around his waist and held to him fiercely. They spoke in hushed voices, almost whispering.

"Mattie—maybe we better not see each other anymore."

"Don't say that! I'd die if we couldn't."

Lad decided that he could very well die if they *did* keep this up. "Really, Mattie, we're in a bad situation. Besides, I'll be going home soon."

"Just once, Lad. I've got to be with you—I want something to remember."

His face rested upon her hair. He smelled perfume and powder and danger as he pulled her softness close. All common sense dictated that he flee as far from this girl as humanly possible. But he had never been a slave to common sense. An extraordinary excitement built and flickered all through him.

She spoke of her husband. "I found out he won't be back for two days. I have to see you tomorrow. Is there someplace we could go?"

In a faltering voice he told her of the bamboo grove by the river, of the trail into it. "By seven o'clock, before sundown, the kids won't be playing there—they'll have gone home."

"I usually go walkin' around then. Ramón's used to that. I'll make sure he doesn't follow." Her eyes shone in the lamplight. "You'll be there?"

"Yes."

After she left the room, he waited, touching the closed door. As she'd anticipated, the footsteps followed her. They paused just outside, and Lad felt the bite of fear. But then they continued, and he heard the creaking of stairboards. He counted to ten, cracked open the door, and, seeing the passageway clear, rushed into the hall.

Lad fled to the end of the narrow hall where he found the window and raised it. Lowering himself slowly, he dropped a few feet to the kitchen's roof, then slid down to its edge. He hesitated before dropping into the shadows. He fell to the ground, rolled over, and struggled to his feet.

Limping slightly, he made his way down the alley and then around the block, making his way through the moonlight to the Tankersley Hotel and his room.

"I won't do it," he said firmly to himself. "I'm not going to act like an idiot. After all, the money should come any day now, and I'll soon be back in Virginia."

The thought of home brought with it feelings of peace, of an overpowering tranquillity. But then a nervous sensation skipped through his stomach. He experienced the feeling a gambler has when he holds a fair but by no means certain hand, when he abandons calculation, when instinct tells him to bluff.

"What the hell," Lad said, falling into his bed. "I'll decide what to do tomorrow." But he already knew what would happen.

Lupe swept the floors of the Tankersley Hotel each morning with alacrity, moving through the two-story structure like a whirlwind—without a single wasted motion. Jabbing the broom into corners, swinging it up to knock down small spiderwebs, she passed through the downstairs lobby—which was the size of a parlor—then went outside. The worn broom whisked small clouds from the porch.

Lad rose from his chair, smiling. "Good morning."

The Mexican woman paused a moment to look at him with penetrating black eyes. "You know Ramón, the one who works for Hudnall?"

Lad nodded uneasily.

"He was here this morning, asking questions about you. I told him you planned on leaving real soon."

"What did he say?"

"Not a word. Just went on his way."

"Where's Mrs. Tankersley?" Lad asked, wanting to change the subject.

"She took sick and had me drive her out to the fort early this morning in her buggy. I waited for an hour, and the doctor, one of them soldiers, came out and said for me to fetch her night clothes, that they'd keep her for a while at the post hospital."

"What's wrong with her?" Shock and concern showed in his voice.

"The doctor didn't say except that maybe he'd have the surgeon come look at her."

Lad frowned as he recalled her comments to him not long before. "She told me her side hurt, but I didn't think it was anything serious."

"When we drove out to the post, she said she had 'a touch of the misery'—that maybe it was her liver or gallbladder. I don't know about such things."

"I'll go see her."

"She feels real bad. When I took her night clothes to her she said, 'Lupe, keep well-meanin' folks away from me. I plan to rest a spell.' She always says just what she means."

Lad went back to his rocking chair. The dust had settled after Lupe moved it from one spot to another on the narrow wooden porch.

"A letter came for you yesterday." Lupe went into the hotel and returned with an envelope which she handed to him. "Miss Annie reminded me to give it to you—and said she was sorry she hadn't got around to it earlier. I think she had some kind of stomach attack around mid-afternoon and took to her bed."

Lad nodded at her, then turned his attention to the letter. "Thank God," he said softly when he saw the heavy wrinkled paper and noted his father's familiar slanted handwriting on it.

His hands shook with anticipation as he opened the envelope.

Dear Ladbrook,

I received the message you sent by telegraph last Wednesday and have given serious thought to your request for funds in order to return to Virginia.

Before responding, I believe it would be appropriate for you to understand my concern for your future, and the reasons I sent you in the first place into the care of John McIntire.

I explained all of this patiently to you before you departed, but you normally do not heed my words. You have, through no virtue of your own, been blessed with certain natural assets. These consist in part of a pleasant personality. You have easy manners and normally get along well with people. In addition, you are aware that many find you to have a handsome appearance, although I'll give you credit for not, at least to my knowledge, being vain about this. But these very attributes have worked to your disadvantage since they have enabled you to live like a vagabond, wandering through life, allowing others to care for you. You have latent talents, I suppose, but have never lived up to your potential.

I do not wish to belabor the point, but I cannot forget the scandal at Washington & Lee College which caused you to be expelled. I have never fully discussed the matter with you, for I was too angry when I received word of it. The Dean of Students wrote me that you had turned your rooms into a gaming house, and had almost ruined several townsmen who lost large portions of their life savings.

It is essential that you be brought to the realization that a man must, in the final analysis, have the strength of character to make his own way in the world. I went over this carefully with you before you left to learn the cattle business. If you had worked industriously, I was prepared to send you the capital necessary to pursue this line of endeavor. However, you have apparently been discharged for slack behavior.

You cannot imagine how distressed I am that you have once again disgraced our family. John McIntire is my oldest and dearest friend, and I'm quite sure that he would not have sent you on your way without reason.

Do not write again to me until you have redeemed yourself. Go back to McIntire and beg his pardon.

You have disappointed me for the last time. In the name of heaven, Ladbrook, be a man. Take charge of your own destiny. Until this occurs, do not expect me to send you money so you can pursue your profligate ways.

Your father,
H.L.T.

Lad's fingers trembled as he folded the pages and shoved them into the envelope. The curt words hurt his feelings terribly. The fact that initials instead of a signature had been placed at the closing, in his opinion, showed a lack of feeling.

For a moment he pictured his father, a man who'd always maintained his dignity so rigidly. Hugh Ladbrook Trimble had kept a distance between himself and all other humans, including his son. Anger had built as he read the clear and brutal message—he was on his own and could expect no further help. Fear now mixed with the anger as full realization of his condition sank in.

He walked upstairs to his room and, on closing the door, leaned back upon it, overcome by a hollow, lost feeling. A single question kept running through his mind: What am I going to do?

He sat on the bed and took out the small purse he carried. He knew its contents but counted the seven dollars within it nonetheless. He returned the money to the purse, snapped it shut, and put it back in his pocket.

If Annie were only here, he kept thinking, I could talk to her, I could get her advice.

He considered returning to John McIntire's ranch. The thought of Beth enchanted him for a moment, but he knew that wasn't realistic. Her parents obviously planned a marriage for her with Harley Bragg, their wealthy neighbor. He recalled his bizarre duel with that man and knew he wouldn't be welcome.

Lad took stock of his situation: he found himself in ranching country, where the only apparent employment available would be for experienced cowboys. It wasn't likely that someone with his lack of experience could get a job. He certainly couldn't get on his horse and ride from ranch to ranch in the vague hope that someone might hire him. The few people he'd run across who lived on Texas ranches had been hospitable, but he knew he had no skills to offer them.

When noon came, feeling intensely vulnerable and desolate, he went down the street to Early Able's Saloon and Gaming Hall. He wanted to sit down and talk of mindless things with the young whores he'd met. He wanted to escape the confusion that enveloped him. He looked about without success for girls in bright dresses. The night before there'd been a host of them wandering about—some with hard eyes and brittle attitudes and others with open, smiling faces. None could be seen at the moment. They obviously remained upstairs. Their workday would begin much later. Midday for those girls, he decided, must be like dawn to others.

Lad paused near the only occupied table in the saloon. A man sat by himself there, spreading cards out before him, turning them up, and then sliding them back into a deck. He wore a striped blue shirt without a coat; black garters around his upper arms held the sleeves slightly above his wrists. He nodded to a chair, and Lad sat down.

"A game of twenty-one?"

Lad inclined his head in assent, feeling the old thrill. This wasn't what he considered his game, but he wondered if fate hadn't drawn him here. Maybe he could build his small stake into enough to get back home.

In a span of twenty minutes he lost four dollars. So he rose and excused himself, leaving the saloon with a haunted feeling. He owed more than the three dollars remaining in his pocket for his lodging at his hotel.

He went to his room and got his things. After explaining to Lupe that he'd run out of money, he asked if she would store his suitcase and saddlebags, saying he'd return for them later when he could pay his bill. Then he went down the street to a building where he'd noted a small scrawled sign which stated that the proprietor had beds available for 25 cents a night.

The room upstairs had seven or eight cots on a dusty plank floor. They occupied the entire slant-roofed attic, a fairly large area for which the building owner had found a use. A single dormer window at one end of the depressing, elongated room gave the only light. Heat hung heavily within the room.

Lad lay down on the prickly blanket of one of the hard, lumpy cots and felt perspiration running down his sides. He thought he'd rest for a time. Mercifully, he fell asleep.

He awoke with a start, opened his eyes, wondering where he was, what time it might be. Then he saw sunlight through the dormer window. Perspiration covered his body, and his clothing clung to him. He stripped to the skin and lay back on the damp bristles of the cheap wool cover. A sour, mildewed odor hovered in the air. Above his head in the attic he saw rough-sawn rafters and the undersides of shingles on the pitched roof. He itched and sat up, scratching, then saw a small black presence on his upper leg. Convulsively, he clawed it, horrified to find its head embedded in his flesh. When he tore the swollen bedbug free, it burst, leaving a large smear of brilliant blood upon the whiteness of his thigh. Gritting his teeth, he touched the slickness.

Revolted, he rose from the cot, ripping off the blanket. At least a dozen other bedbugs crawled slowly on the stained, striped ticking. Stuffed with dried cornshucks, the thin mattress made rustling noises as he tossed it in the air, then knelt upon it, picking through its crevices, searching for the small repulsive, multifooted creatures.

They made soft popping noises when he cracked them between his fingers, and each left behind a spot of bright blood—his own or that of a former occupant of the cot.

Lad desperately wanted to put on clean clothing, but he hadn't brought any of his things from the hotel—and he hated the idea of going back for them. He knew they wouldn't be safe here, that everything he owned would be stolen if left in a place like this.

He had never in his life wanted so urgently to take a bath. He yearned to wash away the blood, bugs, and lice he couldn't see, as well as traces of the filth which he felt must cover him. But there was no tub in the building. Bitterness welled within him, bile stirred in his stomach, and acid came from his throat into his mouth before subsiding.

A few minutes later he stopped trembling. Other people live in these conditions as a matter of course, he thought. Reflecting on this for a scant instant, however, he decided that philosophy was of no use whatsoever under the circumstances. He derived no particle of satisfaction from it.

The mid-afternoon sun glimmered through dust motes from the small window at the end of the room. He stood in this light, checking his naked body carefully, searching for more bedbugs or lice. Something crawled in his hair behind his left ear. For a frantic moment he scrubbed his fingernails through the itching, his jaw clenched so tight it ached.

Lad slipped into sweat-soaked clothing, pulled on his boots, and went to the wagon yard.

A man who identified himself as Owen Cook, the owner's brother-in-law, said, "We can't let you have your horse until you pay us for the feed he's been eatin'."

Lad paid two dollars after a long argument. At the close of it he negotiated the right to sleep for a few nights in a shed near the pens. He knew the hay in it would be a lot cleaner than the cot he'd rented earlier that afternoon. Then he saddled Claude and rode from the downtown area out into the purity and sanity of the barren flats to the northwest of the clustered buildings. Angling through small mesquites, he made his way toward the North Concho River, and found a stand of pecan trees where it made a lazy bend.

Lad tied the long reins of his bridle to a drooping limb in this roughly triangular peninsula and dismounted. Claude leaned his head down, happily pulling up great clumps of grass with blunt teeth, obviously welcoming the change from the dusty hay broken out for him at the wagon yard.

Lad walked through the trees to the river's edge. After looking about and seeing no sight of anyone else, he took off his hat and boots, and strode fully dressed into the dappled surface of the shaded river. The stream ran slowly where he stood but swirled in a rounded darker-looking pool on the far side. Trees on both banks arched over it and their tops swayed lazily in the scorching wind. He sank down in the water, sitting gingerly on the sand and gravel with the river's flow pressing gently around his waist and chest. Slowly he pulled off his socks, then his shirt, pants, and underwear. Determinedly scrubbing them, he used sand as a substitute for soap, and vigorously scoured everything he'd been wearing.

He limped on the sharp gravel through the water to the bank and laid his clothing out in a sunny spot to dry. Returning to the river, he bathed, washing his hair over and over.

A turtle plopped off a mossy log protruding above the river's surface. Sparrows chattered and flitted through the branches overhead, while small waterbugs skimmed about in circles on the surface of the greenish, muddy water. He sat very still, watching them. It seemed that a tension made a film at the surface which allowed them to scurry across it.

Lad leaned back on his elbows, savoring all of this, feeling *clean* again!

The day was intensely hot. The heat felt unlike anything he'd ever experienced before. The breeze against his cheek might have been emerging from a blast furnace. His first summer in Texas, he realized, would be an experience.

Lad, like most young people, never thought a great deal about the weather. In the snow and ice storms of Virginia winters, he had simply put on thick woolen clothing, wrapped a scarf around his neck, put on a heavy coat, and ignored the conditions. During Tidewater summers, along the lazy broad James River, he'd never given a thought to how hot it might be, despite the humidity. Even in the muggy days of August, he'd never paid the slightest attention to it, simply accepting whatever nature offered. But *this,* he decided, was something entirely different.

The sun hung in the west, brassy and intense, radiating a fierceness that absolutely dazed him. Lad told himself uncertainly, I'll get used to it.

He thought of Annie Tankersley and hoped she'd be well soon. Oddly enough, the heat had brought her to mind. He was grateful for her advice to get a hat with a protectively wide brim so he'd avoid sunstroke. He hadn't really understood until today that something as basic as a hat could be, in all truth, a matter of life or death.

He paddled out into the river and sank down into it, trying without success to see in the underwater murkiness. From the surface down two or three feet, the river felt like water in a heated bathtub. But under this ran much cooler currents.

He splashed his way to the far side from the bank where he'd placed his clothes, toward the deep pool where the river made its bend back to the left. Holding his breath, he dove down, kicking his feet, until he reached the muddy bottom. For a few seconds he swam in the delicious coolness. Just as he started up, he felt a slithering, slick firmness slide across his chest.

Horrified, he curled and twisted in the water, urgently threshing his way to the surface—where he gasped for breath. Had it been a fish?

At that instant he saw a long water moccasin. The water snake held its black head just above the surface, and a small wave rippled back as it whipped its supple length rapidly away from him.

Jolted by instinctive fear, still feeling the tingling where it had touched him, Lad swam back across the river as fast as he could. When he reached the shallows, he scrambled to his feet and threw himself on the grassy bank.

My God! he thought. A rustling south wind almost instantly baked the dampness from his flesh and hair more thoroughly than if he'd vigorously toweled himself dry. But almost immediately his skin moistened with perspiration.

Lad stood in the shade, bare feet on twigs and dust, one hand on the rough bark of a pecan tree's trunk. What am I doing here? he asked himself. He leaned forward, sweeping leaves and dry grass from his legs and buttocks, then walked to his clothing.

After dressing, he felt uncommonly relieved—in spite of the fact that, after paying twenty-five cents to rent a cot in that disgusting attic, he now had only seventy-five cents to his name. And he was in debt to Annie Tankersley at least eight to ten dollars. That sum, which once would have seemed insignificant, now loomed impossibly large.

Well, I've got a horse and saddle and a place to sleep tonight, he thought. I'll not part with Claude. After all, he believed the horse came from good stock, and was in addition his means of escape from the trouble in which he found himself.

He'd never really gotten a job on his own. In fact, the brief time on McIntire's Stars and Bars Ranch was the only paid employment he'd ever had. And that had been as a favor granted by McIntire due to family friendship.

People have always liked me, he reasoned. That had been his good fortune all of his life. Without the slightest reason for it, he felt a surge of youthful optimism. In fact, he looked forward to the challenges before him. Phrasing it to himself in a simplistic way, he said out loud, "There's nothing wrong with my circumstances that can't be fixed with a little money."

Heartened by his own encouraging words, he strode to his horse, gathered the reins, and mounted. As he rode along, he thought of the host of people who managed to earn good livings in spite of suffering, in his view, from the undeniable handicap of being hopelessly wooden-headed and ill-informed. His confidence grew, and he felt a certainty that there did not exist one single reason why he shouldn't prosper immediately.

Lad had always felt a distinct sense of superiority to the majority of mankind, despite having no evidence whatsoever to support this theory. While he had no definite plans for launching himself into the world of commerce, he knew that something fine would surely turn up.

Even with his hurt feelings, he grudgingly admitted that his father was right, that he had, up until now, never actually tried to *do* anything. But by God, that was soon going to change.

He said to himself, "I'll show *him* the stuff I'm made of if it kills me."

As he rode southward near the river, he pulled his grandfather's old watch from his pocket. This favorite possession, its gold case worn smooth by generations of use, opened when he pressed the stem. Almost seven-thirty! He couldn't believe the time, forgetting that he'd slept part of the afternoon. The long summer days stayed light until at least eight now that June had arrived.

He remembered suddenly that he'd promised to meet Mattie at seven—and would be late. Spurring Claude into a rocking lope, he sat the saddle easily as his horse wound through trees and bushes. He felt a gnawing hunger, for he'd missed his noon meal. Well, at least he had enough money for a steak tonight and a good breakfast to-morrow, and then he'd find a job. He felt sure of it.

Lad saw the stand of bamboo in the distance and slowed Claude to a trot. I shouldn't be doing this, ran through his mind. But she'd been so insistent—and anyway, this would probably be the last time he'd see her. She'd given him that impression. He composed a few gallant sentences, preparing to say farewell to her in the most gentle-manly of ways—his mind fixed in fact more on the future than on the girl.

Lad said to himself, "I'd be a fool to keep seeing the wife of a brute like Dee Hudnall. Even if he's off on a trip, that mean-looking Mexican who works for him might have followed her."

The recollection of the armed Mexican and the long knife that men said he carried caused Lad's sense of ease to vanish as swiftly as it had come.

Nervously, he pulled Claude to a halt about two hundred yards from the stand of bamboo. He tied his horse in a thicket of hackberry trees where the animal wouldn't be noticed, then walked out through the thorny branches. As he emerged, he saw Mattie sitting at the edge of the river. She wore a long, pale yellow dress and no hat. She was sitting very still, staring at the water.

When he reached her side he saw that she was breathing rapidly and her face was pale.

"You should have worn something to protect your head," he said, but she didn't seem to be listening.

She murmured, "I'm dizzy."

Lad took his hat and filled it with water. Kneeling beside her, he poured a little on her hair.

"Goda'mighty, but that feels good. Pour it all over me."

He did as she asked, then filled the hat again, pouring more river water over her head and shoulders. The light yellow dress turned almost transparent and clung to her like a skin.

"Did Ramón see you come this way?"

"No. He had to ride out to the ranch. He said something about helpin' the men load my things and move them to the new house here in town. I feel a little better now. This day's a real scorcher, ain't it?"

Lad didn't reply.

Mattie said, "My husband will get here tomorrow."

Lad started to think of his gallant farewell speech, the one he'd been mentally composing. But the closeness of the girl interfered with his concentration.

She rose to her feet, clutching his arm. The direct glare faded as shadows fell. The sun couldn't be seen from the river bottom, but he knew it had to be sinking toward the horizon.

"I was afraid you wouldn't come."

"I'm sorry I'm late—I really am." Lad looked about, not seeing any people, only the prairieland lying between the river and the town's low-lying houses and shanties and buildings. Twilight cast a pale yellow light on the scene, painting the roofs.

"Let's get out of sight," he said, leading her toward the bamboo grove.

He drew her into a narrow passageway. Hundreds of tall bamboo shoots, green and limber, crowded together, looking impenetrable. They had to get down on their hands and knees at one point to make it through what seemed like a tunnel, surrounded on all sides by thick round hollow stems with regular ridged joints between their sections. Some of these crisscrossed above them and rubbed against their backs. Then they emerged in a small interior circle. It looked almost like a roofless room lined with waving tall canes with feathery tops. The ground had a thick carpet of bamboo leaves that had fallen through the years as well as a clover-like growth, and they sank down upon the rustling pillowed surface. Around the edges of the enclosure, new conical shoots of bamboo emerged from their roots, rounded tops protruding a few inches into the air.

Mattie began to tell him of the way Hudnall's sons had tried to make advances upon her; how often she'd hear them pushing against her locked door at night. "They were after me," she said in a matter-of-fact way. "That's how men are," she added with a note of resignation.

Lad had heard various stories about the three sons of Dee Hudnall, and everything he'd been told revolted him. But he realized that he and they had at least one thing that was very much in common. Lad knew that they'd have the same normal healthy appetites of any young male, and virtually all of the young women within hundreds of miles were married except for the prostitutes. Tom Green County probably had a thousand or so men, more if the soldiers were counted, and hardly any available women at all.

It made him feel distinctly uncomfortable that he and the sons of Dee Hudnall shared the same problem.

He hadn't been listening to her, and was only vaguely aware of the droning of her words. She continued, ". . . and I just can't stand him. I don't want him to touch me, can't bear it when he comes near me at night." With quick vehemence she whispered, *"I wish to hell he was dead."*

She lay down on her back and unbuttoned the top buttons of her dress. "It's so damn hot," she complained, looking up at his face with the slightest flicker of calculation in her eyes.

She said in a wavering voice, "I need for you to make me feel *alive.*"

Lad tried to speak but had some difficulty. "You'll be better after you rest a minute."

Heatedly she burst out, "You know that's not what I meant."

Lad cleared his throat, but she reached up and pulled him to her. He resisted a moment, then felt a fever overtake him as their lips met.

Fear made chill bumps ripple down his arm and made the hair on the back of his neck seem to raise.

He jerked back to a sitting position. "What if Ramón's trying to trick us? We'd be in a spot if he showed up."

Her face flushed with anger. She snapped, "I *told* you he's gone to the ranch. I watched him ride off."

She said in a cajoling way, her attitude reverting to the way it had been, "You're goin' to drive me crazy if you don't calm down. We've got all the time in the world—and no one to bother us at all."

"Well . . ."

"You're worried about my husband." She waited a few seconds before adding, "Don't think of me as bein' a married woman. I don't think of myself as bein' no wife. I'm just Mattie. That's all there is to it."

He sat beside her without saying anything.

"The fact is, Lad, I got *sold.* I'm *property,* and not by my own choice neither."

She told him falteringly something of her story, of being the eldest of four girls, with their mother dead in childbirth. "Pa farmed a little, but we never had anything at all. You've got no idea what poor is 'til you live like we did. We didn't even have beans or cornbread. There wasn't *nothin'.* So we started out back to East Texas where Pa had some family. But on the way he stopped at Hudnall's and sold me for fifty dollars and a mule. That sounds mighty strange, I know that it does. But it's true."

She said bitterly, "I guess with the money and that mule they got back to where Pa wanted to go. But he never sent for me."

She looked pleadingly at him, as though aching for him to understand what she was trying to explain. "I was so *young,* just barely fifteen, and hadn't really growed up. And Hudnall is such a big bull of a man. He hurt me so bad . . ." Her voice broke off. Then it hardened. "But I got used to it. You can get used to mighty near anything, I guess."

She rose to her feet and paced back and forth for a moment, then sank down on her knees before Lad. "I ran away twice, but got caught both times. Hudnall has his own way of punishment. Mostly he strips me down and whips my little old butt with his belt 'til I bleed. He kind of likes that, I think, otherwise I can't see why he does it so much. But the second time I ran, he went wild. That's when he did this to me. I have to show you or you won't understand."

She unfastened her dress all the way down to her waist and stretched it open. Then she calmly pulled down the wet white chemise, her long shirt-like undergarment.

Lad's heart skipped, and he gaped as she totally bared her small white breasts. They were round, slightly upturned, and pink-tipped.

"Hudnall done that to me," Hattie said, touching long, irregular pinkish scars that went down beside her nipples. "He held me down and slit me with his knife the second time I tried to get away. He said he'd bought and paid for me, and if I ran a third time he'd cut my head clean off with an ax. God, I was so scared. Anyway, after that I didn't fight him or try to run anymore. And from then on when he'd come into the room at night, I just laid there and let him do what he wanted."

She took his right hand and put it on her breast. "Wish *you'd* been the one to buy me," she said.

Lad had never been able to rely on his self-control. Later, remembering what had happened, he recalled that it totally disappeared at the instant his fingers touched her softness.

The sky turned violet with strange red- and orange-streaked rays from the sunset, but the frantic young man and young woman didn't notice this beauty at all.

Thirteen

JULES ORNETTE, the man called "the Frenchman" by his enemies, sat beside Dee Hudnall at his ranch house in its protected
valley. The two didn't entirely trust one another. Hudnall, however,
considered Ornette to be the only friend he had. No one ever knew
what Ornette thought about anything. He had never seen the property in which he held a one half interest before, knowing only what
Hudnall had told him about it on his frequent trips to New Orleans.
This first trip to Texas had a purpose: he wanted to end the Ornette-
Hudnall partnership and split their assets.

Ornette had a withered left arm as a result of a childhood accident
to which he never referred. He habitually held this in a bent position,
and most people never noticed the deformity. A thin man, he had an
aquiline nose and high cheekbones. A carefully trimmed black mustache with some gray in it and an equally neat Vandyke beard gave
him a rather distinguished appearance in spite of the fact that he
stood no more than five feet and four inches. He had black eyes
under hooded lids. This night, sitting under the lamplight, he said
little and, as usual, never smiled.

Many men become happy when they're drunk. Some turn mean,
while others tend to cry. Hudnall, who rarely drank at all, had
downed so much whiskey that he could scarcely stand and, as always
happened upon such occasions, had become morose and enormously
sad.

They had begun the evening by reminiscing, for they shared many
memories. The two had become acquainted in Missouri when they
served as enlisted men for the Northern services during wartime.
Under cover of darkness they had taken twelve thousand dollars intended for the commissary and payroll, and on that same evening

unofficially resigned from the United States Army and the struggle to preserve the Union.

The two deserters found their way to New Orleans a short time after the Yankees occupied it. And in the course of time they met General Butler, commander of the Northern troops there, the man Southerners called "Beast Butler." By virtue of their newfound wealth, they made friends with him and other powerful officers in the occupying forces.

With the help of Yankee tax officials, Ornette purchased two attractive houses—formerly owned by gentlemen serving as Confederate Army officers—for only a fraction of their value. The expansive two-story dwellings, located on charming streets in the French quarter, proved to be extremely popular after Ornette put them to use. He found it quite simple to stock them with beautiful quadroons, girls and young women of one-quarter black and three-quarter French blood. Soon blue-coated officers and Northern civilian officials discovered these discreet and tastefully decorated mansions where they could be provided with quiet but often exotic entertainment. In this way the informal partnership formed by Hudnall and Ornette made a number of important business acquaintances.

These led to contracts to supply beef to the Northern soldiers. When peace came, these contracts continued, and were expanded for supply to army posts across the Southwest.

Ornette conducted his affairs from tastefully decorated offices in an old brick building which housed on its ground floor a highly respected bank. He soon had several dependable bookkeepers who spent their days posting figures in leather-bound ledgers. Ornette controlled the partnership investments and expanded their luxurious houses of prostitution, adding three more of them, employing numerous ladies of the night for the pleasure of floods of Northerners who engulfed the port city during the postwar madness. He added gambling as well and then used the partnership's swelling profits to branch out into other fields of endeavor, buying paddleboats to ply the Mississippi, hauling cotton north and manufactured products south. A few years later, he purchased a large warehouse near the waterfront and in time expanded this extensively.

Hudnall had no patience for the complexities of the growing city enterprises in New Orleans, and attended to the cattle supply end of the partnership.

Any fool could have made money with the beef contracts they

enjoyed during the decades of Reconstruction, for the large cattle herds had, during the course of the war, grown to immense proportions. As a result of oversupply, prices for beef fell like a stone. But Hudnall found that he could make even greater profits if he acquired cattle for nothing. Recruiting men who'd fought for and against Quantrill in "Bloody Kansas," as well as some men he had met in New Orleans, Hudnall swept through the plains of Texas. The long cattle drives were then in full flow to the railheads in Dodge City, Kansas, and his men helped him take charge of cattle while they were in transit.

In the course of these encounters, riders conditioned by years of merciless raids in Missouri and Kansas, trained more as killers than soldiers, bloodied the postwar plains. Taking no prisoners, Hudnall and his heavily armed raiders left more than seventy cowboys unburied in West Texas, Oklahoma, and southern Kansas. But as the trail drives diminished—when railroads entered Texas—and as the risks of these raids increased, Hudnall changed his method of operation.

His first step was to bring his inner circle of outlaws under strict control. Hudnall had a simple philosophy, and knew from experience that the greatest motivator of all was fear, but close behind that lay greed. The few remaining gunfighters he retained in his employ had seen him in action and realized how dangerous he could be—and did indeed fear him. But Hudnall kept their loyalty by raising their wages to the point where they had greater security than any of them had ever known before. With this close-knit body of cold-blooded men as a personal army, he systematically eliminated those less fortunate members of his old organization. A few survivors made their escape, but not many. And those who did get away knew better than to tell what they knew about their former leader.

Ornette never participated in the bloody ventures in cattle country, and although he knew in general the way the partnership had been building its fortunes, he didn't ask questions. Needless to say, he was pleasantly surprised at the sums of money Hudnall brought to their bank accounts in New Orleans. He knew, of course, that Hudnall was probably turning over less than half of his actual profits, but then Ornette only put about that percentage from their New Orleans investments, including the expanding prostitution business, into their partnership accounts in various banks.

The men understood each other perfectly and liked one another as well as it was possible for either to like any man.

But now Hudnall was drunk, on this, the first occasion of a visit made by Ornette to Texas. He leaned forward, holding his great, knobby, bald head in his large calloused hands. He had blunt, thick fingers with wide nails. His hands and arms, like the rest of his body, were virtually hairless.

"Yes, I married again. The first two died, as you're aware. You've always been a bachelor, and I've never inquired into your private life. But I've got to have a woman in the house all the time. Some men need that kind of thing more than others, I guess. The funny thing, Jules, is that she's *different* from the others. For one thing, she's crazy—which in a peculiar way is kind of exciting. I never know what to expect from her."

He fell silent, pouring another drink and sipping from it. Tears suddenly began to run down his face. "Jules, I never thought I'd say this, but I love that Mattie, and I can't understand why. I've always despised weakness, and Mattie's skinny and weak. Makes me so mad that sometimes I grab and shake her 'til her head near pops off. That's one thing. Another is that she's got a mean streak that's a yard wide—and can be cruel and cold as a snake sometimes. That don't really bother me—I understand people like that. But there's sides to her I sure as hell *don't* understand. But in spite of everything, I have this idea that *I want to take care of her.*"

"You're drunk, Dee."

"I know." Hudnall reared back in his chair and tried to sit upright. He said softly, "I just can't bear to be away from her. She's been a bitch, I'll admit, and says all the time that she *hates* me. How can that be? Can you answer that?" A look of dark belligerence colored his swarthy face.

"Many's the time I've had to whip hell out of her—just to keep her in line. But she's *mine.* Now Ramón tells me that she's been triflin' with some town boy, and if that's true, I'm goin' to have to kill her. Jules, that will just break my heart."

More tears flowed as he drank. "Ramón hasn't figured out who the son of a bitch is, but he says he's pretty sure somethin's been goin' on while I was gone on that last trip."

He staggered to his feet. "I got to go to bed, Jules. I'm just too sad about all this." He said in a slurred voice, "I won't really kill her. I want to, but I can't do that. She means too much to me."

The next morning the two men met over breakfast. Hudnall had a severe headache and ate nothing but some biscuits with his coffee.

Later they sat at the dining room table and pored over books of account. They'd been doing this in New Orleans during the last three trips Hudnall had made there, and had finally agreed to what they felt was a fair arrangement. Hudnall had already transferred his share of the money from New Orleans to his bank in Fort Worth. He'd signed over his interests in all of the houses and warehouses and riverboats to Ornette. The Frenchman, in his turn, signed over to Hudnall all of his interests in the huge Texas ranch and the cattle upon it.

With the papers signed, each man leaned back in his chair, quietly pleased. Hudnall felt sure that he had "skinned" his old friend, had done him out of at least three quarters of a million dollars. And Ornette, quietly relishing the moment, felt certain that Hudnall had no earthly idea of the value of the warehouses, riverboats, and other businesses which Ornette now owned all by himself. For one thing, Ornette had acquired a majority interest in the second largest bank in New Orleans over the past six months, a fact he'd neglected to mention. The New Orleans investments turned out dependable income week after week, month after month. And in the years to come, there would be no limit.

On the other hand, the cattle business was subject to wild fluctuations in pricing. The market for beef was controlled by outside forces over which cattlemen had no control whatsoever. In addition, ranchers had the weather as a constant enemy. Cattle died from drouth or from brutal winters. And they were subject to all sorts of diseases that could decimate entire herds. Ornette was frankly delighted with the deal he had struck.

The Frenchman lit a black narrow cigar and drew its smoke into his lungs, feeling totally content to have, in effect, robbed his only friend, to have stripped from him any hope for financial security. None of this showed in his face. He had felt a slight moment of anxiety, fearing up to the last moment that Hudnall would back out of their deal, but this didn't happen.

Ornette stuffed his copies of the contracts into his inside coat pocket and made a studied effort to change the subject.

"You're the sole owner of one of the biggest ranches anywhere, and have one of the largest cattle herds in Texas. On top of that, you have a full bank account in the Forth Worth National Bank. That means you can live anywhere you want. You don't have to stay hundreds of miles away from civilization. Why don't you at least move to Fort Worth or Dallas—why stay out here in this wilderness?"

Ornette couldn't imagine living by choice in such a desolate spot.

"You can't walk away from your holdings, Jules. If you do, the manager you trust to run things for you will start makin' off with your cattle. Rustlers'll come after you. A man has to fight to keep what he has, and there's not a day he can relax and forget that."

Ornette walked to the window and looked toward the west, at the rocky hills and the rolling wide valley between them. "I'd die of loneliness here."

"You've got a point. All of us need to be around others now and again. And it's even more important for a woman. I don't know if I've told you, but I've built a house not far out from San Angelo on the west side of the North Concho. It sits by itself up on a bluff. I'm puttin' Mattie there. She's not all that comfortable around my boys. They pester her."

Ornette's shrewd eyes stared through the rising blue cigar smoke. "I think you'd be smart to keep them apart."

"There's another thing. Last night when I'd had a few drinks I believe I said that Mattie acts a little strange at times. Maybe a change of scene will do her good. That's why I've gone to a lot of trouble to fix a place for her. She sure as hell won't have to worry about anybody botherin' her when I'm away. I've got a house that's not like any you've ever seen."

Hudnall enjoyed talking of his possessions. He went to a red oak cabinet at one side of the room and, opening a drawer, took from it a set of plans. Unfolding these on the table, he talked with enthusiasm about his new house.

"You'll see that I've got some acreage around it, and the property line is fenced with tall cedar posts, about seven feet high. Them posts aren't spaced apart with wire or planks across 'em, but are set deep in the ground with each one snug up against the next. In addition to that, I've got barbed wire strands along the top of the fence. The house itself is a big one, more size than we need, but I like plenty of room. The north side is where I've got a master bedroom that must be thirty feet long and maybe twenty feet wide. Next to it I've built a sewin' room for Mattie that's real nice. There's no windows at all in that wing of the house, which may sound like a bad idea, but it'll be plenty warm during the winter. I've got some big paddle fans rigged to the ceiling to stir the air during summer, and they're hooked up by pulleys to ropes that hang outside. There's some Meskin boys who'll work there, and if it gets hot, they'll by God pull on them ropes and keep us cool.

"Of course, there's a few other bedrooms with regular windows over on the south side, so when I'm home to take care of things, I'll take Mattie over there when it gets real hot so we can take advantage of the south breeze." His face darkened. "But when I'm out of town, I'll keep her locked up in that north wing. She'll have plenty to do there."

"I doubt that she'll find being a prisoner to be pleasant," Ornette observed.

"You don't know Mattie," Hudnall replied shortly. "She's the sort of woman that has to be held with a tight rein. But she won't be a prisoner—I'll get Ramón to take her to the stores now and then so she can look for things she might want. Women love to go shoppin'."

He sighed. "God, she's rare some of the time. Just a few months ago, when I got back from one of those trips to New Orleans, I arrived at the ranch and found my boys out of their heads with rage. They were fit to be tied. We've had an old ewe around the place, kind of a pet. She wandered around but stayed close to the ranch house since my boys fed her and the like. But on the day before I got home, Mattie went outside with one of my rifles and shot the damn sheep. When the boys asked why on earth she'd done that she said, 'That ewe *stared* at me whenever I walked in the yard.'"

Ornette drew back in his chair, making no reply. After a time he asked, "Has she done anything else like that?"

"Not exactly, although a while ago I waked up in the night when I heard somethin' moving. I leaned over and lit the lamp, and damned if Mattie wasn't standing in her nightgown over by the far wall. She had my Colt in her hand. I said, 'Mattie, what in the hell are you doin'?' And she said—just as calm as can be—'I'm fixin' to shoot you right between the eyes.'

"She raised the sixgun and pointed it right square at my head. I jumped out of bed and grabbed the pistol away—damn near broke her wrist doin' it—and then I gave her the worst whippin' of her life. She wasn't able to walk for a day or two after. Later I asked what possessed her, and she acted like she couldn't remember anything at all about it. She swore she never pointed a gun at me. Said she must have been asleep and dreamin'."

"Do you plan to live in San Angelo from now on?"

"Lord no. It'll be sort of a headquarters house for me, and I'll spend a little time there, but mostly I'll be out here, keeping an eye on things, runnin' the ranch. I've made enemies, you have to know a little about that, and I don't like folks knowin' where I'm likely to be. So my plan, like always, is to keep movin' around."

Ornette rose to his feet. He faced a long trip and dreaded it. Outside the window he saw the expressionless black servant he'd brought from New Orleans sitting in the buggy, holding the reins patiently. His baggage had been neatly strapped behind; a padded seat awaited him. His two bodyguards stood by their horses, talking quietly to one another.

"Will we see one another again?" he said.

Hudnall shook hands with him. "I doubt it, but you never know."

Ornette nodded briefly, turned, and walked from the room and away from the man with whom he'd shared an almost twenty-year partnership. He'd always thought he'd have to kill Hudnall, and was satisfied with the peaceful way they'd settled their affairs.

An hour later, Hudnall and Ramón set out for San Angelo. A driver followed in a wagon loaded high with all of Mattie's belongings. They'd reach San Angelo late that day, and by tomorrow would move into the new house.

Lad saddled Claude and rode from the wagon yard where he'd slept on a stack of dusty hay the night before. Last night he'd had the good steak dinner he'd promised himself, and on arising had spent his last twenty-five cents on a decent breakfast. Then, without a cent in his pocket, he rode to the courthouse where he struck up a conversation with a clerk.

"This here," the clerk said, "is the 1880 census report for Tom Green County. You got to understand that it covers a lot of territory —they say they're goin' to bust it up into a bunch of counties one of these days. But anyway, the census lists how many folks live within a few hundred miles of here and what their jobs are. It's just exactly what you're lookin' for, if you want to know what employment might be around these parts. I admire a young fellow like you, fixin' to start out in life and plannin' it in such a thoughtful way."

Lad stood at the counter as the clerk began to read from the list. "The page headed 'Occupation' starts with 'Adobe Worker.' We have three of them. Next is 'Baker,' and I'm surprised to find seven listed, although I'd bet that most are out at Fort Concho. There's a barber, five blacksmiths, one bookkeeper, a buffalo hunter, six butchers, and

God knows how many cattle raisers and herders. We've got one deputy sheriff, who's gone all the time, and a few farmhands, one farrier,
which is a fancy name for a man who shoes horses."

He looked perplexed as he flipped through the pages. "Well, boy,
there's a few hotel keepers, saloon keepers, a few saddlers, some
sheepherders and one goat raiser, a stage driver, a tailor, a well digger
and a wheelwright. Do any of these sound of interest to you?"

Lad shook his head.

"I tell you what. Lonnie Cox owns a slaughterhouse, and he told
me he was lookin' for a hand. You'll find his place out to the southeast—but on this side of the fort. Why not go see if he'll hire you?"

After thanking the clerk, Lad rode to the low-water crossing, made
his way through the river, and, with directions from a number of
people, an hour later finally located Lonnie Cox's small farm.

"I'll hire you for seventy-five cents a day," Cox said, "if you want
the work. To tell the truth, I'd expected to git a wetback Meskin, but
if you want the job, it's yours."

The two walked out the back door of Cox's home to an unpainted
frame building next to some pens. Some skinny old cows and a few
steers stood in the pens, and two boys in their early teens sat on the
fence, staring at Lad.

Cox opened the door of the frame building and preceded Lad into
it. When they walked inside, Lad recoiled from the smell. Green flies
buzzed all around, black blood completely covered the sticky dirt
floor, and great puddles of it congealed in low spots. The stench of
rotting flesh was overpowering. It rose like a pestilent cloud and
assailed his nostrils.

"I'll tell you what we do," Lad's new employer said. "You see how
I built the slaughterhouse—there's a wide door over yonder and a
kind of 'crowd pen' on the far side. Then, leadin' from there is this
narrow chute that you can see. The boys push the cattle into the
crowd pen, and then they take prod poles and git 'em one by one in
that chute. They stick a pole behind and in front of the cow or the
steer when they get one up to this end of it, so they got no choice but
to stand there. Then, all you got to do is this."

Cox picked up a heavy sledgehammer. "You bust out their brains,
and then we drag 'em out of the chute to that hoist you see over
yonder. We wire their hind legs to the hoist, crank 'em up, and we
skin and butcher 'em right here on the spot. After that, we more or
less quarter 'em, and take those parts over to those metal-clad tables

where we carve 'em up for market. Your arm'll git tired at first, 'cause we work hard with them bone saws, and neither them old things or these rusty butcher knives are in as good a shape as they might be, but they git the job done. Naturally, we only slaughter when we've got someone fixin' to buy, or else the meat tends to get a little rank after a few days, 'specially in summer.''

He said, ''I think there's a bright future for the slaughterhouse business. A smart young boy like you can be a big help to me. I'm told that in Chicago they sell the hides for leather. There's a market for tallow, the bones get ground up for bonemeal for feed, and hooves and horns can be boiled down for glue. They just ain't no waste at all if you go at it in a scientific way. So, aside for providin' folks good healthy beef to eat, we got all sorts of other sales prospects.'' He beamed at Lad's back, for his new employee was stumbling through the door leading outside. Cox followed him into the open air.

Several bony yellow dogs dragged a bloated, graying stomach and yards of intestines across the ground. They snarled at one another.

''Haven't figured out how to make money out of the guts,'' Cox said cheerfully. ''I'm told that those crazy Scotsmen eat somethin' called haggis, made of sheep stomachs stuffed with rice and other things, but people out here haven't developed the taste for such things. On the other hand, there's always a market for liver and sweetbread and tongue and brains. Which brings to mind one point. When I said you was to bust out their brains, I want you to do it careful so you don't splatter 'em *completely*. We want to save some, since the cafes buy brains whenever they can git 'em for customers who like 'em along with their scrambled eggs.''

Lad's fine breakfast rose in his throat. Almost choking with nausea, he leaned against the fence.

''Well, do you want the job or not?''

Lad knew that he could probably buy beans and maybe rice if he had seventy-five cents, enough to last him for several days. And by now he was growing seriously hungry in spite of his sick stomach. He decided that he could sleep at the wagon yard for a few days until he could find a better job, and realized he had no choice but to take this one.

Nodding grimly, he said, ''You've got your man, Mr. Cox. When do I start?''

"Right now," Cox said, handing him a blackened stiff apron. "You might want to put this on."

They went back into the small slaughterhouse and in this way the worst day of Lad's life began.

He actually made it through the long afternoon, only vomiting once in the process. His arms were so weary he could scarcely lift them, and his back ached so he could hardly stand it.

As dusk fell, he asked for his wages, collected his seventy-five cents, and said, "Mr. Cox, I know what you're doing is necessary. But I don't feel cut out for this work." He thanked him, and walked slowly toward his horse, listening to Cox mingle muttered cuss words with chuckles as he watched him stumble away.

Claude shied violently away from his blood-covered master. When Lad finally managed to get astride him, Claude bucked with some earnestness before Lad got him under control. A cloud of greenish bottle flies clustered all over him and kept buzzing around his face and ears.

"I've got to get cleaned up," he said to himself through clenched teeth. He urged Claude into a slow rocking canter, and headed for the Tankersley Hotel. After apologizing profusely to Lupe, who tried to deny entrance to him, he forced his way toward the bathtub.

"Lupe, I know that you and Mrs. Tankersley reserve this for your paying guests, but I'll give you fifty cents for some hot water. And please bring me my suitcase so I can change clothes. I think I'll just ask you to burn these."

Lupe shook her head. "You look worse than anybody I've ever seen in my life. It goin' to take me hours to clean up this tub after you get through with it." But she took pity on him, said she'd let him take a bath, and soon brought kettles of steaming hot water and also some harsh soap from the kitchen that she used on greasy pots and pans. After draining the tub and getting more water, cold this time so he could rinse off the filthy suds, he scrubbed every inch of his body. Then he rose from the tub, stepped to the floor, and gratefully accepted fresh towels which she handed through the door to him.

While Lad had bathed, Lupe took his boots out to the kitchen where she took saddle soap and vigorously scoured them until at last she'd removed the coats of dried blood. Then she rubbed them with lanolin so they wouldn't get dry, although now they smelled strangely like sheep. After this, she took them upstairs and put them outside the bathroom.

Lad put on his fresh clothes, left the old ones to be burned, and asked Lupe to keep his things for him. He knew she'd probably let him spend the night, but he didn't want to ask for charity. And he knew she'd feed him, but after all, he'd gone through hell this day in his first effort to make his own way.

Lupe told him that the cheapest place in town to buy food was out past the fort where sheepherders often came. If they could be found, they'd be there to sell mutton or goats to the Mexicans who lived in shacks near the fort. The women who worked as laundresses had little to pay for their meals, she explained.

By the time he made it to the fort it had grown late. He paused a short distance away, watching sentries pace back and forth in front of the main building. Lights in the lines of stone buildings began going out.

A bugle sounded at Fort Concho; a thin blade of sound swelled in the cooling air of night. It soared and zigzagged across the sky and sounded on the ears of lonely men lying restlessly in ordered ranks and files in barracks, and it had a hypnotic effect on Lad.

He reined Claude about and headed to the shacks past the fort. After asking directions, he headed southwest until he made out a campfire.

The sheepherders had a fire going in the darkness. Wind blew briskly, dust whirled through the air, and the campfire made a hazed glow. As he drew nearer, he could see sparks dancing crazily and a charred log glowing dark red, with flakes from it whirling with the unseen wind into the night.

The herders had killed a goat that afternoon, butchered it, and now they would feast. Lad stepped down from his horse, tying him to a tree limb. He approached the men.

Several rose to their feet as he drew near.

Lad said, "I'm hungry."

They didn't seem to understand at first why this well-dressed white man, one who looked to their eyes like a cowboy, one with a fine horse, should be approaching them. They'd had bad experiences with whites, and several put their hands on knives and pistols.

"I'm hungry," Lad said again. Then he realized they didn't speak English. He pointed to his stomach and then to his mouth. He took his remaining twenty-five cents from a pocket and offered it in an outstretched hand.

A fat Mexican with a great mustache smiled slowly. *"Tiene hambre, gringo? Pues, bien, véngase aquí. Puede comer con nosotros."* With that, he took the money from Lad's hand and drew him into the circle of flickering light thrown out by the flames.

The herders sat on the ground about the fire in an irregular circle. One of them had an old guitar and sang a plaintive Spanish song, strumming the strings energetically. After this he leaned it carefully against a tree. The men spoke to one another in their native tongue, paying no attention to Lad.

His stomach growled continuously, and he wondered if he'd ever been this hungry before. The smell of roasting meat tantalized him. Legs, haunches, ribs, and other parts had been stuck on green limbs cut from living trees, and these held the roasting flesh just over the coals. He looked through smoke and flames at what he first thought was an oddly shaped charred log. Then he flinched involuntarily before sinking to one knee, unable to avert his eyes. Fat dripped down on the low flames and sizzled on the fire. The goat's severed head lay in the black and red coals, horns blackened, eyes dark. The skinned head burned slightly, and the herders stared at it in anticipation.

Lad had heard from cowboys on the McIntire Ranch about this practice of Mexican cowboys and sheepherders. They considered the tender flesh of the goat's head a singular delicacy, along with the eyes and the brain and the tongue.

Well, he thought, I'll let them have the head.

A few minutes later he received a metal plate loaded with roast goat and frijole beans with fiercely hot small red chili peppers. He ate ravenously, ignoring the searing peppers. He had never experienced anything more delicious than the wood-smoke-roasted goat flesh.

It seemed that the Mexicans accepted him, telling him stories in rapid, blurred Spanish and occasionally clapping him on the back. He couldn't understand a single word they said. When he unsaddled Claude and curled up on the ground near the fire, they didn't seem to notice. The desert coolness stole over the camp, vaguely surprising Lad after the furnace heat of the day. He found his saddle blanket and put it over him, and moments later he slept.

One of his new friends crept up to the big horse and wondered about stealing him, but when Claude reared straight up, lashing out with his hooves, the herder changed his mind.

The noise waked Lad. He sat up for a few minutes, then put his head back on the saddle.

A coyote howled in the distance as the fire died down. Gradually the men fell asleep except for the one who watched over the placid sheep that stood stoically in the darkness.

Lad lay on his back, looking up at the endless clusters of stars. Every muscle and fiber in his body seemed to ache. But he couldn't go back to sleep. I've got to find a job, he kept thinking. If I don't, I'll starve.

Fourteen

LAD TOOK HIS HORSE back to the wagon yard where he talked Owen Cook into allowing him to clean out the stables in exchange for a meal. He used a shovel and an old wheelbarrow, moving from one stall to the next.

Cook wandered by and said, "In the three years we been in business, this is the first time we've done any cleanin' up. From the loads I seen you carryin' out of here, I guess we should a'thought of this before."

Lad didn't look up from his grim task. It didn't take long before he became accustomed to the sour but not altogether unpleasant odor of horse droppings. Each time he filled the wheelbarrow, he'd take it to a far corner of the property and dump it. Dark beetles fought free of the hay- and straw-filled dungheap and scrambled away.

The noon sun glared down on the little town, turning outcroppings of limestone white, making unpainted frame buildings seem to glow. Heat waves wavered in the air, and color seemed to seep away, leaving only shimmering light and shadows of pale gray. Movement in the town stopped. Dogs no longer barked. No chickens clucked. A heavy blanket of suffocating heat spread over the village.

The bent iron handles of the wheelbarrow seared Lad's hands. He found some filthy rags and wrapped them around the handles so he could hold them. As he struggled, gasping, over the dried-out rough ground with his load, he tried to remember the crisp coolness of October, the cold of December, but it seemed unrealistic. He couldn't imagine that coolness would ever come into his life again.

Lad found it difficult to breathe. He took off his sweat-drenched shirt but after a time felt his shoulders burning, so he put it on again. Salt-filled streams ran down his forehead and into his eyes, making them sting. His shoulders and back kept cramping as he bent to his work, shoveling manure, then moving the wheelbarrow and unloading, repeating the movements, over and over.

Frequently he'd stop during his work, kneel at the horses' water trough, push moss aside, and drink deeply. When he'd finished his work, he cleaned up as best he could in the same trough.

Owen Cook brought him a plate filled with rice and beans as well as a thick slab of bread. Lad sat by the water trough and wolfed down the food. Then he rolled over on his side in the shade under the eave of the main building and rested.

Later, when he sat up, he saw that Cook had returned to his chair in the covered entryway. The sun beat down mercilessly as he crossed to speak to him.

"You're a pretty fair worker, young fella. If you'll help me fix that fence out back, I might be willin' to give you some supper."

By mid-afternoon Lad felt dizzy. The post hole digger he'd been using was old and covered with scaly dark rust. Composed of two steel pipes welded to curved spade-like heads, the pipes connected just above the heads with a sturdy, rusted hinge. The idea was to strike down with the digger, then pull the handles apart, which made the curved blades of the heads close around the earth that had been loosened so it could be extracted from the hole.

Lad's problem was that under about two inches of dry dirt he ran into layers of powdery white caliche, a type of layered rock. By striking repeatedly, he broke through, but as he did, the dull blades grew even duller.

His heart pounded, and he thought he might die if he didn't get some water. He stuck his head in the horse trough, pushing strands of green slickness aside, and drank deeply. Small brown tadpoles with tapering tails wriggled through the murky water, and he stared at them for a moment as his breathing slowed.

Dragging the post hole digger behind him with one hand, he stumbled past Owen Cook, who'd leaned his chair back against a wall. Cook sat in the shade, fanning himself with his hat.

"Where you off to, boy? You got at least eight or ten more posts to set."

"I'm going to the blacksmith's shop. He ought to have a file, and I plan to sharpen these blades."

"Well," Cook drawled, "don't dawdle around too long. You're workin' fer me, and I don't want to git the reputation of pamperin' my hired hands."

Lad moved out into the sun's intensity. He did not waste his energy on an answer.

He moved east down Concho Avenue, not really knowing where he was going, looking around for some sign of a blacksmith. When he came to Early Able's Saloon he felt dizzy and stopped, holding one hand to his forehead. He dropped the post hole digger and slid down to a sitting position by the wall. The overhang from the saloon at the south side of the street shielded him from the sun's rays. He sat below the raised board sidewalk on the ground, and wondered if he might faint.

A gruff husky voice said with a heavy foreign accent, "You better drink some water."

Lad pushed back his hat and looked up. An old Mexican man squatted down beside him on his haunches. He wore light-colored sweat-stained cotton shirt and pants and had a frayed straw sombrero on his head. The tightly woven straw hat had a wide round brim and a conical top with dents in the sides. The hat was grimy, and under it Lad saw an unusual face.

The Mexican had a fringe of wispy white hair hanging down on his forehead, a thick clumpy mustache streaked with gray, and friendly wide-set dark eyes in a wrinkled brown leathery face. *"Me llamo Horacio Escoba,"* he said courteously, adding in English, "that is my name."

Lad accepted the water bottle the man offered and drank from it gratefully. "I met a man a while back who said he knows you—that you're a friend of his."

The old Mexican looked surprised. "How does he call himself?"

"He said most people call him Huérfano DeLong."

Escoba nodded sagely. "I know him well. He used to be a good friend before he sobered up. Now he don't come to town no more. Huérfano was the funniest man I ever knew when he was drunk. But now that he gave up whiskey he's very sad all the time."

The two sat together, leaning back against the braces that held up the sidewalk. Escoba grunted as he moved his legs straight out before him. He wore cowhide sandals over his broad bare feet which looked to Lad as though they were as tough as leather.

Lad noticed that his companion had a bucket of tamales wrapped in cornshucks beside him.

Escoba, seeing Lad's glance, said, "This is how I make my living. I grow corn behind the place where I live on the other side of the river.

I have a sod house, a dugout with a low roof with dirt on it. I found it abandoned and moved in. Then I planted corn, and now I grind the corn and cook the best tamales in Texas. The best times for me are when it gets cold; then the cowboys and soldiers eat all I can make. But during the summers, no one seems hungry. So I stay here by the saloons."

Lad kept looking at the tamales.

"Try one—go ahead, I won't ask you to pay. I can tell that you're like I am. You have no money and you're tired. My tamales will give you strength."

Lad pulled a large firm tamale from the bucket and, peeling back the green cornshuck, tentatively tasted it.

"This is *wonderful*," he exclaimed.

Escoba beamed proudly. "Didn't I tell you?" He offered another free tamale, and while Lad ate, the old man said, "San Angelo is a thirsty town."

"What do you mean by that?"

"There's no place here where they'll give water to a Mexican. Of course, I know that, so I bring my own in this bottle. I don't mind, but I wish they'd let me go inside now and then. I have to stay out here in the street during the heat of summer or the cold of winter. And I wait for customers to come to me. If I could go inside, I'd sell a lot more tamales."

Lad rose to his feet. "You've been good to me, Horacio. I appreciate the food more than you realize. So, why not let me take this bucket inside? I might be able to sell a few tamales for you."

Escoba grinned, his yellow snaggled teeth showing behind his drooping bushy mustache. "Why not?"

"I'll bring you all the money."

"I know you will. I trust you."

Lad walked into the saloon. He stood at the entrance for a moment, unable to see very much after coming in from the afternoon glare. When his vision adjusted he could make out a few of the girls sitting on the stairs, bright long skirts pulled up to their knees, talking languidly to one another, looking with bored expressions of distaste at the men in the saloon. Several of the young whores sat in chairs in a cleared space near the tables. Various cowboys and townspeople stood with their feet on a brass rail which ran a few inches above the floor for the length of the long mahogany bar. Two men, wavering slightly from the effects of their whiskey, stood about four feet away from a spittoon, engaged in a spitting contest. Lad noted that neither was particularly skilled. Four cowboys played cards with a gambler who wore a green eyeshade of the sort used by bookkeepers, and one man sat by himself apart from the others. All of them looked up when he came in the room.

"Is that old Horacio's bucket of tamales?" the bartender asked.

"Yes it is. I'm giving him a hand. Is it all right if I try to sell a few tamales to your customers?"

The thick-bodied bartender's face twisted in a grimace of distaste. "It don't bother me none, if you want to lower yourself to sellin' a smelly old Meskin's tamales. But I'd think anybody would have more pride than to do that."

Having received this halfhearted permission, Lad didn't stop to enter the proffered debate. Instead he went along the bar, holding the bucket up, allowing people to lean over to look at his wares. Several of them bought tamales, giving him a few coins. He'd forgotten to ask Escoba how much to charge. The men had been drinking and didn't look as though they'd be willing to haggle over prices, so he accepted what they offered.

Suddenly the bucket seemed to wrench itself out of his grasp and simultaneously he heard the crashing detonation of an explosion. The man who'd been drinking alone at a table held a smoking Colt revolver in his outstretched hand. A grin covered his face.

"Son of a bitch!" howled the bartender without thinking. "You shot a hole in my bar."

Lad held the fingers of his right hand with his left. They tingled but he hadn't been hurt. He felt a pulse pounding in his temple. A layer of rage swelled within him.

The man who'd shot the bucket out of his hands rose to his feet and, holding the sixgun down at his side, moved toward him.

"Pick it up."

Lad didn't move.

A bullet ripped the boards at his feet. The sound of the explosion reverberated through the room. Splinters and dust flew. Most of the people in the saloon retreated toward the back wall.

The bartender said hoarsely to Lad, "Don't make him mad. Hiram Bork's a terrible bully—he's been known to shoot people for little or no cause. Just do whatever he says." At that he crouched down and moved away to the end of the bar nearest the door.

Bork said again, "Pick it up."

Lad sank to one knee. He scooped the tamales from the floor into the punctured bucket, noticing the jagged hole through which the bullet had exited. Sharp irregular strips of metal flared out from this. Then he rose to his feet and walked slowly toward Bork.

"I hate Meskins," Bork said. "And I hate Meskin lovers." He holstered his weapon, preparing to return to his table.

Lad swung the bucket in a wide hard arc, and it clanged on the astounded man's head. He fell to his knees and the bucket slammed down on his head a second time, making a sound like a strange Chinese gong. The sharp edges at the hole in the bucket peeled ribbons of flesh from the man's cheek and split his ear for almost an inch.

Lad leaned down, pulled the man's sixgun from its holster, and handed it to the bartender, who'd rushed up. "Hold this for me, please."

The bartender nodded dumbly.

Lad went outside and, after retrieving his post hole digger, returned to the saloon. By the time he returned the cowboy had wavered to his feet and was clawing at his empty holster. His face was a bright red mask.

Seeing Lad enter the saloon, he began to make a rumbling noise in his throat, and then he charged, head down, like a maddened bull toward a rival.

Lad swung the heavy post hole digger in a lazy circle, banging the attacker squarely on top of his head. The dreadful sound of steel cracking against bone rang out, and the cowboy fell as if pickaxed.

A girl screamed.

"Jesus!" a townsman cried out.

"You've killed Hiram Bork," the bartender exclaimed.

But Bork rose to his knees. He waved a hand in the air. Blood flowed from a deep cut in his scalp and from the cuts on his cheek and the split in his ear, and it ran in small rivers down his face and into his eyes. "No more," Hiram Bork said.

"I need a dollar to buy a new bucket," Lad said.

"God a'mighty," Bork groaned, pulling a silver dollar from his pocket and flinging it toward Lad. Then he collapsed on the floor.

"Go git a doctor," the bartender said in a conversational tone to a cowboy who approached from the far wall, looking with widened eyes at the sight of the prostrate form.

Lad went outside and found Horacio Escoba. "I'm afraid your

bucket got torn up. Here's money for a new one and what I collected before a cowboy put a hole through your tamales."

Escoba shook his head. "I should have known better than to let you take those inside."

A sense of weakness fell on Lad. He shook hands with the Mexican peddler, and returned to the bar.

While men ran for help, several of the girls took Lad in their charge. He followed them upstairs to a large bedroom where they poured water from a large pitcher into a white enamel bowl on a marble-topped stand. He washed his hands and face, dried off with a towel they handed him, and then sank wearily onto the soft bed.

"Was you intendin' to brain Hiram Bork?" a pretty dark-haired girl asked, her eyes wide with curiosity and excitement.

"No, I wasn't. I tried to swing the post hole digger between us when he charged at me, and he ran into it."

The girl sat beside him. "I seen you in here before. Hardly recognized you this afternoon, though. You was dressed real nice when you came in last week, but right now you're a regular mess."

"I know," Lad said.

Another girl came in with a large stein of beer. "Thought you might like this. Looks like you could use it."

Lad accepted the stein gratefully.

At that moment a middle-aged man in a rumpled brown suit came in the door. He had a large head, a florid face, and wore a string tie.

"Is this the fella that put Hiram Bork on the floor?"

"Yes, sir," the dark-haired girl said, without rising from her place on the bed beside Lad.

"You're just the kind of man I been lookin' for," the older man said. He held out his hand as he introduced himself. "I'm Early Able, and I own this place. Hugh, that's my bartender, told me what happened. We been havin' trouble with Hiram Bork and others like him for a long time. I raised hell with the sheriff before he quit, and now Jim Hislip, the deputy, is the only law we've got. But Jim's always off someplace, never around when you need him. So you can be of service keepin' the peace. Anyone who gets rowdy, you throw 'em out."

Lad rose to his feet. "I appreciate the offer, and there's no doubt that I need a job. But you need to understand that I'm not any kind of fighter."

The girls broke out into peals of laughter. One said, "He's just bein' modest. You never seen nothin' like what he did to old Hiram, Mr. Able. It was *somethin'*."

When Lad left the saloon, he had in his pocket an advance of a week's wages for his new job. He returned the post hole digger to Owen Cook at the wagon yard. He agreed that he hadn't earned his supper and wasn't owed anything for his work on the fence. He gave Cook two dollars on his account for Claude's feed and stabling, and asked that his horse be well fed. Then he collected the few belongings he'd left in the shed where he'd intended to sleep that night, and departed.

A dark cloud built in the west, obscuring the sun, making the late afternoon seem almost like night. Lad walked with a spring in his step, for he'd be staying tonight in the Tankersley Hotel. And he couldn't wait to take a long, lazy bath.

Lad felt a slight sense of uneasiness as he thought of his new employment. But the prospect of a bath, a decent meal that night, and a good bed made him shrug his shoulders. After the jobs he'd had recently, being a combination bouncer and peacemaker sounded like a distinct improvement.

The new house, not painted yet, smelled of rosin and sawdust. It still hadn't been completely furnished and most of the rooms Mattie looked in as she walked down the central hall had no furniture at all. No rugs lay on the freshly sawn lumber that had been laid in narrow strips for the floor.

Dee Hudnall especially liked the porch which overlooked the tree-lined river. The house sat on high ground, and in the distance he could make out the houses and buildings of San Angelo a few miles to the east.

Mattie went into their quarters, into the rooms with no windows. Hudnall followed her, a slight smile on his face.

She looked about her at the immense bedroom, twenty feet wide and thirty feet long. It had a large oval hooked rug, woven with hard fabrics, most of them in harvest tones of brown and shades of yellow and orange with an occasional line of red. The double bed had a patchwork quilt in bright squares of blue and green and white. An upholstered couch with wooden arms sat before a large fireplace on the interior wall, and several settings of furniture, tables, and chairs had been placed in groups in an apparent effort to fill the big room.

No pictures had been placed on the wall, and its flat, rough cedar boards covered the entire northern side of the room.

"There's a sewing room for you through there," Hudnall told her, pointing at an open door.

"It's mighty nice," Mattie said. "Where'd you get all this furniture?"

"Jules Ornette picked it out and shipped it in for me. Do you like it?"

"Yes—I do. To tell the truth, I didn't know what to expect."

"Well, this is your and my house from now on."

"You told me last night that you planned to keep me locked in this room when you weren't around."

Hudnall looked pained. "That was just because I was mad, before you convinced me that Ramón was lyin' about you carryin' on with some town boy."

"Do you believe me?"

"Mattie, after last night I feel completely different about you."

"You'd rather have a lovin' wife than a prisoner, is that it?"

"You're damn right," Hudnall said, taking her in his arms.

He couldn't see the look in her eyes as she gazed over his shoulder.

"We're goin' to be happy here," Hudnall said. "Wouldn't be surprised if we didn't have us some kids."

"I hope so, honey," Mattie said distantly.

He'll be leaving tomorrow, she kept thinking. I'll be able to see Lad!

Fifteen

LAD SHOWED UP for the first day at his new job feeling a considerable amount of apprehension. He entered the saloon a little after ten o'clock in the morning, the time he'd been told to report. The bartender came out from his accustomed station, tying the strings of a fresh white apron around his barrel-like stomach. He had small black eyes and a large lumpy nose which, owing to the network of blue and red veins crisscrossing under its surface, had a somewhat purplish color.

"My name's Hugh Johnson," the bartender said in a rough, graveled voice. "I'm glad to have someone around who'll help keep the damn cowboys calm. Them and the soldiers don't get along. And we got drifters in town who have a few drinks and think they can whip ever' damn man in the saloon."

"Does that happen often?"

Johnson looked at Lad with a pained expression. "About four or five times a night."

"Am I supposed to break up the fights?"

"Mainly I'd just let 'em have it out, but if they start bustin' things, like bottles and chairs and so forth, put a stop to it. Whip their tails, do whatever it takes just so long as you make 'em git the hell outside. Then it don't matter if they choose to kill each other." He studied Lad. "You're not cut out for this work."

"I know."

"Why ain't you carryin' a gun?"

"I don't own one."

"Well, you kin borrow mine. It's a Smith and Wesson six-shooter with a good heft to it."

"I'd rather not," Lad said. "No use running the risk of that kind of fight."

"Folks around here ain't as fair as you might think. They won't care if you *are* unarmed. In fact that might make 'em feel more comfortable about throwin' down on you."

"Well . . ." Lad said, his voice trailing off. He cleared his throat. "I've always been able to talk sense to people."

"Good luck," growled Johnson. Then he added, "Hiram Bork will likely be back today or tomorrow."

"You think he'll be upset?"

"*Upset?* Jesus Christ, boy, he'll be fit to be tied. You humiliated him in front of all them gals and ever'one else. I've known Bork a long time. And the man will surely come in here fixin' to kill you."

"I hope not," Lad said nervously.

Only a few people sat around in the saloon at this hour. None of the girls from upstairs had risen. A few men played cards at a table. Lad looked about and said, "I'm getting a nice salary from Mr. Able, and it looks like I won't have a lot to do most of the time. Are there any jobs around here that need attention—anything at all? I'd like to stay busy and not worry about matters like Hiram Bork coming after me."

"Can't think of a thing," the bartender replied. "Just try to fit in with the crowd."

"All right for me to play cards with those fellows?"

"Don't bother me none, but they'll trim your ears back. You'd be better off playin' a few hands with the cowpokes and soldiers. From the looks of things, you're stone broke. Before you start gamblin', you'll need to have a stake built up. Probably the best thing right now would be for you to hang around watchin' others play."

Lad chose to follow this advice and for the next few days he spent most of his time sitting near tables while the gamblers transferred money from the pockets of cowboys and travelers into their own. He watched for signs of cheating but didn't see any. Even so, the gamblers invariably ended each day well ahead.

Lad had played cards for years, had a sense for them, as well as an uncanny memory for cards that had been played. He didn't think of himself as having any unusual abilities at the card tables but he did consider himself a fairly good observer of his fellow players. He could often detect small signs they made, things that betrayed their thoughts.

In his opinion, everyone sent out signals. No one could keep secrets—they were given away involuntarily—but the signs varied from one person to the next. He had learned that if he had an opportunity to study any individual for a long enough time, he'd gradually observe a pattern.

For example, Earnest, who wore the green eyeshade, rubbed his thumb and forefinger together ever so slightly when he drew cards that helped his chances. Hugo, the man wearing the derby hat, always looked pained when he held a good hand. And the gambler the others called "Slick," the one who always wore a black silk shirt, licked his thin lips when bluffing.

When they weren't playing cards they'd sit about listlessly, waiting for some action to start. During these times they relieved the tedium with a stream of seemingly irrational wagers.

Slick drawled, "It's getting on toward three o'clock. About time for Big Lucy to come downstairs. I'd say she'd be here before three-thirty."

Hugo, the man in the derby, pushed a dollar out on the table. "She won't be here that quick."

Slick put a dollar beside it. "You're on." He added, "She'll be wearing red again. She nearly always wears red."

"What odds you givin'?" Hugo asked.

"Five to one."

Hugo pushed another dollar out on the table, and Slick put five of his own beside it.

Hugo said, "She's got that pretty green dress."

Then the two men leaned back in their chairs, watching the staircase expectantly. Meaning had crept back into their lives. A few minutes later the plump girl called Big Lucy came sashaying out of her room and down the stairs. She wore a red satin dress with bows down one side of her skirt. She grinned and winked at the men, noting their somber stares.

"Damn," Hugo snarled. "You must've seen her fixing to come down when you started leadin' me on."

"Now, Hugo, you think I'd take advantage of a friend? No, indeed. It's just that I know women. Lucy is a dependable gal, and you know as well as I do that she mostly likes to wear red."

During the early morning hours Lad went out on horseback for exercise. He found some clear ground near the outskirts of town where someone had built a few wooden fences around his property. On impulse he spurred Claude into a high lope and headed directly at one of these, laughing out loud as he soared over it. He wheeled about, looking for barriers. Lad took his horse over more fences, a broad ditch, and when he returned to the Elkhorn, he even jumped an old wagon repeatedly, riding around in a lazy circle. As he rode, an idea took shape.

Lad searched out an old rusty saw and a hammer and nails, then pulled some dusty rough posts and wooden rails from a stack of lumber that lay by one of the sheds at the wagon yard.

He began work on the old wagon that had been abandoned behind the pens. It took only a few hours to build a fairly low rectangular panel on top of it. He braced this into place by nailing posts at angles on both sides of the panel and then to the flat wooden bed of the wagon.

He had seen an old tattered cavalry saddle along with other gear stacked in a cobwebbed corner of a shed at the Elkhorn and, after cleaning it, he put this on Claude in place of his own saddle. Then he took Claude over the wagon with the two-foot-high panel upon it without a great deal of difficulty.

He dismounted, looked thoughtfully at his construction, and then went back to work. He hammered nails into boards, and soon it seemed as if he were planning to make a movable sign of some sort. Braced with posts, it appeared to be an improbable short fence made of lumber which some fool had put on the wagon.

The next afternoon he hitched a workhorse to the wagon and drove it to Concho Avenue, the wobbling wheels groaning with protest as they turned on the long-ungreased axle. When he reached his destination, he turned the wagon sideways, almost blocking the road. People from the saloons up and down the street came out to observe the puzzling activity.

Lad unhitched the workhorse from the traces and, riding bareback on its broad back, returned to the wagon yard. Then he saddled Claude with the light cavalry saddle, and returned to Early Able's saloon.

Slick, wearing his black silk shirt, Hugo, the old derby hat set squarely on his head, and Earnest, the man with the green eyeshade, had moved outside. They'd brought their chairs and were sitting on the sheltered board sidewalk, consumed by curiosity.

Lad rode up before Early Able's and dismounted. He said to the assembled men, "Mr. McIntire gave me this horse. His name's Claude."

The gamblers didn't reply to this unexpected announcement.

"Claude can jump higher than any horse in Texas, at least that's what Mr. McIntire told me."

Slick looked at his companions. "Is he talkin' about Mad John McIntire?"

"I believe so," Earnest replied, gazing without expression from under his green eyeshade.

Hugo tipped back his derby. "Why'd you park that wagon sideways in the street? And how come it has a fence built on it?"

"I'm curious to see if Claude can jump it."

"Boy," Hugo said, "you'll break your damn neck. Don't even think of such a thing."

"It can't be done," Earnest said with finality. "For one thing, a horse ain't goin' to kill himself. Even if you try to make him take that jump, he'll veer off at the last second—and you'll fly off into that pile of lumber. You'll get speared on one of them poles you got proppin' that thing up."

He rose from his chair and leaned against a post supporting the overhang. "The wagon is around five feet wide—that'd be kind of an interesting jump even without all that lumber piled on it. The top of that contraption is about even with the eaves of the roof across the way." He squinted his eyes at Lad and said, "You're talkin' pure dee nonsense."

"I agree," Slick remarked. "Ain't no horse can clear that."

"Well," Lad said, "things are kind of dull around here, and I might try anyway."

"I don't particularly care if you bust yourself up, but that's a mighty fine-lookin' animal. No sense ruinin' him." Hugo rose from his chair and walked out beside Claude, who bowed his neck and danced backward a few steps at the stranger's approach.

"I've always loved a good horse," Hugo said. He walked around Claude before adding, "Will you take fifty dollars for him?"

"No," Lad said. "The highest jumper in the state is worth ten times that." He looked up at the barrier uneasily. "What would the odds be on a horse actually jumping right over the top of this?"

"Ha!" Hugo snorted. He sensed some action.

"Hell," Slick said, "they ain't no way that a horse can clear that wagon with all them boards nailed up on top of it. No way at *all*. To my mind the odds are slim and none. But, if we're talkin' what odds I'll give you—I'd say about two to one."

"Don't know if I could risk my life for that."

"What about three to one," Earnest said in a soft oily way. "After all, that *is* a big horse. Got long legs. You're liable to be able to do it. I'll go three to one odds, young feller. And you can bet whatever you please."

"I've managed to borrow twenty dollars from Owen Cook down at the Elkhorn, and my wages for next week are ten, so I'll bet thirty against your ninety that I can do it."

"I'll take that," Slick said.

"Tell you what," Hugo drawled, "I'll bet the same amount, ninety dollars, against your horse that it can't be done. However, if he breaks a leg or gets hurt or killed, then you'll have to find the money and pay me in cash." A slight smile crossed his face.

"I'll accept the bet." Lad turned about and nodded at Owen Cook, who stood nearby. "Owen, you keep up with all of this. You can be the stakeholder."

"I feel left out," Earnest complained, taking off the green eyeshade and mopping his sweating brow with a red handkerchief from his back pocket. "But there's no help for it, since the kid's busted and there ain't no way he can come up with anything so I can have part of the action."

Lad mounted Claude, having to jump a little to get his foot into the high metal stirrup of the cavalry saddle. He said to Earnest, "Give me a minute—I might be able to borrow some more." With that he wheeled the horse about in the windless street and loped down it to the east toward the Tankersley Hotel.

Twenty minutes later he returned. "I've borrowed a hundred dollars from Annie Tankersley who's just got back home from the post hospital. I felt bad bothering her right now, but she said she'd trust my judgment." He paused for a moment. "Do you have the nerve to bet three hundred to my one that Claude can't do it?"

Earnest didn't change expression. "That's an awful lot of money. Let me think about this a minute." He thoughtfully rubbed his thumb against his forefinger. And then he went inside the bar and returned with the small worn carpetbag that the bartender kept under lock and key for him. Opening it, he peered inside. "I've had a good week—and am sorely tempted to take the bet." He looked a bit uncertain. Then he reached a decision. "It'll take you a year to earn up enough to pay back the debts you've run up." He took a deep breath. "It's my opinion that youngsters have to learn by their mistakes."

With that he counted out three hundred dollars and held it tightly in his fist. Softly he said, "Do *you* have the nerve to back up your big talk?"

Slick kept shaking his head. "I been around horseflesh all of my life, and it clearly can't be done." A light came into his eyes as he stared at Lad. "Why, hellfire, you're playin' the fool and have no real intention of goin' through with this."

"You're wrong," Lad said. He turned to the gambler with the green eyeshade. "I'm calling your bet, Earnest."

Owen Cook limped from the sidewalk and collected the stakes from the men, putting the money in a cloth sack. By this time at least thirty or forty people had gathered. A number tried to bet against the chances of Lad's horse clearing the obstacle but didn't find a soul willing to bet on Claude's making it. A gambling frenzy spread, and men began making small wagers as to whether the rider would live or be killed when he ran his horse squarely into the barricade.

A cowboy staggered out of a saloon and, seeing the unexpected excitement about him, began hollering and slapping his hat against his thigh. Claude leaped sideways at the sound.

A voice rang out. "Keep that drunk quiet so he don't spook the horse. Let's give the boy a chance anyways. God knows, the odds against him are high enough."

The crowd gathered on the sidewalks on both sides of the street as Lad rode Claude in a slow walk about a hundred yards back to the west. He pulled him to a stop, then reined him around. The roistering crowd fell silent. Every eye was on him.

Lad clapped his spurs into the big horse's sides. Claude moved into a lope, long legs gracefully moving, his mane and tail flaring back. As they neared the wagon with the ungainly board construction on it, he gave Claude his head. Lad stood in the stirrups and leaned far forward, his head in the horse's mane, almost on his neck.

Claude's muscles rippled. He burst from the ground into an almost perpendicular leap. With his forefeet gathered, he surged into the sky.

Cheers resembling screams carried through the air as the big horse barely cleared the barricade and came down on the far side, quickly recovered, and galloped forward—neck curved, head held high as Lad hauled back on the reins.

The crowd cheered and screamed, men waved their hats, slapped their knees, hit one another on the back. A man with a deep voice hollered, "Have you ever seen such a sight in your born life?"

The onlookers surged into the street, waving their arms and shouting with excitement. Claude reared and began to crowhop, terrified by the mob. Lad backed him from the men, and then turned him around, riding down the street away from them. When he'd reached a safe distance he stepped down and tied him to a hitching post.

Slick turned on his heel and went into the saloon. Earnest, red in the face, followed him. Hugo took off his derby hat, threw it on the board sidewalk, and kicked it as far as he could. Then, reconsidering, he picked it up, repaired the dents, clapped it on his head, and followed his friends into Early Able's Saloon and Gaming Hall.

When Lad met Owen Cook at the wagon yard, the two grinned at one another. "Here's the twenty I borrowed from you, Owen, together with another ten for your help. And thanks for driving the wagon back."

Owen said, "You ran kind of a risk sayin' you had a hundred dollars from Annie Tankersley. She's still out at the post hospital. If you'd a'lost and I hadn't had that stake, them fellas might've killed the two of us. Don't do to fool around with them gamblers, especially Earnest."

"We weren't going to lose."

Owen rubbed his hand over the stubble that covered his chin. "I been watchin' you practice takin' that jumper of yours over the contraption you built on the wagon. I seen you try it with the boards about half as high as they are now, and then you got down and put on some more. You worked him good yesterday afternoon, and I seen that he could make it—looks like the horse *enjoys* that jumpin'. But still, what with all them people yellin' and raisin' hell, it might've affected him. I got a jumpy gut anyways, and for a minute there it like to of went out of control."

Lad unsaddled Claude, rubbed him down, and curried him. He fed him oats before he broke out some hay.

"Guess I'll go back to work. I'm getting ten dollars a week to keep the peace there."

"Lord a'mercy," Owen babbled, unable to keep his face straight. He chuckled as he sat in his accustomed chair at the wagon yard's entrance. "God a'mighty, you won four hundred and eighty dollars —less the ten you gave me." His eyes widened. "Many's the cowboy who counts himself lucky to earn a dollar a day and his keep. You just made yourself quite a stake."

"That's exactly what I need," Lad answered.

*   *   *

Lad walked down Concho Avenue to the Tankersley Hotel. He had paid the bill he owed for lodging to Lupe and made arrangements to stay there again. The big upstairs room at the end of the hall, the one that Annie had built for herself before her bad hip made it necessary for her to move downstairs, seemed like home to him now.

He'd been to see Annie Tankersley at the post hospital two days before. Before going into her room he spoke to an officer who stood near her door. This man, a captain, was no longer young. He had pure white hair and a long white mustache. He identified himself as the senior doctor on the post and told Lad that he knew Annie had something seriously wrong. He led him outside where they talked for a short while.

The captain tamped tobacco down in his pipe and lit it. After drawing smoke into his lungs, he said, "The only way to find out what the trouble might be required exploratory surgery. When I opened the abdominal wall I saw right off that she had a diseased gallbladder—it had to come out. And by ding, I got it. There's no reason why she shouldn't be up on her feet in a few weeks. Maybe less."

As they walked back into the stone post hospital he said, "I've done this procedure before. There's a danger of infection and fever after any operation, especially one like this. But so far she's doing well." He added, "By damn, it's fine havin' chloroform. I sure wish we'd had it available durin' the war. You can't imagine how many legs and arms I sawed off with four or five men holdin' the wounded down. Didn't even have much whiskey to give those poor boys before we worked on 'em."

Lad spent a short time with the old lady. She lay very still on her pillows, looking at him with her pale blue eyes. "I'll be back home in a while," she promised. Her voice sounded weak. "I'm glad you have a new job—and that you're back at the hotel."

He thought of her as he walked down the street. He felt tired tonight. There had been only one fight and he'd managed to calm the men down by offering to buy them a drink on the house.

His time at work passed slowly and usually without a great deal of excitement. The disturbing rumor circulated that Hiram Bork had recovered and was going to come after him, but he'd heard that for the last two weeks and decided he'd stop worrying about it.

Business on Tuesdays at the saloon was usually slow, so he left early. He walked up the stairs, down the hall, and turned the knob.

He never locked the door. But on walking in he sensed the presence of someone else in the room.

A spasm of fear wrenched through him. A single thought blanked out all others: It's Hiram Bork. He froze, standing just inside the door. He heard a floorboard creak, then the sound of someone approaching.

Lad reached to one side and his hand fell on the water pitcher. He raised it, prepared to defend himself.

A long wooden match popped and flared, he smelled burning sulphur, and a hand lit the coal oil lamp.

Mattie Hudnall stood beside the lamp. She wore a white blouse and a long blue skirt. "I've been waiting for you a long time," she said. Her dimple deepened as she grinned at him, her eyes dancing.

Weak with relief, he put the pitcher back on its stand. "How did you manage to get away from your husband—and from Ramón?"

"My husband's at the ranch, and I figured out how to handle Ramón. He's got a weakness for tequila, so I've laid in a store of it. Tonight he passed out, so I rode into town."

She rushed into his arms. "God, but I've *missed* you," she said. She held him tightly, raising her face to his, pulling his head down. She kissed him fiercely, desperately.

An hour later she dressed and sat on the edge of the bed. "I worry all the time about Hudnall. I dream about stabbin' him with a butcher knife—anything to get rid of him. I've talked to you about him. He just scares me so much and . . ." She didn't seem able to finish her statement. After a deep breath she said, "I've got to protect myself. Once I almost had the nerve to shoot him, but I couldn't. You've got to do it for me."

"We talked about that once before. You know I wouldn't ever kill anybody. If you want me to, I'll help you get away from him."

She sounded hopeless. "He'd find me. He'd hunt me down no matter where I went."

She curled up on his lap. "Do you love me?"

He hesitated. "You're the most exciting girl I've ever known."

"That wasn't much of an answer."

"I think about you all the time."

"That's more like it," she purred. "I think of you, too. I guess that you're shy—some people don't know how to talk about lovin' and things like that. Men especially. I understand that. But I ain't never had anything like we have when we're together. Never had feelin's so strong."

Her voice sounded husky and urgent. "It's like I just got shown somethin' that I never knew about. I get all wild when I remember it. Hudnall never made me feel nothin' at all e'cept pain and hate."

She trembled as she clung to him. She said with intensity, "You just *got* to help me. If we get rid of him, we can be so happy."

"No."

She leaped from the bed, eyes glittering. "If I have to, I'll do it alone." A quivering silence surrounded them. Then she murmured, "He'll hurt me so bad if I try. That's what scares me."

He took her hands and pulled her along. He stopped at the doorway and drew her against him, holding her. "I don't think we should see each other anymore. I really don't."

"Please," she said. Her words were muffled as she buried her face against his chest. "I can't get you out of my head—you're there all the time. Don't say things like that."

She broke away and ran from the room.

Sixteen

PUCKER AND RAMSEL entered Early Able's Saloon on a white-hot Saturday afternoon. They had ridden to town from the McIntire Ranch through stinging windblown sand across arid semi-desert country. Their journey had one objective: they sought an oasis. The two tall, broad-shouldered men clumped with single-minded concentration up to the bar and stood before it.

"Johnson," Jim Pucker cried to the bartender, "bring us a big pitcher of beer."

"We're near death, Johnson," Ramsel rumbled. "Drop that damn rag, stop whatever the hell you're doin', and attend to your customers."

For a full half hour the two cowboys gulped down one foam-topped mug of warm beer after another, complaining ceaselessly in low monotones about the terrible quality of the product made by the local Rock Bluff Brewery.

"In San Antonio they *know* how to make beer," Ramsel said morosely as he refilled his mug. "There's more to it than fillin' a vat with creek water and malt and hops and then watching the damn mess ferment and heave about. Them Germans who settled in San Antone have a special recipe that the folks around here would do well to copy."

He warmed to his topic. "I've seen herders dip sheep in stuff that looked and smelled exactly like this. In fact, sheep dip is considerably clearer." He held his mug up toward the light that came in from the door as it opened, and squinted his eyes, trying to look through it. He considered his case proven. "A good German brew is golden, it ain't near this murky," he said emphatically. "This is kind of greenish yellow. I'd switch to whiskey, but the last time I drank that I was blind for two days and came very close to death's door. There's a fine line between our local bar whiskey and the purest of poisons. But considerin' the quality of this beer, it's a hard choice."

"True," Pucker said, signaling for another pitcher. "I keep hopin' I'll get drunk so the taste will go away."

"Come to think of it," Ramsel observed, "it don't seem quite as rank as when we first started." He nodded thoughtfully. "In another hour or so, it may smooth out."

"You can't go through life hopin' for miracles," Pucker said.

"You're wrong," Ramsel replied. "I tend to *rely* on 'em."

They were surprised and delighted to see Lad in the bar.

"You mean to say you *work* here?" Ramsel couldn't keep the perplexity out of his voice. "What on earth do you *do?*"

"My job's to keep the peace, since there's rarely a lawman around."

Pucker's head drew back from his mug. "You're the new bouncer?"

"I guess you'd say that."

"The last one in here, old John Haygood, had his skull busted. Two cowboys got into a fight and John stepped in between 'em. They both got mad and attacked him. One hit John with a whiskey bottle and the other cracked him up the side of his head with the barrel of his sixgun."

"I heard about that," Lad said after a momentary pause. "My strategy is to keep an eye on things, and when people look like they're getting on edge, I buy them drinks on the house. So far it's worked every time."

"You git *paid* for hangin' around a saloon?" Pucker asked with a note of sadness in his voice.

The bartender said to Ramsel, "The kid's got the boys in here buffaloed. It happened when he took on Hiram Bork."

"He *what?*" Ramsel sounded incredulous.

"Them two got into a fight that you'd have to've seen to believe, and when it was over they had to *carry* Bork off. The kid almost killed him. Hit him with a post hole digger, can you believe it?"

"No, I can't." Ramsel turned his back to the bar and looked about until he located Lad. The young man stood near the gambler named Earnest, who as usual wore his green eyeshade pulled low over his eyes. Earnest dealt from the deck to five men sitting in chairs at his table, and then leaned back to examine the cards in his own hand.

At an adjoining table some cowboys and off-duty soldiers sat while

Hugo, the gambler who wore his old derby hat squarely on his head, shuffled cards and called for them to put their antes on the table. Slick, in his customary black silk shirt, hosted a similar group not far away.

Until the gunshot boomed in the street immediately outside the saloon, it was an ordinary Saturday afternoon. The slamming jolt of the explosion froze every man in the bar.

A scant instant later the swinging doors burst open and a man stood in the entrance, a dark figure framed by brilliant sunlight.

"I've come for the Virginian," the apparition announced in a loud voice.

Chairs scraped in jittery screeches on the board floor as drinkers and gamblers and brightly clad whores rose as one to their feet.

"Lad Trimble, I'll be outside—waitin' for you to come face me." Hiram Bork turned about after roaring his challenge. The men inside heard the thudding of bootheels and clinking of spurs as he stalked down the board sidewalk and descended to the street.

All eyes in the big room swiveled toward Lad. He walked to that section of the bar nearest the door and hesitated a moment.

Hugh Johnson hitched his filthy apron up about his formidable waist and approached him. The bartender leaned down behind the polished mahogany and came up with a heavy sixgun which he clapped on the well-worn surface of the bar. The sound of metal striking wood rang through the trembling silence.

Johnson shoved the pistol toward Lad. "You're unarmed. Take my Smith and Wesson—it's loaded."

Lad ignored the offer and started for the street.

Pucker appeared beside him. "Hold on. You may have been able to settle down a few upset gents with the offer of free drinks on the house, but this is a different situation. I can't let you go out to face a man like Bork. You have no idea what you've got yourself into."

A lazy smile drifted across Pucker's face. He drawled, "I've never liked Hiram Bork. Maybe I better go in your place."

Lad shook his head and without speaking a word went through the doors. Early Able's Saloon had few windows and in consequence was always dark and shadowy. The contrast between its interior and the glare on the street was vivid. He hesitated on reaching the sidewalk, narrowed his eyes, waiting until they became accustomed to the brightness.

He saw before him at least thirty horses tied to the long hitching rail in front of the saloon. Most of them stood quietly, occasionally flicking their tails sharply, slashing them like limber wire whips at large bottle-green horseflies. One bay mare with a bad disposition strained her neck sideways and took a sharp bite on the shoulder of the bony gelding next to her. That animal emitted a squealing whinny of pain and instantly retaliated with a sharp kick. The mare jumped sideways, bumped into the horse on the other side, then jerked her head, only to find it firmly tied by the reins. With ears drawn back and a vicious stare at her antagonist, she fell silent, biding her time until she could try another bite.

Lad saw several rifles poking their wooden butts out of weathered leather saddle scabbards. He stepped between two horses and pulled out a carbine. It was a Winchester much like the one he'd used for hunting in Virginia.

Looking over the backs of several horses, he saw Hiram Bork waiting. He stood squarely in the middle of Concho Avenue, feet planted wide apart, boots on the crusty dirt of the road. Both hands dangled down at his sides, but his right was crooked up just a little, leaving his hand only inches from the grip of his holstered pistol.

Bork cried out, "You think you can make me look like a fool?" His face turned a shade of splotchy red. His throat swelled and its veins stood out as if they might pop. He stared at Lad, who stood with only his head showing in the midst of the tethered horses.

"Come out and face me, you cowardly son of a bitch!"

The entire population of Early Able's Saloon shoved and pushed and fought their way out the doors to the sidewalk, straining for a vantage point. Men in other saloons, hearing the commotion, also emptied outside, forming ragged, surging lines. The large crowd assembled, their blood heated, lusting for violence.

They lined the sidewalks and spaces between frame buildings on both sides of the dirt road, turning it into an outdoor theater. Unlike the noisy day not long before when Lad had jumped his horse over the wagon with the barricade on it, the onlookers stood in absolute silence. The town huddled in a cathedral hush. No one yelled or cheered or spoke. Men waited, mesmerized by the prospect of sudden death.

Lad levered a cartridge into the Winchester's firing chamber. He heard the oily metallic ratcheting noises as if in a dream and then sidled through the horses into the street.

Moving quickly, Lad turned his back on the waiting man and began walking away from him.

Bork stood stock-still, glaring, confused, and obviously furious. *"God damn it, turn around and fight like a man."*

Lad ignored him until he'd reached a distance of some sixty or seventy yards. Then he turned about, sinking as he did so to one knee. Very deliberately he thumbed back the hammer, felt it click into place, then lay down on his stomach in the dirt.

Bork's face twisted into a terrible frown, his bushy eyebrows meeting over his nose. He reached for his Colt but must have realized his disadvantage with a sixgun at that distance. His hand wavered away from the gunbutt.

In a prone position, Lad put his left elbow down, providing a steady support for the rifle. His right arm flared out slightly as he sighted carefully along the Winchester's unwavering barrel. The crook of his right index finger gently touched the hard steel curve of the trigger.

Bork stared at him, as still as if he were frozen.

Lad kept his cheek on the edge of his right hand, wrapped about the rifle's smooth wooden grip. He called to Bork, "Unbuckle your gunbelt. If you reach for your gun, I'll shoot you."

Bork's red face gradually turned purple. His lips parted to show an expanse of clenched teeth. And then the pressures within him seemed abruptly to explode. He charged forward, clawing with his right hand as he started his draw.

The cowboys and soldiers strained forward on the sidewalk. As Bork's boot hit the ground on his first step, with the Colt coming out of its holster, Lad's Winchester rang out.

Bork went down head over heels. His Colt flew into the air. As he struck the ground he began writhing and screaming. Blood shot from his lower leg, and he grabbed the wound with both hands. Rolling onto his back, he began bellowing like a wounded bull.

The street, sketched in black and white with shades of gray, had almost no color except for the scarlet that spurted from Bork's leg. The people stood as still and stiff as if they'd been captured on a daguerreotype. The only movement was the man who rolled on the street, bright blood pulsing from an artery. His screams were the only sounds. Even Lad remained in his prone position, transfixed, staring at Bork. Then the picture broke apart as men began yelling and crowding into the road.

Lad rose to his feet and walked forward, ignoring the soldiers and cowboys. Bedlam broke loose. Lad retrieved Bork's Colt from the street with his left hand, holding the Winchester with his right.

The onlookers formed a large circle around Lad and the man on the ground. Bork stopped rolling back and forth, and looked up, fear in his eyes.

"I'm going to keep your pistol, Mr. Bork. I don't plan to give it back to you this time."

A sudden harsh gust of wind blew sand down the artificial canyon between the ramshackle buildings. Lad turned his head and closed his eyes until the gritty whirl of dust and sand passed by. The late afternoon sun stretched shadows darkly to the east.

"We've only met twice, Mr. Bork. So far I haven't been angry. But if you try me a third time . . ." He paused, then turned from the street.

A whiskered soldier with a big belly said, "That wasn't no fair fight."

Lad's face turned pale as death, and he faced the man. His eyes narrowed. Speaking softly, he said, "Are you suggesting that I have a fair fight with you?"

The whiskered soldier stepped back. "Well, no," he replied.

Lad shoved the Winchester back in the saddle scabbard from which he'd taken it.

The crowd parted, forming an aisle as he walked through it. Subdued men followed him into Early Able's Saloon and Gaming Hall. They spoke quietly to one another, glancing in Lad's direction with an attitude of mixed fear and awe. They seemed to see the young man in a different light.

Pucker and Ramsel remained for a time on the sidewalk after most of the others entered the various saloons along the road. Pucker said, "I'll say this, the boy got Hiram Bork's attention."

Several soldiers carried the wounded man down the street toward the doctor's office. Bork moaned and cursed at every step they took.

Pucker said, "In fact, he got the whole town's attention."

"He looked kind of calm the whole time," Ramsel noted. "And the curious part was explainin' to Bork that he hadn't got mad yet."

Pucker grinned. "Every man in San Angelo is likely to walk soft around that kid for a while. They'll be askin' themselves what he'd be like if he *did* lose his temper."

Ramsel's big laugh echoed down Concho Avenue as they strode side by side into the bar.

Jim Pucker and Boots Ramsel, exhausted by the tension, no longer stood at the bar. They slouched in chairs at a table, their long legs stretched out at full length. Lad joined them and pulled up a three-legged stool.

"We gave the local businessman a fair chance," Pucker said, "but I'm not prepared to die to advance the cause of San Angelo's commerce."

"What?" Lad asked. "What did he say?"

"He's talkin' about the green beer," Ramsel explained. "We figured that we might not see the light of another day if we drank one more pitcher of it." He tugged the cork from a whiskey bottle and poured a few inches of its amber liquid into a thick glass tumbler before him. "This stuff is only dangerous if you overdo it. We're merely goin' to sample a few sips." His voice sounded vague.

"Understand you got into a big poker game a few nights ago," Ramsel said. "The way we heard it, you had a chance to play with the big boys."

He spoke of the private poker group that met at the Nimitz Hotel once a month. The game as a rule accepted as players only the area's men of substance, most of them owners of large ranches. They didn't permit the town's professional gamblers to join them and rarely invited any outsiders at all.

"Mad John told us about it when he got back to the ranch. He said that you'd built up a stake with a bet as to how high Claude could jump."

Lad said, "Mr. McIntire talked the others into letting me into the game. The cards fell just right for me all evening, and before long I found myself a good bit ahead."

"That's what Mad John said," Pucker responded. "Was it then that Louis Farrar offered to bet you his herd of sheep against what you had at the table?"

Lad grinned. "Mr. Farrar had spent the evening cussing his sheep. He'd bought them on the advice of J. S. Pierce who ranches out toward Devil's River. Anyway, Mr. Farrar said he had Mexican herders who followed them around—and he claimed they fouled the watering holes so that his cattle wouldn't use them. Anyway, to get back to the bet, it was a simple match. We decided to draw for high card, my three thousand dollars against his sheep.''

Pucker's eyes widened. *"Three thousand dollars?"*

"As I explained, I'd had quite a few good hands, and on the last one I'd filled an inside straight. We'd been playing stud poker, and I'd have dropped out except I was so far ahead I felt reckless. Anyway, toward the end one man had three of a kind showing, and a couple of others had two pairs, so as the cards fell, they kept making raises. When I took my last card, the eight of hearts, they began to wonder if my hole card was the nine. Then I made a heavy bet—as if I were bluffing. They started laughing, and said that if I *really* had filled my straight I'd try to sucker them to stay in with a small bet. So they raised me, and I raised them back—which made them stop laughing. But in a minute they talked to each other and convinced themselves that I was trying to buy the pot. So they met my final raise. Of course, when I turned over my hole card, they almost had a fit.''

Ramsel slapped his hand on the table. "You're the luckiest youngster that ever walked the face of the earth.''

"Anyway," Lad continued, "that's how my stake built up. And that's when Mr. Farrar made his offer. I *knew* that he couldn't stand those sheep—that he wanted to get rid of them. So I said, 'Well, if I win, I want the right to keep them on your ranch for one year, then I'll get them off of it permanently.' For some reason he took me up on it. I suppose the main reason was that he thought he'd win—but it may be that he'd had quite a bit to drink and it clouded his judgment.''

"All I knew was that you'd made a killin' at the card table. I didn't hear about all the rest," Pucker said. Then he sighed. "I can't imagine havin' three thousand dollars. And the idea of bettin' it all on the turn of a card makes me downright sick," he tapped his middle, "right here in the pit of my stomach.''

Lad smiled. "I felt that way myself. After we made the bet, John Loomis, who ranches east of here, shuffled the deck and fanned the cards out face down on the table. Mr. Farrar drew the jack of clubs. I drew the king of diamonds.''

Lad didn't explain that he'd seen that this particular card had a dog-eared corner. He always noticed small things. He wondered if he'd been unfair, but shrugged. Maybe Mr. Farrar had earlier spotted something that enabled him to select the jack.

"Well, by God," Ramsel said, "I never thought I'd sit at the same table with a damn sheepman."

Pucker shook his head. "You got outsmarted. Louis Farrar has got rid of all them hollow-horned woollies. Now they're your responsibility. How you goin' to pay your herders? Where will you take your stock when the year's up?"

"I've still got the three thousand dollars and don't plan to lose it playing cards. I'm dropping out of the gambling business while I'm ahead." Lad added, "As for the sheep, I have a plan."

The girls had a busy night upstairs. Cowboys crowded the stairs, impatiently waiting their turn. Several brief fights broke out, but Lad would walk up to the angry men, speak softly, and the combatants would part. Lad wondered how long this newfound respect would last—and decided it wouldn't be for long.

By midnight most of the soldiers went back to the post, and the cowboys who remained were too drunk to stand, much less cause trouble. Lad picked up the Colt he'd taken from Hiram Bork, put it in his belt, and walked down Concho Avenue until he reached the Tankersley Hotel.

The wind died, moonlight silvered the buildings, and a dog barked in the distance. Lad stood before the darkened hotel. No lights shone at any of the windows. He entered, walked up the stairs, and turned to the right toward his room.

When he entered, a match flared in the blackness. He grasped the Colt's butt, then hesitated as a slender hand holding the match lit the lamp. In the swelling glow of light he saw Mattie Hudnall.

"I didn't think you'd *ever* get here," she said, her voice shaking. "I've been crazy to see you. *Something's happened.*" She seemed to be in a fever.

"They ran into trouble. It was bound to happen." She couldn't continue.

"What are you talking about, Mattie?"

"About Loftin, Hobie, and Julius," she said. "Hudnall's boys, the ones that made my life such hell on earth. Well, they won't never bother me again."

"I don't understand."

"The three of them and four of Hudnall's men had been makin' raids, rustling cattle for the most part. They got caught last night driving cattle off the Shannon Ranch out west of here. A bunch of cowboys and a ranger were waiting for whoever was rustlin' out there, and they caught the whole pack.''

"Are they in jail?"

"They're dead. Whether they got shot or hanged, I don't know yet. A rider came from the ranch to tell Hudnall, and he and Ramón rode off. But he'll be back before morning, and I have to get back. I was afraid you wouldn't get here in time for me to let you know about this.''

"Mattie—I've told you before that you and I can't keep on seeing each other."

"You don't mean that. Don't you realize what this means, Lad? Now I'm the *only one* left to inherit Dee's money. He's *rich*—there's more than you can imagine. When he's dead all that will belong to you and me.''

Lad took her hands in his, to calm her. "Don't talk that way, Mattie.''

She wrenched free and began to pace back and forth. "If you won't help me, well, I'll do it alone. When he comes home, I'll be waitin' for him.''

Her eyes glittered. In a whisper she said, "He won't have a chance.''

She left the room abruptly, slamming the door behind her. Lad hadn't seen her horse, but supposed she'd have hitched it down the street from the hotel.

He undressed and lay down in his bed for a while but couldn't sleep. The events of the day tumbled through his mind. He kept seeing images of Hiram Bork starting toward him, pulling at the Colt, and then he saw the man writhing with pain as he rolled in the dirt.

Finally, one thought crowded the day's events from his head: Mattie's going to murder her husband. I've got to stop it.

He rose from the bed, pulled on his shirt and pants, then put on his boots. He decided to run down the street to the Elkhorn Wagon Yard, saddle Claude, and ride west to the low-water crossing of the North Concho. He had to get to the Hudnall house before anything happened. At the last moment he decided to take the Colt revolver. He'd put it in one of his saddlebags.

Seventeen

LAD SADDLED CLAUDE near the shadowed stalls. He could make out several men curled up on blankets not far away, sleeping beside their wagons. One of them snored moistly through his wide-open mouth. The moon's pale glow outlined shapes of the structures, corrals, and randomly parked wagons. A horse nickered in the main corral as he led Claude out the front way.

As he stepped into the saddle he calculated it must be around one in the morning or maybe a little later. He'd lain in bed for a time after Mattie left. At first he'd thought that her statements about killing her husband had been idle threats, her rambling words merely summoning up unreal daydreams like those of a child living in a fantasy world. After all, she's only seventeen, he'd told himself, and hasn't really grown up. But then the chilling realization came to him that Mattie really might be out of her mind, as insane as people said.

He directed Claude to the west and followed the bend of the river a half mile toward the north until he reached the crossing. On the other side he leaned forward as the big horse gathered under him and jolted up the steep slope.

Feeling on edge, he turned and reached back into the saddlebag hanging on the right side until he touched the butt of the Colt he'd taken from Hiram Bork, just to make sure he could grasp it quickly if necessary. I could be going into a dark house, he told himself. As a precaution he fumbled in the saddlebags again until he found the small oilskin packet that held a bundle of matches. He took out several of these and put them in his shirt pocket.

Lad stopped and listened, but heard only silence. He spurred his horse forward into a trot, with anxiety gnawing at his stomach.

He didn't really have a plan but knew he had to keep Mattie from committing murder. At the same time, a picture formed in his mind of how it might be, walking into a house he'd never seen.

Disquieting thoughts kept running through Lad's mind. Hudnall would be wild with rage and grief after hearing of the death of his sons; he surely wouldn't be asleep. Lad shuddered to think of Hudnall's reaction if he saw a man slipping onto his property in the dead of night. Especially on this of all nights.

I must be as crazy as Mattie, he decided. But he knew he couldn't rest until he stopped her.

From what she'd said, Hudnall would be coming back *later,* and this comforted him. Surely he won't be here yet, he thought. Lad hoped he could find Mattie, convince her to abandon her plan, and get away before her husband showed up. Mildly relieved at this vague strategy, he urged his horse forward.

Wryly he told himself that, in a short life filled with unintelligent actions, this one stood out as the dumbest of all. But even as he tried to still his uneasiness, his nerves tightened.

Mesquite branches with sharp thorns rasped across his legs as he rode through a thicket. Then the stockade-like cedar post fence around the Hudnall place loomed before him. Behind its barricade, the house sat on a high raised bank overlooking the North Concho River.

Lad stepped down and tied his reins to the rough-barked limb of a mesquite. Taking the Colt .45 from the saddlebag, he put it in his belt and cautiously started forward toward the only entrance—a wide double gate. He felt sure it would be bolted from the inside but could see in the moonlight that he'd be able to climb over it.

No sounds came from the protected compound. He put his hand on the rough cedar posts and on the boards of the gate. He pushed it slightly. To his surprise he felt the gate creak open.

He slipped through it, realizing that he could easily be spotted in the light of the full moon. His feet slipped as he sprinted across the grounds toward the windowless northwest wing of the house. With his back pressed against the wall, he stood quietly, breathing rapidly, but heard only the sound of his heartbeat.

He'd noticed a light through the windows on the south side of the house when he'd run from the gate. He slipped along the wall until he reached the four wide steps that led to the darkness of a covered porch. As he ascended, the boards creaked and his spurs jingled. My God, he thought, I should have left my spurs behind, they'll give me away. He leaned down, unbuckled them, and slipped them into his pants pockets, one on each side. After this he waited, nerves tingling, but no sounds came from inside the house.

He looked at the outline of a barn toward the west inside the fence and a small shed-like shelter built beside it. He remembered Mattie telling him Ramón lived in the shed.

As his heart slowed, he moved away from the door and flattened himself between two windows. Then he moved his head slowly until he could make out the interior. He saw an empty living room, one that had been sparsely furnished. A few chairs, one throw rug, and a table with a coal oil lamp shedding its light on a sewing basket next to it.

Lad withdrew the Colt .45 and cocked the single-action revolver. Holding it in his right hand, the barrel pointing up, he opened the door, left it ajar, and made his way into a long hallway. He hesitated a moment, then turned to his right and entered the living room. He slipped to the table and leaned forward to blow out the lamp. In the darkness he retraced his steps, proceeding on tiptoe toward the doors he'd seen along the hall on the north side of the house. Mattie had told him her bedroom lay there.

He opened the first door and looked into blackness. "Mattie?" he whispered. He stepped in, touched the empty bed, and went back to the hall.

He thought, If I walk into a room and find Hudnall in bed with her, he'll kill me. There's no doubt about it.

But surely, he decided, Hudnall can't be here. Lad took a deep breath to summon his courage, and told himself, If he's just arrived, he probably wouldn't have had time to go to bed. If he were around, I'd hear something.

Not convinced at all by this logic, Lad moved silently toward the only other door leading into the unwindowed wing of the house. He opened it, went in, and found it as empty as the first.

When he reached the porch once again, Lad stood uncertainly. If Mattie wasn't in the house, where could she have gone? Would they have left for the Hudnall ranch? Of course. That's what must have happened.

Relief swept through him. If that's the case, she hasn't committed murder.

He saw no corral and figured they must have stalls in the barn.

Before leaving, he thought he'd check to see that the horses were gone. Then he could go back to his room and rest easily.

He heard the wind sweep from the south, heard the sound the trees made, branches snapping against others. The force of it struck the barn as he neared it, and the barn door groaned as it swung back and forth on its hinges. Lad entered the darkened structure, not able to see a thing. He found a lantern hanging just inside the door and took it down from its nail.

Lad reached into his shirt pocket, and a moment later his match snapped and flared. The smell of sulphur reached his nose, and a brief circle of yellowed light from the coal oil lantern puddled on the dirt floor about him. He walked forward slowly, boots rustling at times when they went through a thin cover of hay on the ground.

Lad held the lantern before him while he checked the stalls. He saw Mattie's sorrel mare in one and in another saw a bay. Both seemed startled by the light and raised their heads abruptly, ears pointing forward.

They must have taken a buggy, Lad told himself. Then he saw something, a darkness, a strange still sight higher than the lamplight reached.

He walked forward, bewildered—then stunned. It took a moment to realize what he'd discovered.

He raised the lantern slowly and saw the awful sight of Mattie's body dangling from a rafter. Baling wire around her neck cut into her throat. It had almost decapitated her. A sturdy table rested a short distance under her feet—the murderer must have stood on it when he executed her. He would surely have been drenched with blood, for the thick-topped pine table glistened with a covering of slick, dark scarlet.

Lad stood stock-still, breathless and frozen by horror, and then he felt a terrible rush of nausea that made him sink to one knee. He put the lantern on the floor beside him as he retched. Recovering, he rose, grasped the lantern, and backed away.

Hudnall did this. A rigor ran through him. Has he been watching me? Is he waiting outside?

Moaning noises came from the barn. It creaked under the force of the wind as Lad blew out the lantern, put it down, and ran. He tried to stay in shadows, then made his way out the gate and to the trees where he'd tied his horse. He stood by the side of the big animal, uncertain and afraid. Instinctively he reached for the heavy revolver he'd stuck through his belt, but it was gone. It had fallen out at some time, probably when he got sick. He couldn't stand the thought of going back into the barn. But without the Colt, feeling even more vulnerable than ever, panic struck him. Once mounted, he clapped his unspurred heels into Claude's sides. A short time later they splashed through the Concho, at a point where the warm river only reached the horse's knees.

When he reached the community, he made for the house owned by Jim Hislip, the deputy sheriff, and pounded on the door. A groggy woman, clutching a cotton robe about her nightclothes, came to the door.

"Jim's out of town somewheres, like always. I don't have no idea when he's likely to git back."

Lad went to the Elkhorn Wagon Yard, waked Owen Cook, and told him what he'd found.

"Damn!" Owen croaked. But he offered no help or suggestions.

He left his horse with Owen and went on foot to the Nimitz Hotel, and then to the Tankersley Hotel. At least ten men reacted in the same way. They looked at him with blank faces as they listened to the horrible story. All of them were obviously terrified of Dee Hudnall—and refused to get involved.

Lad didn't sleep. He sat in his room, then washed his face, and went downstairs. When he went out on the veranda the day was dawning. Not a soul seemed to be up and about. The street was deserted. He heard a horse's hoofbeats and saw a man approaching at a lope. He pulled up in front of the Tankersley Hotel and sat there, waiting.

Lad rose to his feet, hesitated, then took a few steps forward where he faced Ramón, the Mexican gunman who worked for Hudnall.

"I told him about you and his wife. How she went to the room where you sleep." The man's swarthy face broke into a grin. Except his eyes weren't smiling, they were cold and black.

"Hudnall took care of things at his house. His wife had a knife and tried to use it, but he took it away from her." The smile left his mouth. "After that she told him everything, all about how the two of you were going to kill him and she'd inherit his money."

His eyes glinted. "She made a big mistake, trying to use that knife on him. He paid her back for that."

Lad stood without moving. Finally he said, "Why are you here? Why are you telling me all of this?"

Ramón ignored the questions. "Hudnall's sons got killed, maybe you knew about that. He hated them and they hated him. But after he heard what happened to them, he wasn't in a mood to waste much time on his wife." He shifted in his saddle and said, "He asked me to watch what he did to her."

"You did that?" Lad's voice broke with anger.

Ramón backed his horse, seeing Lad's expression, and he put his hand on his sixgun. "Yes, I never seen nothin' like it before. Hudnall was really mad, *enojado,* but he said all along she was crazy. He decided later—after he'd done with her—that the whole thing must have been your idea.

"I never saw him like he is now. He sent me to tell you that there's no place you can run, there's no way to hide. He wants you to know this so you'll sweat while you wait for him to come after you."

The Mexican whirled his horse about and clattered away.

Lad's blood ran cold. He remembered seeing knife cuts in Mattie's half-nude body as it hung so grotesquely from the rafter. Hudnall must have tortured her before hanging her with baling wire. She would have confessed everything as she begged for her life to be spared. She'd have told him about going to Lad's bed. And now Hudnall planned to kill him.

Lad went behind the small counter at the hotel where he knew Annie Tankersley kept her double-barreled Greener. He found it propped in a corner. Breaking it open, he found the shotgun wasn't loaded. With a sinking sensation, he began pulling out drawers in a tall maple cabinet, looking for cartridges. Panic built as he pawed through the clutter of papers in his useless search.

Lupe came down the stairs, but said she never touched the shotgun and had no idea where cartridges might be.

Annoyance showed in her voice. "Don't pry through Señora Tankersley's things."

He pushed ledger books aside, pulled books from their shelves, searching for shotgun shells. Then he went to the kitchen with Lupe trailing behind, angrily telling him that she intended to tell Mrs. Tankersley what he was doing.

"There are men coming after me with guns, Lupe. Maybe I didn't make that clear before."

"Why wait around? Why don't you make a run for it?"

He rose from his crouch by some wooden boxes along the kitchen wall, stared at her a moment, and said, "That sounds like good advice."

Leaving the unloaded shotgun behind, he went out the back door. A dog started to bark and wag its tail, prepared to play. Lad rubbed the shaggy animal's ears and managed to quiet him. He heard the sounds of wagon wheels creaking and jolting on Concho Avenue. The town had come to life.

Lad wanted to make it to the Elkhorn Wagon Yard, get his horse, and head west. He slipped behind the adjoining frame structure and peered around it.

A voice called out, *"There he is!"*

Lad saw Dee Hudnall then, sitting on a big red roan horse. The two gunmen with him dismounted and walked toward Lad, drawing pistols as they advanced. He saw that they were both Anglos. He wondered fleetingly where Ramón might be. As they neared him the butterflies fluttering in his stomach made him physically sick. He stared numbly at them.

One of the men, with a gun pointed at Lad's stomach, said, "We're takin' you with us."

"Where are we going?"

"Out to the ranch."

"I'll need to go get my horse."

"We got one saddled. He's hitched right over yonder."

Lad saw a swaybacked gray gelding tied to a rail behind Hudnall. His head turned back to the men holding guns on him. His knees trembled, and when he tried to speak, he couldn't. Without thinking, he raised his hands over his head and began walking from beside the building out into the street.

The two men holstered their weapons but kept their hands on them. One of them said, "Put your damn hands down. Don't try to call attention to yourself. Just git on that pony. If you try to run for it I'll put a bullet right in your spine. You understand me?"

Lad nodded and lowered his hands. When he reached the hitching rail he looked at the red brick building behind it. A sign with large letters stood on a shed roof supported by four wooden posts. It said "H. Wolters & Co." and underneath this, "Star Saloon." Windows on either side of the front door were open, and he saw gun barrels on the sills—seemingly pointing at him.

He flinched and looked quickly at other buildings. Pistols and rifles poked through windows to the right and the left. He turned around and saw the same thing in windows on the other side of the street. At least fifty armed men crouched behind cover, prepared to open fire. Looking up, he saw several men on top of frame buildings, craning their heads around false fronts.

Dee Hudnall and his two gunmen saw all of this as he did. Instinctively they reached for their guns but as they did so a large man came out of the Star Saloon. He wore a Colt at his side but hadn't drawn it. A tall, heavyset individual, he wore a wide-brimmed Stetson squarely on his head. A star shone on the lapel of his faded blue shirt. Lad noted the man's calmness, saw his large features and his long flowing mustache.

"Don't move a muscle," the tall man said. "Raise your hands, real slow. That's right—just like that."

He stepped down onto the road and approached Hudnall. He told him, "The whole town is here to give me a hand if there's trouble. I'm arresting you for the slaughter of your wife. I can see her blood all over you, Dee. No use denyin' anything. You're goin' to trial, and then we'll hang you. And we'll try these gunhands with you for attempted kidnapping."

Dozens of men came into the street, holding their weapons on the three mounted men. Others followed, forming about Dee Hudnall and his two men.

A man called out, "Why not hang 'em right now?" But the sheriff said, "Not without a trial." He nodded to a deputy and said, "Take 'em to jail."

Later, gulping down a drink of bar whiskey in the Star Saloon, Lad sat surrounded by a number of his saviors.

"Who was that man? Where did he come from?"

"When you told folks what happened, we didn't know what to do." He acted embarrassed and his voice lowered. "You know, Hudnall has all those gunfighters workin' for him. He's got away with a lot of meanness through the years. But then we ran across the sheriff from Ballinger who came to town late yesterday to do some shoppin' for his wife. He went with us out to the Hudnall place."

He screwed up his face in revulsion. "We saw what happened when we got to the barn. Most awful thing I ever seen in my life. The word went all over. You know how fast news travels in a small town."

"What's his name?"

"The Ballinger sheriff? Why, ever'one knows him. That's Mortimer Mertz. He don't put up with no foolishness. And you're damn lucky he was here. He told us exactly what to do—like this was the sort of thing he sees all the time. That helped us get our nerve up— and we backed him."

He spoke proudly. "I ain't never goin' to forget this day—the time we finally put a stop to Dee Hudnall." He looked around at his friends. *"I was part of it."*

Lad saw a familiar face and recognized Jap Turner, one of Mad John McIntire's cowboys. He greeted him and Jap said he'd come to town for supplies.

All the men in the saloon seemed to be talking at once, when a cowboy burst through the front door. "The sheriff and his deputy and several others have decided they better take Hudnall and his two gunfighters to some other town, or they're likely to git lynched."

"Have they left yet?" a man asked.

"Yep. They're on their way. Got Hudnall and his men hogtied in a wagon, and they're on their way to Austin."

"Damn!" a voice complained. "I was lookin' forward to the hangin'."

Another said, "Well, you'll have to travel to Austin to see it, I reckon."

"Thank God it's over," Lad murmured. He didn't try to find words to express his true feelings. He'd felt certain that Hudnall was going to kill him. Still weak from fear, he sat silently as waves of relief washed over him.

Jap Turner came to his table and pulled up a chair.

"I'm going to be looking for land to lease," Lad told him. "I'm now the owner of almost three thousand sheep. I've got range for them for almost a year, but at the end of that time I'll have to move the herd."

Jap looked pained. He took a drink but made no reply at first. At last he said one word: "Sheep." He closed his eyes as he spoke, and shook his head, obviously distressed at the idea of a decent man getting involved in such a foul business.

"I was thinking that Mr. McIntire might be able to give me some advice."

"I don't know that I'd go to Mad John for advice," Jap finally drawled.

"He's the only stockman I know around here."

"Well, you can ride back to the ranch with me tomorrow if you like."

"That sounds fine," Lad said. "I'll look forward to it." He looked at the cowboy and at last asked about Beth McIntire.

"Well, funny you should ask. She's broke off her engagement with Harley Bragg and don't do much but moon around." He grinned. "Maybe you can cheer her up."

Lad felt his spirits rise. "I'll certainly do my best, Jap," he replied.

Eighteen

LAD FELL BACK into an easy companionship with the men he'd known during the brief time he'd worked for Mad John McIntire. On arriving at the ranch he moved into his old place in the bunkhouse, renewing his acquaintanceship with Pucker, Ramsel, Jap Turner, the cook named Joshua, and the others. He breakfasted with the cowboys, rode through long hot days at their side, and, after cleaning up in the evenings, enjoyed dinner at the big house with the owner and his family. Mrs. McIntire, who reminded Lad to call her "Miss Ellen" as the others did, had been especially happy to see him, saying repeatedly, "Beth surely was pleased to hear you'd be spending some time with us again."

If this was true, Lad decided, it certainly hadn't been apparent. Beth hardly spoke to him the first week, treating him instead with the stiff courtesy she might accord a stranger. And when she did address him, she didn't venture far beyond polite comments on the weather. When he replied, she'd look away, her gaze fixed on something off to one side.

Lad began to believe that her shyness was contagious. Throughout his life he'd always had the ability to carry on spirited conversations with pretty young women under any circumstances, but suddenly he found himself feeling tongue-tied and awkward. He couldn't account for his nervousness around the slender dark-haired girl, and wondered if she simply didn't like him.

While he was lying in bed one night, thinking of Beth, a possible explanation for her apparent coolness occurred to him: she probably had heard of his relationship with Mattie Hudnall. The scandal would surely have spread far from San Angelo. But she never mentioned anything about it.

As time passed, they relaxed and began to enjoy each other's company once again. One night Beth said, "I look forward all day to seeing you." Lad didn't know how to respond, although, an hour later when he'd returned to the bunkhouse, he thought of the perfect response.

He looked forward to the evenings spent in her company and to the days spent with the cowboys. As he rode with them, he observed the care with which they made their plans, and began to see a pattern in their activities that at first hadn't been at all apparent to him. When he'd begun work on his arrival at the Stars and Bars spread it had seemed that each day's ride was random, but now he gradually became aware of the foreman's systematic way of working the ranch. He learned the different tasks that came and went with the seasons. He listened to plans being made to move stock, and precautions against overgrazing. He had, he realized, a great deal to learn.

He paid close attention to the foreman, an angular man named Lew Cutter, and heard few wasted words. Yet when Cutter spoke, he passed on the wisdom of a lifetime. Gradually Lad felt he was absorbing knowledge, he was getting an education.

At times Lad rode with the foreman, and during the long days listened to his comments. Cutter once told Lad that as a boy he'd wanted to go to sea—that had been his dream. He'd had visions of himself on shipboard, looking out over vast ocean expanses. They stopped near a tree so the foreman could roll a cigarette, a difficult task since the third finger of his right hand had drawn up and curled strangely into his palm.

"This finger gives me hell," Cutter said dryly. "Can hardly rope anymore. My pa had the same thing happen, seems like a tendon pulls tight, and there's nothing to be done about it." By this time he'd finished rolling the cigarette and lit it in cupped hands, protecting the flame from the wind. Looking out over the limitless prairie, he asked, "What do you see when you look out there?"

Lad gazed at rolling land, rocks, some shinnery and greasewood, a few clumps of sumac and lotebrush. "I don't know what you mean," he finally answered.

"There's a world to be learned about this land. It looks kind of like a desert, a wasteland, but it has strong grasses—and when you put cattle here, it turns out food for people."

A sudden breeze bent the grasses, and their tops flowed almost like waves. "Sometimes I see things like that," Cutter said, "and it makes me feel that this is kind of like being at sea." He paused. "I like the peace out here." He didn't say another word for about fifteen minutes.

The two men dismounted, and Cutter walked stiffly, limping as he moved. From time to time he'd sink down on one knee and speak patiently to Lad. He said, "This buffalo grass is common, so's the mesquite grass. But there are so many others. We've got black grama and hairy grama and sideoats grama. Over that hill you see right over yonder you'll run into what we call little bluestem, and it stands two to three feet high. There's some silver bluestem that grows almost to that height too. Lord, son, once I drove a herd up to Chase County in the flint hills of Kansas, and there's a different bluestem grass there that stands as much as eight feet high—I had to stand in my stirrups to see over the top of it. I've seen Indian grass in this part of the country that stands five or six feet, but it wasn't anything at all like that sight I saw in Kansas."

During that day he talked about special places he'd seen. He told Lad about the Marathon Basin, out near the Glass Mountains on the way to Fort Davis. He said, "You'll see green sprangletop grass there —that the cows like. There's threeawn grass and rescue grass, and hooded windmill grass, clumpgrass, and sand dropseed, and bush muhly grass—there's maybe ten kinds of that—not to mention slim tridens and vine mesquite, and Texas cupgrass."

He stopped for a moment, looking at the young Virginian riding beside him. "Not many people are real interested in things like this."

Lad soaked in his words, and Cutter, like so many older men, absolutely loved having an apt pupil at his side.

Lad looked forward to dedicating his daytime hours to learning the cattle business, even though during this entire time he dreaded the nights. At first he had vivid, horrifying dreams of Mattie's blood-drenched body, waking from them in the darkness sitting bolt upright, his heart pounding. He never permitted himself to think of her during the day, but the dreams kept recurring. However, after two weeks on the Stars and Bars Ranch, the nightmares blurred and gradually ceased.

The cowboys wanted to talk about the murder, but on seeing his reaction, they fell silent. At times he'd enter the bunkhouse to find them in a lively discussion, and they'd suddenly stop, looking almost ashamed as they clumsily changed the subject.

On one occasion Lad rode west to the J. S. Pierce Ranch on Devil's River and spent a week there getting acquainted with the old-timer and with his children. One of these, a youngster named Victor, took him out on a long ride to see the sheep Lad had won in the poker game.

These were followed by Mexican herders who carried with them a piece of canvas as their shelter, some bread and beans, and little else. At times they'd go before the sheep, leading them to water. But usually, they simply followed wherever the flock might wander. Lad learned that, at lambing time in the spring, more Mexicans would be sent for to help the few herders who worked for Mr. Pierce on a full-time basis.

Then he returned to the McIntires' table, telling them about the things he'd seen and heard. "The herders are paid an average of eighteen dollars a month, and I understand they're dependable. Mr. Pierce's son says he thinks that a man ought to fence a pasture and leave the sheep alone, that they don't need herders following them all the time."

"Fences? I hope we haven't come to that," said Mad John McIntire.

Lad had heard the cowboys in the bunkhouse talking about their boss. Pucker had said, "You know, Mad John had a touch of the misery for more than a month, and Miss Ellen threw out all his whiskey. Busted ever' blessed bottle on those rocks behind the house. Made Mad John mad as hell—he was fit to be tied. But now that he's gittin' better, he hasn't taken up drinkin' again. And he ain't near as crazy as he's been since I've known him. In fact, he seems downright normal."

Ramsel had said, "I liked it better when he was drinkin'. Never knew what the hell he might be up to next."

The cowboys in the bunkhouse had laughed at Ramsel's remark.

Now, sitting by his father's old friend, Lad saw how much steadier John McIntire's hands were. He seemed to be a different man.

McIntire turned in his chair and addressed Lad. "I wrote your father that you'd managed to accumulate a stake, and furthermore that you'd come into possession of a large herd of sheep."

Lad felt his face grow warm. In spite of his hurt feelings, he valued his father's good opinion.

"I hope you didn't mention anything about my winning that stake in a card game."

"No, I left out that part. Although I did say that the seller was glad to get rid of the sheep as he felt they were the stupidest of all of God's creatures.''

"When I was on his ranch," Lad said, "he was making arrangements to buy more of them."

"Joe Pierce always complains about sheep, but he's a good businessman. I think I told you that Harley Bragg and I bought a good many of them. Well, Harley has decided to look for a cattle ranch up toward the panhandle, and has found one he likes near the Canadian River. He says it gets better rainfall than we do, and told me once again that sooner or later the drouths will put us out of business in this part of the state. Anyway, as a result, he's offered to sell me his ranch together with his interest in the sheep."

Lad looked at him, fascinated by this development. "Are you going to accept the offer?"

"It'll take a good bit of money, and I'd have to go into debt," the elderly man said, "but I'm sorely tempted, for it's a fine piece of land —and it adjoins my property. When I wrote your father about the new developments in your life I made mention of my dilemma."

Lad laughed. "He doesn't think anyone should invest outside of Tidewater Virginia."

McIntire chuckled. "I know."

In September, with the wind still hot from the south but with the promise of fall in the morning air, Lad received a letter from home. A cowboy from a neighboring ranch delivered it early that Sunday along with a bundle of newspapers to which John McIntire subscribed. Lad took his letter and carried it to the yard. Inside the picket fence, two once white wooden chairs sat under a rough-trunked elm tree, and Lad sat down in one of them as he opened the envelope.

Dear Ladbrook,

I've received word recently from my old wartime companion, John McIntire. He said that you are once again working at his ranch, as I'd encouraged you to do, and that you are learning how to become a stockman. He also said that you had in some fashion acquired a herd of sheep, and that he intends to offer to allow you to keep them on his range if I have no objections.

One should not take undue advantage of friendship. It wouldn't be appropriate for you to accept his generous offer.

On the other hand, I understand that a neighboring ranch is for sale at the price of $1 per acre. This is a good bargain, even for the type of barren prairieland that I understand is available in West Texas. Accordingly, I've made the decision to send the funds necessary for you to purchase the ranch now owned by Harley Bragg, but in what I consider a prudent manner. In a separate letter to John, I've set out my recommendations. In addition, I'm sending an additional sum in order to provide more livestock and operating capital.

Naturally, all of this depends on John's approval, and if he wants to purchase the Bragg ranch on his own account, I'll certainly understand.

This advance on your inheritance is being made on the condition that you act under the guidance of John McIntire and his advisers. Quite frankly, I'd hoped that we could ultimately work side by side in Virginia. But your going into the ranching business in Texas is certainly intriguing.

If my attitude seems to have changed since my last letter, it's owing to the fact that I've had some health problems recently and want to take action while I still am able to do so in order to see that you are in a position to have a productive life.

Don't worry about me—I've recovered. It was a matter of some pains in my chest that disabled me for a time. But the doctor has brought me some medicine that seems to be effective.

It is difficult for me to imagine a landholding of 200,000 acres. If I follow my doctor's orders, I hope one day to be able to see this ranch.

It has always been difficult for me to express my feelings in words, but please understand that I do care for you.

The letter ended with a hastily scrawled, "With affection from your father."

Numbed by the news, dumbstruck in fact, Lad sat with the sheet of paper in his lap. He reread it several times.

Then he went to the house and sat for several hours with John McIntire. He learned of his father's suggestions that an offer be made by Lad to purchase 20,000 acres, including the main house and pens at its site on a creek, and that he enter into a lease-purchase agreement with regard to the remaining 180,000 acres. His father had sent a proposed contract to be executed by Lad as buyer and Harley Bragg as the seller. His father had this drawn up by his lawyer in Virginia. By its terms, Lad purchased the main house and 20,000 acres located on the creek, and with regard to the remaining 180,000 acres, Lad had the option of leasing the land for a cost of 10 percent of the purchase price, or ten cents an acre per year, for a period of ten years. At the end of that time, the land would be his. In a separate note from the lawyer they read that in the event the venture should prove not to be profitable, the instrument had been so drafted that Lad could withdraw from the lease agreement at any time without penalty, but that Bragg was bound by it.

At their meal that evening, the prospect of Lad going into the ranching business as their neighbor was the sole subject under discussion. McIntire said, "I have plans to see Harley in San Angelo later in the week, and I'll take the contract to him and we'll discuss it. He filed on that land not long after the war—and I doubt that he has much invested, if anything. He's determined to move and needs cash real bad right now, so I think he'll accept your offer."

McIntire explained once again that, since Bragg was moving to cattle country, he wanted to sell his interest in the four thousand sheep he and McIntire owned in partnership. He said to Lad, "If you're interested in stocking the ranch alone, that's fine with me, and you can buy my share too. But if you'd like a partner while you're learning the business, then you and I can own those sheep together just like Harley and I did, and we can add more to them."

Lad quickly stated that he'd like a partner very much, and the matter was settled.

Lad and Beth sat in the parlor along with McIntire, who seated himself in his accustomed chair which sat by a table with a lamp. He unfolded the newspapers delivered that morning, grumbled that he hadn't taken the time to see the news of the outside world, and began turning pages. Miss Ellen stood at the door and, saying she was going to bed early, excused herself.

Beth had learned to crochet as a child and when she'd sit with Lad after their evening meals she'd often bring this handwork with her. Tonight her needle flew while an intricate white oval design took shape between her hands. She was making a set of doilies, she said, and later she wanted to start on a big bedspread as a special present for her mother. Feeling Lad's gaze upon her, she stopped her work and looked up.

Lad stared into her dark hazel eyes, noting tiny golden flecks in them. She smiled and he heard soft contralto laughter, saw the laugh lines crinkle at her eyes. He saw her in a new light, as if for the first time. She had a small, almost black spot, perhaps a tiny birthmark, high on her left cheek. He found it bewitching. Her hair was tied back with a deep red ribbon, and soft brunette curls escaped from it.

"Well, I'll declare," McIntire said abruptly, crackling the newspaper folds so that he could hold an article in the light. "Says here," he announced, "that Dee Hudnall has not only not been hanged yet, but the prosecuting attorney has announced that the case has been dismissed for lack of evidence. The scoundrel has been released!"

Electrified, Lad sat on the edge of his chair.

"How can that be?" McIntire demanded.

After a silence of some moments, Lad said, "I understand Hudnall has friends with political influence."

"Everyone in San Angelo knows he committed murder!"

Lad didn't comment.

"Could you excuse us a few minutes?" McIntire said to Beth.

When she had left the room, Lad's host said, "I understand that he swore to kill you."

"Yes, that's true."

"You think he'll try it?"

"I don't know."

The next morning at first light, Lad intended to ride twenty miles to the north to see part of Harley Bragg's land. The ranch house lay another twenty miles from there. He couldn't wait to go see it but felt it would be best to wait until invited by Bragg. However, he could at least look over part of the land he hoped to acquire and come back to the McIntire Ranch by nightfall.

Upset by the news about Hudnall, Lad didn't sleep well and was glad when the time came to rise. When he'd dressed, he ate some bread and had a cup of coffee from the big pot that Joshua had just made, then left for the corral.

When Lad finished saddling Claude, he heard the noise of horses' hooves drumming in the corral. He walked to the fence and saw them moving in a tight circle in the big pen. Beth, dressed in a loose-fitting white blouse and denim trousers, stood in their midst as they whirled about her, and he saw her throw a loop over the head of a dun gelding called Ross. He knew that she liked to ride him on long trips, for he had long legs and an easy gait. And, of importance to Beth, he had a good disposition.

Lad had mentioned the night before that he planned to make the trip, and she'd commented that it would be fun to go with him. He hadn't realized that she really intended to join him.

They rode to the house and Lad tied their horses while Beth ran inside to the kitchen to make sandwiches for their noon meal. "We'll have a picnic," she said excitedly. "I'll make sandwiches. We've got baked chicken left over from last night's supper, and I'll slice some of the bread that Rose baked yesterday."

Around eleven o'clock that morning they reached a narrow boulder-strewn valley that folded into the rolling land. "I've been here before," Lad said, leading her along the trail.

A hawk floated over them, wings outspread, seemingly serene—an ordinary sight—yet carrying the promise, the certainty, of violence.

Earlier they'd crossed a small creek where the horses had stopped, leaned down their heads, pawed the clear water until it was muddy, and then with deep uphill gulps, drunk water until they'd had their fill.

They rode with the sun hot on their backs until they reached a deep arroyo. Lad turned to his right into it and Beth followed. Riding on the rocky bed of the dry creek, they made their winding way a few hundred yards.

The arroyo gradually widened from its width of six or seven feet to an elbow where it curved to the south. Lad could see where the runoff water from rainstorms had eroded the bank at the turn, widening the dry creek until it measured at least twenty feet across. At one side, under an overhanging tree which leaned precariously over the edge of the ten-foot-high bank, was a low mound covered by soft dry grass.

Lad pointed it out to Beth. "Let's have our lunch here."

They moved up the arroyo until they reached a few cedars growing near the steep walls of the gully, and dismounted. Hidden from sight, they loosened the girths of the saddles.

They walked hand in hand, stumbling over rocks and dead logs, to the small grass-covered promontory, a shaded island in a dried-out watercourse. Lad brought his canteen along with him and sank down on the short dry weeds and grass. Beth had retrieved their lunch from her saddlebags, and she unwrapped this, placing warm chicken sandwiches on red and white checked napkins upon the ground. She had picked watercress that grew profusely by a spring they'd seen when watering the horses. She'd noticed it and jumped down, not minding that her boots had gotten soaked. Now she put the watercress in their sandwiches.

She leaned against him, raised her head, and he kissed her. Then she pulled away from him.

"I shouldn't have done that," Lad said, his voice husky. "Are you mad at me?"

"Yes," Beth replied. She grinned and handed him his lunch.

They talked about the ranch as they ate. Beth had been there with her father and mother a number of times, and she described it to him. She seemed flustered when she mentioned the house, saying only that it was large but sparsely furnished.

Lad had almost forgotten that at one time she'd been engaged to Bragg, and realized now that she obviously must have thought of her life in that house with him.

"Does it bother you that Harley Bragg's moving away?"

"No," she said emphatically. "It's not that I have anything against him, but I was so unhappy with the idea of his being my husband." Her voice broke off. "It really was Daddy's idea at first. I suppose he liked the idea of our having an interest in both ranches."

Lad said, "And now *I'm* the one who'll own it."

Beth blushed almost crimson. At last she said, "Well, I'm surely not going to marry *you.*"

"Why not?" He spoke in a joking way, teasing her.

Her eyes sparkled. "Oh, I don't know. I was going to say 'too young and inexperienced,' but then I remembered some of the stories I've heard about you."

This time Lad felt *his* face flush. "What did you hear?"

"The past doesn't matter to me," Beth said.

Relieved to have the opportunity to change the subject, Lad told her of the time he and Pucker and Ramsel had a noon meal of canned tomatoes and hardtack in this same general area when they'd been riding along with Jap Turner. And he related how Turner had led him through Bat Cave.

"I've heard about that place," Beth said. "But I never saw it. My daddy told me it was dangerous and allowed that he'd switch me if I ever went in it."

"I can't imagine his ever hurting you."

"I can't either—he just teased that way."

Lad rose to his feet suddenly and listened intently for a moment. Turning to Beth, he asked, "Did you hear something just then?"

She looked puzzled. "No."

"Sounded like horses whinnying. I thought I heard hooves on rocks a second later. But now everything's quiet."

He saw that her face was pale. He said, "Stay here—I'm going to take a look around."

Lad climbed up the steep side of the bank, pulling himself up by clinging to roots and a few rocks and cedars. When he reached the edge he peered over it. Looking slightly downhill toward the valley where he and Beth had ridden earlier, he saw three men approaching on horseback. The rider in the lead, a thick-bodied man, wore a long duster that reached almost to his boots. Lad stared at him. His mouth went dry. Then he was certain who this was, and his blood froze within him.

Nineteen

BETH WATCHED as Lad slid back down the dirt bank, digging rough bootheel furrows as he struggled to slow his descent.

Face pale, shaken by his grim expression, she asked, "What did you see? Who is it?"

"Hudnall and two of his gunmen."

"My God."

"They've probably been following us all morning. I guess they came to get me at the ranch, then saw the two of us ride out. They've let us get beyond the reach of help, and now it looks as if they're coming in for the kill."

"What will we do?" Beth looked at him, waiting for guidance.

Lad didn't have any idea what they should do. As the man who should be protecting her, he was supposed to be decisive. Except he didn't know what decision he ought to make.

He looked at the girl's wide, frightened eyes, held both of her hands in his, and took a deep breath. "They'll never be able to keep up with Claude. I'll make a run for it and they'll chase me. You wait here until they've gone by, then double back and head for home."

He touched her cheek, looked at her an instant, then ran toward their horses. He tightened the girth on Beth's saddle and then on his own before mounting. At the instant he found his seat in the saddle, as he pushed his foot trying to locate the right stirrup with the toe of his boot, he wheeled about. He headed Claude toward an angled gully cut by runoff water in the far wall of the arroyo—and leaned forward as the horse surged up it.

Emerging onto the floor of the narrow valley, Lad put his mount into a slow lope to conserve him for a long ride. He saw no signs of the men he'd spotted in the distance. He knew they'd have no trouble following the fresh tracks of his and Beth's horses.

Lad turned in his saddle and saw all three of them coming up from the arroyo at about the place where he and Beth had entered it. One of them gestured, and he knew he'd been spotted.

He spurred Claude into a run, ducking through a stand of hackberry and cedar trees. A dozen antelope, startled at his branch-snapping passage, fled across the rocky prairie. They had white faces and bellies, light brown backs with an orange cast, and they sailed gracefully over bushes and small mesquites, short tails held high like small flags, heads erect as they floated over obstacles, smoothly moving with surprising swiftness. The antelope rushed in front of the three men who thundered in pursuit. Startled, they reined back momentarily, enabling Lad to gain ground.

Outcroppings of craggy limestone and numerous small boulders cluttered the land before Lad and also the slope of the hill on his right. He had to angle down to the left, to the north. The men, about a half mile behind him, kept going dead ahead. Lad could see them narrow the gap between them. He reached an even part of the prairie, and felt Claude's strong rhythmic movements beneath him as his strides lengthened.

Lad saw Hudnall veer to his left, and the two hired gunmen swerved slightly to their right. They were going to make sure he couldn't get away. A shot cracked over his head, and he leaned down low as his tall rangy horse seemed to fly, hooves clattering over the ground. He touched the wooden stock of the Winchester which protruded from the saddle scabbard just in front of his right knee. He thought of stopping and making a fight, but the odds of three against one made him think better of it.

Lad jolted up an incline, came over a crest, and drew back convulsively on the reins, hauling Claude's head back sharply. The horse jarred into a sliding, stiff-legged, gravel-throwing stop which ended at the brink of a precipitous drop-off—a cliff that fell at least thirty feet to the valley below. Reining about to his right, he ascended the ridge at the edge of the bluff until he stopped in the shelter provided by a stand of mesquites.

Instants later the two gunmen labored over the hill, and did as he had—pulling up frantically just short of the bluff.

Before they could get their bearings, while they were staring over the edge, Lad slammed his spurs into Claude's sides and headed directly for them. The two men, slightly downhill from him, were on the other side of a small mound. They sat on their heaving horses, side by side, facing ahead.

Lad used his reins as a quirt, leaned forward as the big horse pounded into the flat, approaching the men from their flank. He saw them jerk their heads toward him, saw the horrified whites of their eyes as Claude thundered up the mound. He would use that small inclined promontory as a takeoff pad.

Lad stood in his stirrups, body angled forward, holding his head by Claude's muscular neck, his face flicked by the flying mane. He attacked instinctively, but at the last instant had second thoughts—and a single question ripped through his mind: My God, what am I doing?

Claude went at the two horseback men as if they were a form of living fence, a barrier to be cleared. As his front legs bent and he surged high and fast over them, the horse on the near side reared in terror.

Lad's world turned into a crashing kaleidoscope. He felt himself fly free from Claude, saw the horses and men beneath him, heard the sounds of flesh and hooves and bones smashing, and then he tumbled in midair, felt himself making a complete flip before striking through the splintering branches of a bush just short of the edge of the bluff. He crashed through this, which broke his fall to some extent, and tumbled onto the ground where he bounced and rolled until he lay still on his back with the wind knocked completely out of him.

Fighting desperately for his breath, panic surging, he only faintly heard crashing noises followed by sliding sounds, screams of men and horses, and, far below, a series of dull dreadful thuds.

He gasped, caught a breath, choked for an instant, and then sat up dazedly as he caught his wind, almost sobbing as the quick inhalations began. He struggled to his knees and looked over the edge of the bluff. Down below in the rocks he saw two horses, one on its back, the other on its side. They lay grotesquely, feet splayed, bodies bent. They stretched over the bloodied remains of the two gunmen who'd pursued him. Then he saw Claude lying a short distance away, his head raised as he sought to move.

Lad heard the wind coming from a distance, moving over the narrow valley, bending trees before it. And, though it was too far, he thought he could hear Claude's labored breathing. He watched the horse's head sink to the ground. For long moments he stared at Claude's unnatural stillness.

Shocked and weak, he stood at the edge of the cliff, looking down. A grim certainty grew that Hudnall would find him in a few minutes, and he forced himself to action.

Lad tested his legs and arms and gingerly touched his ribs with his fingers. Miraculously, he hadn't broken any bones. But every inch of his body felt bruised.

He started to go up the ridge to his right, but saw only cactus and low rocks and bushes. Without a rifle, he'd be helpless there. A ripple of fear curled through his stomach. I've got to find a place to hide, he thought.

He walked rapidly to his left, to the north. Then he began to jog, taking deep breaths as he passed through stunted cedar trees on his way downhill. He stumbled up a slight incline and saw a stone-crested flattened butte—and at that instant knew where he was.

Straining forward, he scrambled around rough rocks and outcroppings of cactus, weaving through soto, catclaw, and prickly pear as he headed toward the big cave Jap Turner had shown him. He kept thinking, If I can get into it before Hudnall sees me, I'll be safe.

Lad climbed as rapidly as he could, fell once, then rose. He didn't notice the tear in the fabric at his knee but felt something warm and, looking down, saw a bloodstain.

The bullet struck a boulder right beside his head before he heard the deep bark of a sixgun. Chips of stone sprayed into his face, cutting it in a dozen places. His heart slammed like a triphammer as he plunged into full flight, running the remaining few yards up the hill and then floundering down into a great irregular dark hole. He had found the thirty-foot-wide entrance to Bat Cave.

Slipping on loose stones and sand, he climbed down to the first level of the crater, then made his way to the narrow rocky chute that dropped perilously into the main cave. It angled at about seventy degrees, winding steeply down like a rough-walled stone flue. He held to rocks as he blindly sought footing. The sharp edges of the handholds tore his palms and fingers, but he paid no more attention to them than he did to the deep bleeding on his knee or the various tiny cuts on his face.

At the bottom he found almost even footing and ran down a narrow passageway that led away from the light.

A pistol shot exploded from high above and ricocheted off the stone floor behind him. He looked about and in the shadows caught sight of a strange living tapestry above and beside him. A wave of disgust, of revulsion, caught at his throat as he saw thousands and thousands of bats hanging head down from the cave's ceiling and walls. Some were close enough for him to see their wrinkled bodies, their folded leathery wings. They hung everywhere, in clumps and clusters, veined and hideous. A few curled up and took flight as he brushed near them, wings blurring as he glimpsed rodent-like heads, bright eyes, and small-toothed open mouths.

"God!" he cried out through gritted teeth. Repressing a shudder, he hurried on while unmistakable sounds from the flue above told him that Hudnall had begun his descent.

The roof of the passageway became much higher as he came into what he remembered as the main cavern. This formed a large room with a relatively level floor. Faint glints of jewel tones, faint amethyst and rayed opal, shone from the stalagmites rising from the floor and the weeping stalactites hanging from the rocky ceiling. Some of them, at their tips, seemed to have slick milky deposits. Incredulously, he rushed into the bizarre cathedral-like room, hidden through the ages underground, beneath the faceless rough hills and prairie on the surface above.

His footing felt strange and oddly soft. It crunched slightly as he walked on it, as though he were treading through an ankle-deep layer of feathers.

He glimpsed a radiant flickering in the passageway behind him and realized that Hudnall must have a torch. He had probably brought some greasewood with him, and perhaps some rags from his saddlebags.

Lad sank back into a deep recess in the rough wall.

Hudnall entered the main cavern, holding the torch over his head. It formed a brilliant luminous disc, a circular band of colored lights with bright rays within it. Shadows beyond its reach turned even darker, blacker than the dead of a moonless night. Shining flames from the torch fell down in a glowing yellow and white puddle upon a thick-bodied man walking forward carefully, holding a long-barreled Colt in his outstretched right hand.

"I said I'd come after you," a deep bass voice boomed out. "I can't forgive what you done with Mattie. She's paid the price, and now it's your turn."

Lad took off his hat and frantically slapped it against the walls behind and above him. At first a few dozen bats took flight and then, as he kept hitting at them, more began to wheel and dip and dart through the cavern. Their movement stirred others to life, and in an instant, thousands and thousands of bats swirled through the air. A whirlwind of bats, an incredible, satanic cloud, blurred and diseased, swarmed madly about the flames held by Hudnall.

Hudnall cried out in astonishment, backed toward Lad and then beyond him, striking reflexively at the diving shadowy bats with his torch, moving without realizing it to the blackened edge of the pit, the one Jap Turner had told Lad was bottomless.

Lad lowered his head and charged. Hudnall saw the movement, fired once, then twice, as Lad's shoulder made contact in a bone-jarring collision.

Hudnall's big body swayed and he lost his balance. His horrified roar turned into a long-drawn-out shriek as he plunged over the side and down, deep down, into the waiting pit. He fell for a very long time before the faint sound of a splash could be heard.

The violent explosions of the cartridges inside the ancient cave kept bouncing wildly in a deafening drumbeat, echoing from one side to the other, and these reverberations threw the rest of the bats into a mad spiraling frenzy. The hazed frantic flapping of thousands of wings joined an incredible high-pitched frequency, a trembling chorus of squeaking as a whirl of them surged from the cave, up the flue, and erupted in a dark surging plume from the cave to the outer world.

The dropped torch guttered out in the deeply layered floor, in the thousand-year-old crumbling dryness of the droppings of millions of bats.

Lad's ears rang from the concussive explosions of the big Colt .45. He rose unsteadily to his feet and turned to the faint glow that came from the sunny day outside. He hurried toward the cleanness, fleeing the foul-smelling scene of death inside Bat Cave.

He struggled for what seemed hours up the steep stone flue. When he reached the ground outside, he kept climbing away from the crater-like entry to the maw of the cave until he reached the hard clean dirt of the hill. Then he collapsed to his hands and knees.

When Beth found him, he was sitting under a small tree, leaning against its trunk.

She came cautiously into the clearing on foot. She had retrieved his Winchester and carried it like a hunter, ready for action. She stopped when she spotted him, then dropped the rifle to the ground, running forward with a small cry.

"Lad!" she gasped as she threw herself into his arms. "Are you badly hurt?"

"No," he lied. "I'm fine." In spite of the warmth of the day, he felt cold. His stomach and his arms trembled ever so slightly, but he hoped she didn't notice that. He wanted so much to comfort her.

She buried her face against his shoulder. "I saw the three horses—there were bodies . . ." Her voice broke and she paused for a moment. "Your horse was there . . . I thought you were dead." She began to sob almost noiselessly, her shoulders shaking. Tears streamed down her face. Then she rubbed them away with both hands. Again she spoke as a child might, one who'd been hurt, telling a parent of the experience.

"I climbed down, looking for you, praying and hoping against hope that you'd still be alive. When I saw you weren't under those horses, I decided you must have jumped before they went over the side."

With difficulty she told her story in fits and starts. She had found a way down the bluff, and had taken his rifle from its saddle scabbard. Then she'd climbed back up the slope a few hundred yards away from the rocky ground where the horses lay, finding an animal trail at a place where the bluff wasn't so steep. When she reached the top she saw an odd sight, as if a prairie fire had started on the edge of the flat-topped butte not far away. She went toward it, and saw that the smoke was the outpouring of bats.

"That's when I came on you—leaning against this tree."

He held her tight to him. They didn't say anything for a long time. Gradually his heartbeat slowed and the dizziness passed away. But still he felt disoriented, as though in a dream.

At last she asked, "Where's that man? The one who threatened to kill you?" She couldn't bring herself to use Hudnall's name.

"He's dead."

She clutched her hands about his waist, not wanting to hear about it; not wanting to know how the other two pursuers came to be lying under horses at the foot of the bluff.

"You're *safe,*" she murmured. "Everything's going to be all right." Shuddering, she clutched him. "Let's go home," she said softly. "We'll send the men with a wagon tomorrow. Let someone else handle the burying. They'll get your saddle." She swallowed. "I don't want to think about it."

Lad felt her softness and warmth. He saw Hudnall's horse tethered to a greasewood bush on a slope across the way. He'd ride him back to the ranch. "I don't want to think about any of this either," he said.

He looked down from the side of the hill toward the north, toward his new ranch. Then he put the fingers of his right hand gently upon her cheek. The two young people stayed very still, holding one another, surrounded by the horizon-to-horizon immensity of the southern plains.

A hawk floated high above them, riding the air currents, but they didn't notice.

About the Author

H. B. Broome was nominated for the Medicine Pipe Bearer's Award for Best First Novel by the Western Writers of America for *The Meanest Man in West Texas*, the first novel about the reluctant gunfighter Tom English. His subsequent novels include *Gunfighters, The Man Who Had Enemies, Violent Summer,* and *Dark Winter.* Mr. Broome's great-grandfather was a U.S. Marshal in West Texas. His grandfather was a director of the Texas Sheep and Goat Raisers' Association, as well as an early member of the Texas and Southwestern Cattlemen's Association.